D0914214

The Pistol Poets

Also by Victor Gischler

GUN MONKEYS

The Pistol Poets

Victor Gischler

DELACORTE PRESS

THE PISTOL POETS
A Delacorte Book / February 2004

Published by Bantam Dell
A Division of Random House, Inc.
New York, New York

This is a work of fiction. Names, characters, places, and incidents either are the
product of the author's imagination or are used fictitiously. Any resemblance to
actual persons, living or dead, events, or locales is entirely coincidental.

"Anecdote of the Jar": From *The Collected Poems of Wallace Stevens* by
Wallace Stevens, copyright © 1954 by Wallace Stevens and renewed 1982 by
Holly Stevens. Used by permission of Alfred A. Knopf, a division of
Random House, Inc.

Book design by Lynn Newmark

Delacorte Press is a registered trademark of Random House, Inc.,
and the colophon is a trademark of Random House, Inc.

Library of Congress Cataloging in Publication Data

Gischler, Victor, 1969–
The pistol poets / Victor Gischler.
p. cm.
ISBN 0-385-33724-8
1. College teachers—Fiction. 2. Accident victims—Fiction. 3. Oklahoma—
Fiction. 4. Death—Fiction. I. Title.
PS3607.I48P57 2004
813'.6—dc22
2003055373

Manufactured in the United States of America
Published simultaneously in Canada

10 9 8 7 6 5 4 3 2 1
BVG

For all of my parents (biological, in-law and step)
Thanks for being there.

Acknowledgments

Time to whip some gratitude onto some people, lather them with niceness. Beer and Skittles to Anthony Neil Smith, Sean Doolittle, and Scott Phillips for sage advice on rough storytelling. Many thanks to Irwyn Applebaum for bringing me on board. Thumbs up to Bill Massey for kick-ass editing. A bouquet of tulips to Andrea Nicolay for keeping things organized. And many thanks to bionic, super, turbo-agent Noah Lukeman.

Finally, it must be noted that some folks will inevitably try to draw comparisons between the fictional Eastern Oklahoma University in Fumbee, Oklahoma, and Rogers State University in Claremore where I teach creative writing. Don't bother. The denizens of this novel are in no way based on the fine faculty, staff and administration of Rogers State. Relax, people. You're safe.

The Pistol Poets

Prologue

Moses Duncan was in the barn up to his elbows in the fried engine of his Harley-Davidson when he saw the girl driving too fast down the dirt road to his ranch, her Toyota pickup kicking dust, the dogs barking. He knew who it was. The girl, one of those college kids. Sexy.

He looked at himself. Wiry arms sticking out of his sleeveless AC/DC T-shirt, greasy jeans. It was freezing in the barn, but he couldn't work on the bike in a jacket. He hadn't shaved or bathed in two days. Damn, he hated to look so shitty when the pretty ones came around to make a buy. He pushed back his shaggy dishwater hair, accidentally smearing grease on the side of his head.

He wiped his hands on a rag, stepped out of the barn just as she parked her truck. Moses squinted at the sky. Clouds rolling in. It would rain soon, sleet maybe if it got cold enough.

"Hey," she called. "Remember me?"

"Of course." The name came back to him just in time. "Annie."

She smiled big and electric. "You have time for me right now?" She hugged herself in a leather jacket, huddled against the cold.

"Come on in the house."

Inside, they were immediately hit with the heat and stuffiness. He'd left the thermostat up too high again. The house smelled like old beer and socks.

"Have a seat." Moses gestured at a badly stained sofa.

"It's okay," Annie said. "I'll stand." She peeled off her leather jacket, wiped sweat already forming on her forehead and neck.

"Sorry about the temperature," Moses said. "The thermostat's a tricky bastard. It's either freezing or hot as hell." He walked to the wall and flicked the heat off.

She stood, one hand on a hip, the other swinging the leather jacket over a shoulder. "It's okay. I won't be here too long. I was just hoping for maybe a little grass."

He looked at her. Nice. Red hair cut short and mean. Long legs. With her jacket off Moses could see she wore a cut-off tank top that exposed her flat, smooth stomach. Nice curves. A gold belly-button ring. Yeah, he had her figured for one of these wild college chicks. She could probably fuck his dick raw all night.

Sometimes when one of the college girls would come in looking for a bag of weed, he'd trade the stuff for a blow job or a quickie. But he was pretty funky at the moment. He doubted she'd go for it. Better just to take the cash.

"Just a minute."

He went back in the bedroom, opened the closet door, looking over his shoulder to make sure she wasn't snooping. He pried up the floorboards and fished out the old suitcase where he kept the merchandise. The crystal-meth boys were big in this part of the country, but they left Duncan alone. As long as he sold everything *but* crystal meth, they chose not to notice. He picked out a Baggie of marijuana and took it back to her.

She paid him. She shuffled her feet.

"Anything else?" he asked.

"Big night tonight," Annie said. "I thought I'd see if you had anything special."

He scratched his head, spread the grease around. "What do you have in mind?"

"Dancing, drinking, partying." She put her hands in her back pockets, arched her back. "I want to get this guy in the mood. You know?"

"Party drugs. Got it."

He went back to the suitcase, looked at his selection. What did these kids think? He had special custom drugs for every occasion? He had weed, uppers, downers, and now and then some coke. Pretty much the basics. Nothing fancy.

He picked some random pills, shook the plastic bottle, and looked at them. Where had he gotten these? They'd been in the case for a while. What the hell? The girl would never know the difference.

He took them back to her. "Here you go. Perfect. Pretty colors. Hot times."

"Yeah?" She took the bottle, held it up to her eyes.

"You bet. Party all night with these," Moses said. "Makes your orgasms like fireworks." Sure, why not? "Good for orgies."

"Okay to take with booze or will it fuck me up?"

The hell if he knew. "No problem. Alcohol ramps up the effects."

"How much?"

"Fifty."

She balked.

"For you, thirty-five bucks."

"Okay." She handed him the cash.

Moses watched her butt as she walked out. If she didn't like the pills or got sick, he'd apologize when she came back, give her a discount on the next bag of grass. Hell, it wasn't like he was selling kitchen appliances.

Moses Duncan didn't give money-back guarantees.

Part 1

one

Morgan's eyes flickered open, and he realized that his naked ass was touching another naked ass under the covers.

Annie.

Visiting Professor Jay Morgan sat up in bed slowly, tried to remember how he'd hung himself over. The slim girl in a fetal curl under the covers next to him, Annie Walsh, didn't wake. A whole semester had slipped away on his one-year contract at Eastern Oklahoma University before he'd struck pay dirt.

She was nice, young and fit. Eager.

Morgan was short and soft around the middle. His black hair, sharpened into a deadly widow's peak, was long, pulled into a tight ponytail. But he had good cheekbones, and his eyes were a haunting blue. Morgan knew how to flash those eyes at young students.

Last evening's dark blur streaked with neon. The dance club on University Drive. Annie packed tight in denim and a black tank top, red hair shaved close. First-year master's student, a Sharon Olds wanna-be.

Morgan found boxers on the floor, slipped into them. He crept to the kitchen, tile freezing under his bare feet, started a pot of coffee, and watched it drip itself into existence. He filled a mug, drank with his eyes closed.

The phone rang. He grabbed it quickly. "Hello."

"Morgan? It's Dean Whittaker. We had an eight o'clock appointment."

"That's Wednesday."

"This is Wednesday."

Morgan's wristwatch said 8:37. "I'll be right there."

Morgan ran in and out of the shower, threw on black pants and a green Hawaiian shirt with a picture of flowered Elvis playing the ukulele. Brushing his teeth almost made him puke. He grabbed his pea coat, shrugged into it.

Oklahoma winter, not so much snow but plenty of ice and cold rain. How had he ended up in this redneck backwater? Oh, yeah. He needed the job. Every year a new campus, the life of a gypsy professor.

A flash of skin caught his eye as he passed through the bedroom. The girl.

He cleared his throat. "I have to go."

Nothing.

"There's coffee."

More nothing.

"Lock up when you leave, okay?"

He pulled the door closed behind him, groaned his way down the sidewalk, and climbed into his twelve-year-old Buick. He pointed it toward Eastern Oklahoma University's main campus, muttering inventive curses at Dean Whittaker in which the word *cocksucker* figured prominently.

Morgan stopped at the secretary's desk on the way into the English Department. "We have any aspirin, Tina?"

"I have Motrin in my purse."

"Okay."

He took the bottle from her, spilled five pills into his palm, and swallowed them dry.

"There's a girl here to see you," Tina said.

Morgan turned, fear kicking around in his gut. He thought Annie had somehow—impossibly—raced there ahead of him, coiled to spring charges of sexual misconduct.

It was a different girl, compact, tan, round-faced, and fresh, with black plastic glasses perched on the end of her nose, brown hair wild and shaggy. She bounced out of her chair and offered her hand to Morgan. He took it and shook, squinting at her, hoping to figure out what she was, if he was supposed to know her.

"Professor Morgan, I'm Ginny Conrad."

"Oh." Who? The voice was silky, familiar.

"I'm supposed to do a ride-along." The edges of Ginny's mouth quivered, hinted at a frown. "I'm supposed to follow you around. A day in the life of a poet—for the school paper. Remember?"

"Yes, of course I remember." No he didn't.

Morgan rubbed his temples with his thumbs. He looked at Ginny again, tried to make himself interested. But she had too much on the hips, too fleshy around the neck and cheeks.

"This isn't a good day, Ginny." He didn't have the stomach for questions right now. His head pounded.

A real frown this time from the girl, panic in the eyes. "But I have a deadline. My editor—"

Dean Whittaker leaned out of his office. "Morgan."

"Yeah."

Morgan left Ginny standing there, the girl flowing into his wake, "but, but, but…" like an outboard motor about to stall. Morgan pulled the dean's office door closed and cut her off.

"Sit down," Whittaker barked. He was a huge man with a big voice. His full black beard, barrel chest, and concrete shoulders made him look like a bear. Whittaker was also interim chair of the English Department until a search committee could find somebody permanent. Whittaker's dissertation had been on ladies' costuming in Elizabethan theater.

Morgan began to lower himself into the overstuffed chair across from Whittaker.

"Not there!" Whittaker yelled.

Morgan leapt aside like he'd been hit with a cattle prod. He looked into the chair to see why he shouldn't sit.

The reason was an old man.

"I'm terribly sorry. I didn't see—I'm just out of it today."

The old man scowled but said nothing. His thin, nearly transparent skin clung to his skull like wet tissue paper. Bald. Small, shrunken inside a brown sweater and a pair of khaki pants pulled up almost to his armpits. A red stone the size of a doorknob on his pinkie finger.

"Take the seat by the bookcase." Whittaker glared.

"Sorry." Morgan squeezed between two giant bookcases. A narrow chair without armrests.

Whittaker sat, pulled at his tie, and fidgeted with a pencil.

"Morgan, this is Fred Jones. He's very generously donated enough money to keep *Prairie Music* operational for the next ten years."

"That's extremely generous," Morgan said. "Extremely."

And surprising as hell. The university had slashed the budget from under the third-rate literary journal, and it looked like they might have to go from a quarterly to an annual. Or maybe even scrap the journal altogether.

"Mr. Jones is a lover of fine literature and an amateur poet himself," Whittaker said. "He's been working quite hard on his own project, a volume of very personal poetry."

Whittaker was nailing Morgan to the back of his chair with his eyes, and Morgan realized he was supposed to say something about this but hadn't a clue what it should be. He took a shot at it.

"That's great." He nodded, raised his eyebrows to convey deep sincerity. "Absolutely great. I wish more people would develop their creative sides."

It was a fantastic lie. The amateur poet was a cancer. Morgan's brief stints as an assistant editor for a number of literary journals reinforced this belief. Every day he'd arrive at the office greeted by a towering stack of hideous verse. *Everyone* wrote poetry. Schoolteachers and teenage girls and spotty adolescent boys who couldn't catch a girl's eye. Christian crusaders who dumped their message into abstract verse, old men who committed the birth of the latest grand-offspring to rhyme. Housewives who scrawled their bland, unhappy lives into greeting-card drivel and refused to believe that their lives were as ordinarily miserable as everyone else's. They pressed on, relentless, minds clouded with the delusion that their agonies were somehow special or interesting and must therefore be shared with the world.

And the poetry came in like a flood, a tidal wave. It arrived dozens of pages at a time, folded into sweaty, smudged thirds and overstuffed into flimsy #10 envelopes that burst at the corners. It arrived as a wad of Scotch tape, or held together by string, handwritten in red pen, *i*'s dotted with little hearts.

"I said, what do you think of that, Morgan? Sound okay?" Whittaker eyed him, clearly annoyed.

"Uh...that might be okay," Morgan said. He hadn't heard a word. He was too busy picturing a group of beret-clad amateur poets being run down by a team of Clydesdales.

The old man shifted in his seat, glowered at Whittaker, spoke for the first time. "Is this guy on the dope? Don't saddle me with no dopehead." His voice strained like an old sedan trying to crank. A deep Northeastern accent. New York? Philadelphia? Morgan had no idea, but the old man wasn't an Okie, that was for sure.

"You can count on Morgan, Mr. Jones. He's rock solid." Whittaker shot a look at Morgan that said *or else*.

"That's right," Morgan said. "I was just deep in thought, trying to figure the best way to approach the project."

Fred Jones stood, joints creaking. "It ain't goddamn rocket science." He made for the door.

Whittaker and Morgan stood as well. Morgan opened the door for Jones.

Whittaker said, "Morgan and I will work out the details, Mr. Jones."

"Don't take forever," Jones said without turning. "I'm only getting older." And he was gone, shuffling out of the office and down the hall, an old man a lot bigger than his bones.

"For Christ's sake, Morgan, you could show a little interest." Whittaker flopped back heavy in his chair.

"I'm interested," Morgan said. *What the hell did I agree to?*

"Jones doesn't think so. You better act fascinated as hell when you see him again. It's not like folks walk in and hand the department a big fat check all the time."

Morgan wondered why he was going to see Jones again. He couldn't ask. Whittaker would know he hadn't been listening. "So how do you suggest going about, uh, the project?"

"The hell if I know. Just keep him happy. Maybe the old buzzard will put us in his will. Don't you have a class?"

Morgan looked at his watch. He did have a class. It had started three minutes ago.

Outside the dean's office he saw Ginny the reporter coming for him with her hand raised. Fortunately, the department was crowded with undergrads trying to get their schedules changed before the end of the drop/add period. Morgan ducked into the flow of students, pretended not to see Ginny as he scooted down the hall. He didn't quite run. But he walked very, very fast.

"DelPrego." Morgan looked up from the roll sheet, saw a bored youth in a T-shirt and jeans lift his hand. Hair shaggy and over his neck, dishwater strands falling over his eyes.

He went through eight grad students like that, all dripping attitude. One actually wore an ascot. A goddamn ascot! What the hell was that kid's name? He scanned the roll. Timothy Lancaster III. Christ. Morgan made a mental note to humiliate and demean the kid soon.

He called the last name on the list. "Annie Walsh."

Morgan marked her absent, then asked the class, "Has anyone...uh...seen Annie Walsh?" *Good one, Jay. Nobody suspects a thing.*

"She wasn't in my eight o'clock class." The kid in the white T-shirt. DelPrego.

The Lancaster kid cleared his throat. "It's been my experience that Annie Walsh has some sort of allergic reaction to early-morning classes."

Morgan wondered if the girl was still home in his bed. He supposed she might have a whale of a hangover.

Morgan pulled Lancaster's poem from the bottom of the pile. "Okay, let's start with you, Timmy."

"Timothy, sir."

"Eh? What?"

"I prefer Timothy to Timmy."

The DelPrego kid snickered.

Morgan's predatory smile didn't touch his eyes. "Your poem's called..." He squinted at his copy. "What is it?"

" 'The Fallible Quiescence of a Wrathful Jehovah.' "

"Uh-huh."

"It's about the disparity between free will and—"

"What's this about in line seven?" Morgan asked. "Fuzzy nut sacks..."

Lancaster's lips moved as he counted lines. "Nut soldiers. It concerns—"

"What the hell are you talking about?"

DelPrego squirmed in his seat, bit his bottom lip. He couldn't stand it.

Lancaster had a little sheen of sweat on his forehead. "I use *rodentia* to symbolize the lower societal strata—"

"Squirrels?"

Lancaster said, "It's really a metaphor for a much broader—"

"It's squirrels, isn't it?" Morgan said.

"Yes, sir, but—"

"Your poem's about squirrels, Timmy."

DelPrego's face had purpled, his shoulders shaking with barely controlled laughter. He stuck the heel of his hand in his mouth to stifle himself. Others in the class giggled openly.

Morgan sifted the pile of poems, moved DelPrego's to the top.

two

Harold Jenks was one tough nigger, and everybody knew it. You had to be tough to work for Red Zach.

Jenks liked to call himself the King of East St. Louis, but that was sort of a joke too many of the neighborhood folks took seriously. More accurately, he was king of about seven square blocks between the bus station and the Missouri State Welfare Offices. But everyone knew Jenks was Red Zach's boy. That made Jenks important.

Jenks and Spoon Oliver hung out in the alley near the bus station. They sipped beer and smoked and waited for something to happen. It was after midnight. When you worked for Red Zach, you didn't keep regular hours.

Jenks's boy Spoon nudged Jenks in the ribs and pointed down the alley. "Check it out."

Some nigger coming down the alley, carrying big suitcases. Jenks watched a minute, puffed his cheap cigar, a Philly Blunt he bought at the convenience store along with a sixteen-ounce can of Bud Light in a little paper sack.

"So what?" Jenks drank his beer.

"Toll," Spoon said.

Jenks shrugged. "Shit."

"I say we toll him. This our alley or ain't it?"

"We ain't charged toll since we was sixteen," Jenks said. "We work for Zach now."

"I'm cash short," Spoon said. "I say we do it."

Jenks sighed, tossed down the cigar stub, and stamped it out. "Okay, but don't go all crazy."

Jenks backed up behind the Dumpster, gave the "stay down" motion to his partner Spoon on the other side of the alley. *Let that nigger get closer, then we jack his ass good. Only I got to keep an eye on Spoon. He's over the edge lately.* Jenks suspected his boy had developed a coke twitch, dipping into the merchandise.

When the victim got between them, Jenks and Oliver leapt. Poor nigger dropped the bags and tried to run, but Jenks had a fistful of his jacket, and Oliver tackled his legs. They all went down in a pile.

Jenks saw the kid was about his age, maybe twenty-two. He yelled, but Jenks twisted, got on top of him. He punched down hard across his face, twice. A third time broke the kid's lip open, and dark blood smeared down his chin. Jenks let up when he saw the blood.

Oliver stuck a knife to the sucker's throat. "Give it up, boy."

"Let me go," the kid said. "Take the bags. I got money. Take it."

"Shut up." Jenks gut-punched the kid. He pulled the wallet out of the kid's jacket, counted the bills. "Eighty fucking greenbacks. Shit."

He pulled the kid up by the shirt. "All you got is eighty fucking dollars, motherfucker. Shit. Not even worth jacking your ass."

"Please—"

"Shut up, nigger."

"Aw, shit," Spoon said. "We got to kill this boy."

"Please, no, I—"

"I said shut your cunt mouth." Jenks rapped him on the nose.

"I know this boy," Spoon said.

Jenks shook the boy by the shirt. "You know us?"

The boy nodded.

"Who's that?" Harold pointed at Spoon.

"Spoon Oliver."

"Shit," Jenks said. "Who am I?"

"Harold Jenks."

"Who are you?"

"Sherman Ellis."

"He live three blocks over," Spoon said. "Pappy in prison. Momma died of the cancer last year."

"You gonna die now, Sherman Ellis."

"I won't say anything. I promise." He was shaking. Tears.

"Can't take that chance," Jenks said. "Nobody to cry for you anyway. All alone in the world. Say good night." This always scared them good. Jenks had even seen a few motherfuckers piss themselves.

"W-wait," pleaded Sherman. "I'm leaving. What if I promise I'm never c-coming back. Never returning to Missouri. That would be okay, wouldn't it?"

"Shit," Spoon said. "A motherfucker about to die will say any shit."

"It's t-true," Sherman said. "I've got a scholarship to Eastern Oklahoma. Grad school."

"Bullshit."

"The letter's in my pocket," Sherman said.

Jenks pulled the letter out of Sherman's coat pocket. It had been folded into quarters. He opened it and read by the dim light of the streetlamp.

"You gonna be a *poet*?" Jenks couldn't believe it. Of all the fucked-up things.

"Please." Sherman's face contorted with anxiety. "I've worked hard. Straight A's in high school. I worked two jobs to get through Truman State. Please, brother. Not like this."

As Sherman talked, Jenks felt himself deflate. He let go of the kid's shirt. This nigger was on his way out. On his way to something better. He and Spoon always said that shit about killing. Kept the suckers scared. Make them keep their mouths shut. Hell, maybe they should let the kid go, give him his damn eighty dollars back. Maybe just this once—

Spoon moved forward, stuck the knife into Sherman's chest, slammed it down to the hilt.

"Goddamn!" Jenks fell back.

"Motherfucker," Spoon yelled.

Sherman twitched, clawed at the knife still in his chest, arched his back, eyes open to the night sky. He worked his mouth, no words. A trickle of blood welled up over his lips, stained his teeth red.

"Nigger thinks he can give us that *brother* shit," Spoon said. "Who the fuck he think he is? He think he better than us. Fucking scholarship motherfucker."

A long, strained breath leaked out of Sherman, and he went slack. Steam floating up from his open mouth, drifting out of the alley like a soul.

"Damn." Jenks stood, looked down at the body, and shook his head.

Spoon grabbed Sherman's bags. "Come on, Harold. Let's go."

Spoon jogged to the end of the alley where his Eldorado was parked.

Jenks stood a moment looking at Sherman, then followed Spoon. They put the bags in the trunk, then climbed in the front seat. Spoon started the engine, and they drove away slow without the lights on.

After three blocks, Spoon turned onto the big four-lane and switched on the lights. "I'm going to Wendy's. You want something?"

"No." Jenks still had Sherman's wallet. He flipped it open, looked at Sherman's picture. He and Jenks were both very dark, same hair, same long nose and square chin. He was only a year older than Sherman. There was a Greyhound ticket folded into the wallet. Sherman had been on his way to the bus station. "Nigger was gonna be a poet." He hadn't meant to say it out loud.

"Fuck that," Spoon said. "My cousin Jimmy busts rhymes at the Starlight Lounge Thursday nights. Don't need no bullshit college for that. You sure you don't want a Frosty or something?" He turned into the Wendy's drive-thru.

Jenks put the wallet in his own pocket.

"You crazy?" Spoon asked. "Toss that out."

"I got an idea." The way Jenks said it frightened Spoon.

"Now hold on, Harold," Spoon said. "You know that ain't smart, keeping something like that. Cops hang a murder on you."

"Nigger, I said I got an idea."

And Spoon shut up. He ordered a triple with fries and shut his mouth.

three

Professor Morgan dismissed the class, stepped foot into the hall, and immediately saw Ginny the cub reporter waiting for him at the other end. She lifted her hand to wave, and Morgan turned, fast-walked around the opposite corner. He could hear her *cloppity* footfalls on the tile behind him.

Morgan zigzagged a labyrinth of office corridors, past a heretofore unseen set of rest rooms, a water fountain, some kind of tutoring room.

Where the hell am I?

The sound of Ginny's blocky shoes pursued, dogged, relentless.

Hath thou slain the jabberwock? Morgan scrambled. Looked side to side.

A stairwell.

He darted up and around, into the dark, dusty reaches of the third floor. The door was nailed shut, but the stairs kept going. Dry, wooden, creaking with each step.

He climbed.

A fourth floor. A fifth.

How many floors does this goddamn building have?

Morgan shoved open the fifth-floor door and found himself in a dim hall, murky with yellow light. Faded rectangles still remained where nameplates had been pried from office doors. He walked the hall, stale and silent like a ghost town. He stopped, cocked his ear down a cross hall. Listened.

What was that? He strained to hear. Music. He walked toward it. A smell. Sickly sweet.

He recognized the album now. *Bad Luck Streak in Dancing School* by Warren Zevon.

Who in God's name is up here? This floor had obviously been abandoned, light fixtures empty, no blinds on the windows, dust.

Morgan glanced behind him. He'd shaken off Ginny. He could find another stairway down and go home if he wanted to, or find his own office and hide. But the smell and the music drew him on, the nagging tickle of curiosity.

He turned down a long hall. The music came from a door at the far end, and the smell grew stronger as Morgan approached. Yellowing pages had been taped to the door: news articles, poems, *Far Side* and *Bloom County* cartoons. Also a class schedule and office hours for fall semester 1983.

Morgan lifted his fist to knock, stopped, tried the knob. It turned. He very slowly pushed open the door and went in.

The office was long and dark, the music loud. The room was thick with smoke. Bookshelves lined with assorted tomes from floor to ceiling. Near the window sat a large brown globe of the world like it had fallen there from orbit, more books stacked around it like the edges of an impact crater.

A black-and-white poster of Freud on the wall. Some wag had drawn a penis head at the tip of his cigar with a red Magic Marker.

Morgan waved at the smoke, coughed. This smoke seemed familiar. He inhaled deeply, tried to remember.

Ganja.

The music stopped abruptly, and a voice from the dark recesses of the office said, "Close the damn door."

Morgan jumped. "What?"

"You're letting the smoke out."

Morgan shut the door behind him, peered into the haze. "Who is that?"

Slowly, as if from a long way off, from the other side of a Scottish moor, a reedy, bearded man, round spectacles, pointed frame draped in threadbare tweed, emerged from the smoke like he was walking out of an Arthur Conan Doyle mystery.

In his gnarled hands he held a bong the size of a clarinet.

The old man exhaled as he spoke, eyes narrowed to dreamy slits. "I'm Professor Valentine."

Morgan's jaw dropped. "Valentine? *Tad* Valentine?"

"The same."

"I thought you'd gone on sabbatical." Valentine was the professor Morgan had been hired to replace for a year, but it was Morgan's understanding the old Pulitzer Prize–winning poet had rented a studio in Prague. It seemed unlikely to find the man smoking weed from a giant bong in a remote office on an abandoned floor of Albatross Hall.

Perhaps this wasn't Valentine. Maybe it was an old derelict junkie who'd wandered in from the cold. Morgan could think of no tactful way to ask.

"Please, please. Have a seat," Valentine said. "Make yourself at home. I haven't had visitors since . . . well, I don't suppose I've ever had any. Not since moving up here."

Morgan cast about the room. No chairs. He remained standing, hands folded demurely in front of him. "Uh . . ."

"Want a hit?" Valentine offered him the bong.

"Oh . . . uh . . ."

"You're not a cop, are you?" Valentine pinned Morgan with wild eyes.

"No, no, I . . . Um . . ."

Valentine frowned. "Is there something wrong with you?"

"I'm Jay Morgan."

"Well, that's hardly your fault, is it?" Valentine mouthed the bong like he was in love.

"No," Morgan said. "I mean, I'm the one-year-contract professor teaching your classes. Why aren't you in Prague?"

"Ah, Prague." Hazy nostalgia washed over Valentine. His eyes narrowed to slits, and he looked off into the dreamy distance. "Yes, I had a glorious few months there, and this wonderful studio apartment overlooking the Charles Bridge." He shrugged. "I got kicked out."

"Out of the apartment?"

"Out of the Czech Republic," Valentine said. "Some leftover Iron Curtain nonsense. All ancient history really, but these chaps evidently have a long memory."

"Does anyone know you're here?" Morgan asked. "Whittaker never mentioned you'd returned." Morgan worried he was out of a job. Would the old poet want his graduate workshop back?

Valentine lunged forward, took Morgan's elbow into his bony fist, maneuvered Morgan into the smoke. The spindly professor's grip was iron.

"Now listen, old sport," Valentine said. "I'd really appreciate it if you could keep my presence here on the hush-hush side. Understand?"

"No."

They arrived at a low leather couch, and Valentine dropped Morgan at one end. Valentine perched down at the other. "It's just that I am still officially on sabbatical." He sucked long on the bong. "I need rest. I couldn't stomach a mob of ghastly students and their dreadful writing."

"I understand."

"Do you?" Valentine leaned forward, squeaking the sofa leather. Shaggy brows knotted with stress. "I can't write anymore, Bill. My head is cluttered with student writing. Insipid, cliché, rhyming excrement."

"My name's not Bill."

Valentine didn't hear. "I sit down at my desk and nothing comes out. My pen is an impotent noodle."

Morgan nodded, sunk into the vast, deep swallowing womb of the leather sofa. He'd just been making the same complaints. His mind drifted. If he'd had a chance to take a year off and write in Prague, he damn well would have made good use of it. He day-dreamed himself to cobblestone streets. Perhaps the ganja smoke had gotten the better of him.

"I won't tell anyone," he told Valentine.

Valentine grinned, eyes brightening. He patted Morgan on the knee. "That's a good fellow, Bill. I appreciate it. I really do. Let's smoke on it, eh? Seal the deal."

"I'd prefer a beer," Morgan said, more a wish than an actual request.

"Certainly." Valentine waved his hand like he was casting a spell. "In the refrigerator behind the desk."

four

Harold Jenks crouched on the fifth-floor fire escape of the abandoned building and smoked a Philly Blunt with one hand, the other hand in the warm front pocket of his Cardinals sweatshirt. He scanned the alley below. He puffed quick and nervous, watched the smoke spiral away on the cold wind.

He was always nervous picking up a delivery from Red Zach. Anything could happen. Only two years ago, the cops had shot Jenks's cousin in a drop just like this. Those undercover fuckers could be anywhere—on the roof, in the old buildings, disguised as homeless drunks sleeping in a Dumpster. Anywhere.

Sherman Ellis's wallet still hung heavy in Jenks's back pocket. Jenks sighed out a long, gray stream of smoke. He hadn't wanted Spoon to kill that boy. His heart hadn't been in it. Hadn't been in a lot of things for a while now. If Spoon hadn't been there . . .

Jenks had told Spoon his wild idea, but in a flash of sanity, Jenks figured it just wouldn't work. Spoon told him he was crazy and should throw the wallet out. If he did this thing—if he was crazy enough—he'd keep it under wraps. He would tell no one. Jenks would simply slip off quiet into the night. He made Spoon swear to keep it secret.

A flutter of noise off to his right. Jenks jerked, his free hand going to the Glock at the small of his back. But it was only pigeons. Damn sky rats sawing on Jenks's nerves.

He smoked the Blunt down to the end, flicked the glowing butt into the alley.

Then he saw Red Zach's white limousine enter the alley. It approached slowly, parked under Jenks's fire escape. Five men got out. Four big motherfuckers, hands deep in the pockets of expensive overcoats, stone faces, sunglasses. They spread out and kept watch.

Red Zach craned his neck, looked up at Jenks. Jenks waved. Red Zach climbed the fire escape. Jenks watched him come. Zach carried a small canvas gym bag.

Red Zach had hair the color of a fire engine. Not natural, of course. Zach was a broad-shouldered, light-skinned black man with a pencil-thin beard also dyed red. He had sharp features, a pointed nose. Story around was Zach had some white blood in him somehow.

Jenks heard Zach clanging halfway up. Red Zach wore an impressive collection of gold chains and bracelets, a brown pin-striped suit that cost more money than Jenks saw in a month.

By the time Zach reached the fifth floor he was huffing and puffing pretty good.

"You know I'd climb down," Jenks said.

"Better up here," Zach said. "We can see if the cops come in either side of the alley and have plenty of time to dump the stuff. Besides"—Zach grinned big, capped teeth, white—"I need the exercise once in a while." He patted the beginnings of a slight paunch under his suit.

Zach opened the gym back and showed Jenks the contents. It was full of little clear Baggies of white powder, prepackaged for street distribution. Jenks's job was to ferry the stuff to the bartenders and hairdressers and street pushers who distributed the stuff in his area. Jenks knew he was looking at a hundred thousand dollars' worth of junk.

"Here you go, Harold." Zach handed over the bag. "You know what to do with it."

"Right."

"You okay?"

"I'm good."

"You don't seem like yourself," Zach said. "You down? Got some kind of woman trouble?" He nudged Jenks, laughed.

"I'm just tired."

"Uh-huh. Where's your boy Spoon today?"

"I didn't bring him."

"Shit, I know that. That's why I asked where he is."

"Went to see his sister and her kids. Going to eat Chinese with them."

Zach leaned on the rail, looked down into the alley, then out across St. Louis. "You know I been keeping an eye on you, Harold. You're doing good work, and I've noticed that. I need loyal men on my team. You keep clearheaded and put in your time, and I'll do right by you. You know what I'm saying?"

"I know."

"I could send one of my boys up the ladder with the stuff if I wanted, but I come up here to talk to you personal. I'm bringing you along. You hear what I'm saying?"

"I hear you." Jenks looked up at the gangster. "You know I appreciate it, Red."

Zach nodded, squeezed Jenks's shoulder. "Okay. You stay cool and I'll check you later."

Red Zach climbed back down the ladder. Jenks watched him get back into the limo with his boys. Jenks lit another Blunt, inhaled long and slow, watched the limo glide quiet out of the alley like smoke on the wind.

Back at Jenks's shabby apartment, he threw the gym bag on the bed, looked at it for a long time.

For two years he'd been Red Zach's boy. He knew Red was right. If he stayed tight, he'd eventually have a fine ride, a Caddy or a BMW. He'd have fine clothes, bitches that did whatever he said simply because he was Red's boy.

But Jenks kept seeing Ellis's eyes when Spoon had stabbed him. In one angry motion, Spoon had taken away everything the boy was, everything he'd worked for. And Jenks was to blame too. He'd been there.

Jenks pulled his big army surplus duffel bag out from under the bed. He packed his clothes, packed everything he valued, and threw away the rest.

And he took Red Zach's gym bag too.

Red Zach sat in the back of his limo, mute goons on either side of him. The limo cruised the decay of East St. Louis's side streets. He had more stops to make. A big day of pimping and gangstering.

He pulled out the latest copy of *Esquire* from between the seat cushions. There was a clothing advertisement which featured a square-jawed black man in denim. Stonewashed. Snakeskin boots. The jacket matched the jeans, and the black man had one leg up on some rocks, a mountain view in the background with an SUV off to the side. Zach couldn't decide if the man in denim looked rugged or like a fag.

He thought about elbowing one of his goons, showing him the ad and asking what he thought. Never mind. It was no good talking to these guys. They didn't do talk. And Zach couldn't risk his image anyway. These boneheads expected him to strut around in ridiculous outfits and spit out homeboy talk. Fine. He'd put on the act for the troops. Whatever.

But Zach didn't bust his hump to clear a high six figures a year just to waste away in the hood. He had reservations in Aspen. He wanted to catch *Don Giovanni* before the season ended. He'd recently become a gold-level member of the St. Louis Art Museum and there was a cocktail reception at the end of the month.

He *needed* some new clothes.

And some new acquaintances. He was surrounded by troops and his crew, but not pals. These leg-breaking motherfuckers were useful, but not good company.

Harold Jenks was a little different. That boy had something. A quality. But Zach noticed something was off. Jenks had something on his mind. And when a brother didn't have his mind right, things could go bad.

five

Three beers later, and Morgan left Valentine's office, drifted back down to the inhabited floors of Albatross Hall. No sign of Ginny.

Morgan felt woozy. Beer on an empty stomach, and he still wasn't in top shape from the night before. He needed to go home, get a bite to eat. He needed to shower again after the cloying experience of Valentine's smoke-filled office.

On the way out of the building he heard Ginny's high, clear voice chasing after him. "Professor Morgan!"

He ran to the parking lot, started his car, and almost smacked a coed while backing out of his space. In his rearview mirror, he saw Ginny fumble with car keys, gallop toward a half-rusted, silver Toyota. Morgan gunned the Buick, squealed the tires, and scraped pavement on his way out of the parking lot.

He tangled himself in traffic on Garth Brooks Boulevard but thought he could still see her a dozen cars back. He yanked the Buick down a side street, found himself in a maze of student slums. He came out on Old Highway 12 and made the long, slow curve back to the house he rented. Morgan kept an eye in the rearview mirror, lips curving smug and satisfied when he didn't see Ginny's car.

Not today, junior newshound.

Morgan shuffled back into his little house. Not even 11 A.M. and he was beat, a little nauseous, skin slick with alcohol sweat. He'd begun the semester recklessly, unprepared. He didn't even have syllabi finished for his two undergrad classes.

Sleep. He'd sleep away the rest of the day and start fresh tomorrow. And exercise. Sit-ups. He'd start doing sit-ups. He was a wreck.

"You look like shit, Doc."

Morgan leapt back against the door, yelped, a high-pitched bleat like a puppy or a little girl.

"Take it easy, Doc." It was Fred Jones. He perched like a ghost in the shadowy corner of Morgan's living room, a bony apparition in a billowy sweater, sitting in a wooden rocker but not rocking.

"You can't just barge into a guy's house," Morgan said.

"Whittaker sprang the deal on you," said Jones. "I understand that. You wasn't ready, so I figured I'd come talk to you one-on-one."

Morgan had almost forgotten. He'd agreed to participate in something and wasn't sure what it was. Still, Whittaker might have wanted him to humor the old fart, but if he couldn't escape this shit in his own home, well, something would have to be done. First thing was to toss this old bag of sticks out on his ear. He started to tell the old man to take a hike when the giant walked in from the kitchen.

"Hey, boss, you want a beer? Imported." He was six and a half feet easy, shoulders carved of granite. His blue-stubbled chin was an anvil. Sleepy eyes. He chewed slowly, half a sandwich still in his fist. Morgan reconsidered his plan. Maybe he should politely ask what he could do for these fellows.

Jones craned his neck, looked up at the bruiser. "You know my doctor said to lay off, meathead."

Assorted protests tumbled in Morgan's brain. The one that came out was "That's my beer."

"Your cheese went bad," the giant said. He looked mournfully at the rest of the sandwich, then finished it in one bite.

"I can't digest dairy," Jones said. He handed Morgan a manila folder filled with loose paper. Thick. "How long to look at those?"

The folder was heavy. Morgan opened it. Poetry. Tons of it. Handwritten in feeble, shaky scrawl. "What the hell am I supposed to do with this?" He felt hungover—sick and confused. His stomach boiled. Head swimming.

Those beers in my stomach. I need food. The thought of the bad cheese put him off. He rubbed the bridge of his nose.

Jones leaned forward, frowned, put his gray hands on his knobby knees. "Dammit, man, are you on the dope? You can't seem to focus on what we're doing here. I'm getting impatient." He pulled a handkerchief out of his shirt pocket, shook it open, and blew his nose. "By the way, you got a dead girl in your bedroom."

"What?" Morgan felt hot in the face. His ears buzzed. He took halting steps toward his bedroom.

"Hey, Doc." It was the giant.

"I'm not a doctor. I have an MFA from Bowling Green." He was trying to think.

"I just wanted to tell you—"

"Don't tell me anything. Just shut up a second." He felt dizzy, blood pumping in his ears, mouth pasty. Did he just tell that hulk to shut up? What had happened to the girl? Annie. Was she . . . ?

"What's the matter with you?" asked the old man.

Had Morgan done something to her? No, some kind of misunderstanding. But he couldn't feel his legs. Head . . . spinning . . .

The giant said, "I just thought you'd want to know that there's this chubby girl looking in your front window."

Morgan turned. Ginny Conrad had a hand cupped against the glass, trying to see into the dim living room.

The room tilted. Morgan's mouth fell open, his jaw working but nothing coming out.

Darkness.

six

Morgan blinked, moaned, belched acid. His eyes focused on the giant kneeling over him.

"You fainted."

"I didn't faint," Morgan said. "I'm not feeling well."

"You look like you're gonna barf."

"Look, Mr.— Who are you?"

"Bob Smith."

Morgan sat up. "Where's Fred Jones? I want to know— Wait a fucking minute. Fred Jones and Bob Smith?"

"The boss went to get help. He says we got to smooth over some of your problems for you."

You are one of my problems.

Morgan swallowed another belch, rubbed his head. "The dead girl."

"And the live one." Bob jerked a thumb over his shoulder at the rocking chair in the corner.

Ginny sat forward. "Professor Morgan, will you please tell this enormous wad of muscles that I know you?" Her chin was out, defiant. It was a good act. Morgan could hear the little tremor in her voice.

"For Christ's sake," Morgan said. "She's a reporter for the university paper."

"I know," Bob said. "We searched her." He looked at her, eyes narrowed. "She threw her shoes at me."

"They took my notepad and my tape recorder," Ginny said.

Morgan climbed to his feet, swayed a little, then headed for the bedroom. "Back in a minute."

Ginny made a little disgusted noise. "Professor, what's going on? This guy won't let me leave."

"Just shut up a minute, okay?"

He kept his eyes averted from the girl in his bed and went to the bathroom. He splashed water in his face, leaned on the sink.

He went back out and looked at Annie. Eyes closed, lips slightly apart. She could have been sleeping. Somebody's child gently napping. Perhaps it had been a mistake. Maybe she was fine, and Morgan moved toward her as he thought this, hand outstretched to touch her cheek. If she was warm . . .

But he jerked his hand back. If she was cold, he wouldn't be able to stand it. It would break him. He'd lose it. Had she still been alive earlier or not? Had she been dead when they were under the covers together?

He went back in the bathroom, closed the door, and sat on the toilet.

What in holy hell was he going to do? After that business with the provost's daughter at UNLV two years ago, Morgan was lucky to be working at all. Another disgrace might relegate him to a community college in backwoods Mississippi for the rest of his career. He hadn't published a collection in seven years. He hadn't published a single poem in two. All he could do was teach. The thought of a nine-to-five job in some Dilbert office twisted his stomach again. A dead coed would seal his fate.

A knock on the bathroom door startled Morgan. "Yes?"

The old man pushed his way in, frowned down at Morgan like he was looking at a dumb little kid. He handed Morgan an empty pill bottle. "Found this on her side of the bed. Looks like she couldn't handle her shit. You give this to her?"

"Of course not."

She'd overdosed. Pills on top of the alcohol. Crazy. But the more Morgan thought about it, the more he wondered. He did feel pretty goddamn awful. Had she slipped him something? Last night was hazy at best, especially toward the end when they closed down the pool hall across from campus. Stix, it was called.

Oh, hell, if somebody saw me with her . . .

"Come on," Jones said. "I've got some plastic. Let's get her out of here."

Morgan followed him into the bedroom.

Giant Bob turned Annie on her side, a big roll of clear plastic over his shoulder. It was an awkward arrangement. Annie's arms flopped.

Ginny stood off to the side, eyes big, watching them wrap Annie in the plastic. "Oh my God."

"What's she doing in here?" Morgan's voice had climbed two octaves. Almighty God, Morgan realized, was finally getting him. An old man with reams of tattered poetry. A fearless reporter ready to expose his scandals. Plagues upon Egypt.

"We'll handle that later," Jones murmured in his ear.

Bob wrapped Annie in the plastic, sealed her up with duct tape.

Ginny stood near the chair, hands clasped in front of her. "Why do you need the plastic?" Curiosity fighting anxiety.

"Routine," Bob said.

"Would you shut up," Jones said. "This ain't routine. We've never done this before."

"Right, boss."

Jones nudged Morgan with a pointy elbow. "Get her feet."

"What?"

"I can't carry her with my back. Grab the feet."

Morgan took Annie by her plastic-bound ankles, Bob at the other end. Morgan's breathing went shallow. The girl was heavy. They made sure nobody was looking, then quick-walked her out to the trunk of an old Plymouth Fury. Jones explained that they'd swiped a car specifically for this errand.

Morgan turned green as he listened. Sweat on his forehead.

"There's two shovels in the backseat," Jones said. "There's a peach orchard six miles south of town. Take the dirt road and bury her in the middle."

Morgan choked. "Me?"

"For chrissakes, Doc, I can't be involved," Jones said. "I'm in a very delicate situation. Besides, she's your dead girl, not mine."

"But—"

"You'd think you'd be grateful I was fixing this up for you."

"But—"

"Make sure you ditch the car someplace out of the way when you're done."

"But—"

"And don't worry." Jones jerked a thumb at Ginny, who watched from Morgan's porch. "We'll take care of the kid." He made a trigger-pulling motion with his finger.

"No!" Morgan's eyes bulged. "Let me worry about her."

"Want to do it yourself, huh? Sure, put her in the same hole as the other one." Jones slipped something cold and hard into Morgan's hand.

Morgan looked. A little blue-metal revolver with a stubby barrel. "What the fuck's this?" He'd wanted to sound tough and outraged, but it came out like a squeak.

"It's a .38. You said you'd handle her."

"Right." Now wasn't the time to argue. He'd take Ginny with him and figure what to do with her later. But he wasn't going to shoot her.

Maybe himself, but not her.

Morgan waved Ginny into the Plymouth. He took the keys from Jones and climbed behind the wheel. The car's interior reeked of stale cigarettes, and he told Ginny to roll down the window. The cold wind steadied him.

They were a mile from the peach orchard when Ginny spoke.

"They wouldn't give me back my tape recorder, but I have my notepad."

"This will not be a newspaper story," Morgan said. "You must know you can't say anything about this to anyone ever." And how do you shut up a chatty undergrad newspaper reporter? The old man's revolver nudged cold against his thigh in his front pocket.

"I know. It wasn't your fault, right? I mean, you'd be fucking ruined if they found out. I mean, with a student and everything. Not that *I* find it offensive, but a lot of the establishment types like to maintain this artificial hierarchy."

"Right."

"Besides, I figure if I help you, you might be able to help me, right?"

"Maybe."

"I asked for this assignment specifically because I wanted to speak to you," Ginny said. "What I really want to be is a novelist."

Maybe Morgan would shoot her after all.

He turned the Plymouth into the peach orchard. The narrow road petered out, and he found himself zigzagging among the trees. He parked in an arbitrary spot. He and Ginny took the shovels and started digging.

Morgan began sweating again, rings under his armpits, stomach queasy. His hands ached with the cold, fingers rubbing raw on the shovel's handle. He hadn't done anything this physical in a long time. He stopped digging, leaned on the shovel. His chest heaved, short breaths puffing out like fog. "Okay, good enough."

"That's way too shallow," Ginny said.

"It's fine."

"I'm telling you it needs to be deeper. One good rain and up she comes. All that topsoil will wash right downhill."

Morgan sighed. He looked at the shovel, back at the hole. They kept digging.

When Ginny was satisfied, they muscled Annie out of the trunk and dropped her facedown into the hole. Morgan thought she looked unreal in the plastic, a dime-store mannequin. He could still fish her out of the hole, unwrap her. He wasn't too far into this yet. He could explain. Take her to the police or a hospital.

But there would be questions. What had happened? Who had she been with and where? Morgan leaned on his shovel, eyes unfocused with thought.

Ginny grabbed a shovel and started scooping in dirt.

And it was as if his hands lifted the shovel on their own, scooped the dirt. It was the heaviest thing in the world. He tossed in the dirt, and it landed on Annie's back. The second scoop was easier, then a third, his problem returning to the earth. He wondered how long it would take him to forget he'd done this thing, that he'd crossed some line from which there would be no return.

Soon there was only the moist mound of fresh soil. Ginny flattened it down hard with the bottom of her shovel. Steam came off her.

Morgan thought about Ginny. Jones had made it clear what he wanted done, but Morgan had no intention of killing the girl. But she was a time bomb. Morgan's hand slipped into his pocket, fist closing over the revolver's handle.

Ginny turned, saw him watching her. "What is it?"

"Just thinking." He let go of the gun, put his hands on his hips.

She searched his eyes, moved toward him. "I'm not going to say anything."

"I know."

She stood very close to Morgan, her erect nipples brushing his belly. "I want you to believe me."

"I believe you."

Ginny shrugged, lowered her eyes. "Maybe we can seal the deal. Some kind of show of trust."

She unzipped his pants and reached in for him. He stiffened, and she stroked him, the cold air washing over his groin.

Morgan cleared his throat. "I think we can work something out."

Her hands were very soft, her mouth warm.

seven

Harold Jenks got off the bus, took one look around, and said, "Fuck this."

What the hell was he doing in this one-horse, Okie shithole? He stood with his duffel over his shoulder, took another look up and down University Boulevard hoping it would seem better this time.

It didn't.

Pickup trucks, flannel shirts, and feed caps. Redneck city. No place for a brother like Harold Jenks. He pulled his coat tighter around him. What was it, twenty degrees? Colder? Fumbee, Oklahoma, was the asshole of the planet.

Maybe Spoon was right. Maybe his plan was insane in the head, and Jenks was just asking for an assload of trouble.

Fuck that. Jenks could pull it off. Nobody else would dare.

Jenks crossed the street to the campus. He pulled a folded wad of paper out of his back pocket and read until he saw what he needed. The administration building.

He stopped a slender white girl with blond hair in the court-yard, asked her which way to Administration. She was polite, but took a step back, eyes wary. *Like you never seen a black man before.* She pointed down the sidewalk to a gray, domed building.

"Thanks," Jenks said.

The girl frowned and walked away fast.

At the main administration desk, Jenks was shuffled to the registrar. The gray-faced bureaucrat in that registrar's office said that since he was a week late for classes, his schedule had been forwarded to the English Department.

"Where's that?" Jenks asked.

The lady sighed, dramatic, shoulders slumped. She handed Jenks a folded map. "Albatross Hall," she said. "Building 41 on the map."

"Thanks." *Bitch.*

He found Albatross Hall and ducked inside, stood a moment in the entrance letting himself get warm. A sign on the wall said ENGLISH DEPARTMENT and pointed him left. He followed the arrow.

The English Department office was barren of life. Jenks stood in front of the outer desk and waited in case a secretary or some-one official happened along. Nobody did. He shuffled loudly, dropped his duffel bag with a heavy *whuff.* Nobody heard. He looked for a bell to ring, or a sign-in sheet or anything. He didn't have a clue.

Just left of the front desk was a door marked WHITTAKER. It also said ENGLISH DEPARTMENT CHAIR and was slightly ajar. He pushed it open, looked in.

A big white guy with a heavy black beard stood wearing a woman's hat and looking at himself in a hand mirror.

"Aw shit." Jenks stared, scratched his head.

Whittaker glanced over his shoulder. "Who is it? Can I do something for you?" As he spoke, he turned back to the mirror, cocked the hat at a jaunty angle on his head.

"I'm—" He almost said he was Harold Jenks. "I'm Sherman Ellis."

Whittaker put down the mirror, went to his desk, and began leafing through a stack of papers. "Ellis, Ellis, that name sounds familiar."

"I'm supposed to be paid for," Jenks said. "My school is free."

"Yes." Whittaker pulled a list from the stack. "Sherman Ellis. You have a graduate assistantship in the tutoring lab. You're a week late."

Jenks didn't say anything.

"We thought maybe you'd forfeited the assistantship. We almost assigned it to someone else. The waiting list is pretty long."

"What about the free schooling?"

Whittaker frowned, cleared his throat. "That's what I'm saying."

"And a place to stay," Jenks said.

"You'll have to take that up with graduate housing. Their wait-list is even longer. Might be a problem."

"Hey, man. I got it right here I'm supposed to have a place to stay. For free." He shook the letter in the air, one of the documents he'd taken off of Ellis. He'd get all up in this guy's business about his rights and shit.

The gun in his coat pocket hung heavy. A .32 revolver with a short barrel, the serial number filed off. Spoon had given it to him, told him the little heater would be easy to hide when he was on campus. The Glock was in the duffel. Harold Jenks wasn't planning on letting any of these white college motherfuckers get over on him.

Whittaker's face hardened. "Nobody's going to take away your entitlement, Mr. Ellis." He said it through gritted teeth.

"I'll get a lawyer." But Jenks took a half step back. The guy was big, lady's hat or not, and Jenks saw he was getting mad. Jenks's hand dug into his coat pocket, closed over the butt of the pistol. He didn't like the way the dude's face twitched when he said *entitlement*.

"Here." Whittaker handed Jenks a manila folder stuffed with paper. "You need to see Dr. Annette Grayson about your one-hour comp-rhet practicum. They'll start you in the tutoring lab, I imagine. Pair you up with one of the veteran tutors until you learn the ropes. Your schedule's in there as well. I'd find all of your professors soon, get syllabi, and find out what you've missed."

"Right." Jenks had no fucking idea what he was talking about.

"If you have any more questions, I suggest you talk to Professor Jay Morgan. He's been assigned as your faculty advisor. Or ask Professor Grayson. You'll be working closely with her too."

"What about the place to stay? I'm supposed to have a free place to live."

"The housing office."

"Where's that?"

"You have a campus map?"

"Yeah." He handed it to Whittaker.

The dean unfolded it, squinted at the small print. "Building 9." He gave the map back to Jenks.

"Later." Jenks left, grabbed his duffel on the way out.

*   *   *

After Ellis left, Whittaker reminded himself that he was *not* a racist. But the sheer arrogance of these kids! Still, he'd have to tread lightly. The university was in a delicate position. He pulled the memo from his desk drawer, the one university president Lincoln Truman had sent directly concerning Sherman Ellis. He read it again.

He did not need the brief overview of the university's checkered past, but he read it anyway. Enrollment just fifteen years ago had been over twelve thousand. But bad choices and bad administration had caused the school to fall on hard times. At its worst, enrollment had fallen to a catastrophic thirty-two hundred students. Instructors had been laid off. Crusty, tenured professors had been strongly encouraged into retirement. Funds had been slashed in every department. The football team, the fighting Buffalo Skinners, had been reduced to a Division III joke.

Indeed, the university had almost been closed altogether. There had been serious talk about turning it into a branch campus for OSU.

But superadministrator and divine savior Lincoln Truman had turned the school around. Enrollment had been up the last four years in a row, and the student body was now a healthy 6,857 students. Eastern Oklahoma University was entering a glorious new renaissance.

In only one area was the school drastically behind the rest of the nation. Diversity.

They weren't. Diverse. At all.

Out of nearly seven thousand students only forty-one were Native American, the school's largest minority. Twenty-three were Hispanic.

Eastern Oklahoma had only five African-American students. Now six with Sherman Ellis.

Granted, it had been hard to attract black students after the lynching. But that was nearly ten years ago. Still, Lincoln Truman had vowed to erase the university's stained reputation as a "Klan Kollege" as one muckraking newspaper had put it.

Whittaker pulled Ellis's file. His grades were solid. His GRE scores were through the roof. He returned the file to the cabinet.

Okay. A smart kid with a bad attitude. Whittaker had seen it before. Once Ellis realized he was among people who wanted to see him succeed, he'd ease off the tough-guy routine.

If not, well, Whittaker was known to be rather a tough cookie himself. He picked up the hand mirror again and went back to adjusting the hat.

"I've told you already," said the woman at the housing office. "We didn't think you were coming. We gave the room away to somebody else."

"I'm supposed to get a free place." Jenks waved the letters like a magic wand.

"But there's simply no place we can—"

"I'm black," Jenks said.

The woman's shoulders slumped, and she picked up the phone.

eight

After Morgan dropped Ginny at her apartment, she thought about him all night. The next morning she found herself getting into her car, driving toward the professor's house as if she were hypnotized. Not that Morgan mesmerized her, not completely. She was in love with the scheme developing in her head.

Ginny determined that she would weasel her way into the professor's life whatever it took. He was the most interesting thing to happen to her in a long time.

It rained hard, the sky black with fat clouds. The slap of the windshield wipers contributed to her hypnotized feeling.

Morgan was a *real* writer. Just a poet, sure, but a published writer. Not like the pussy posers in her fiction-writing classes. Morgan knew publishers, editors. He could help her launch a real career, guide her past pitfalls, introduce her into the right literary circles.

She parked in front of his house, ran through the downpour to his front porch. Her knock was almost lost amid the thunder and sheets of cold rain that pelted Morgan's tin roof. He opened the door, ushered her in, and shut it again quickly against the wind.

"I didn't expect you," Morgan said.

"Is it okay?" She shivered, stood dripping in his living room, shrugged out of her coat, the thin fabric of her blouse clinging to hard, thimble-sized nipples.

"You're soaked." Morgan found towels, brought them to her. She dried her hair.

"Your clothes."

"I need to take them off," she said.

"Okay."

She peeled off the blouse in front of him, slithered out of the wet jeans.

Morgan put his arms around her, and she stood on tiptoe, forced her open mouth over his. She was eager and hungry and they tripped and tumbled into the bedroom, fell in a grabbing, rolling pile. She pulled off his pants, took him in her mouth briefly before climbing on top.

She rode him during the lightning, the flashes making her pale skin blue. His hands sank into her round softness. She was warm and deep and she covered him with herself, back arched, mouth open.

Thunder crashed. Rain fell. The storm swallowed their moans.

Morgan didn't know what to think of her.

"I came back to tell you it will be okay," she said.

She sprawled across the bed, trying, Morgan supposed, to spread herself over every possible square inch. A leg and an arm draped over him too.

"What do you mean?" he asked.

"That I won't say anything. I thought you might be worried. I know you and that girl—"

"I wasn't worried." Yes he had been. Someone would miss Annie Walsh sooner or later, come asking hard questions. And what about Ginny? Strange, soft, bouncy, eager Ginny. Was this some kind of kick for her, bury a body and bed a professor? Yeah, he knew women like that. You could find them at writers' conferences, chasing after the latest young, hot novelist. Flavor of the month.

She nuzzled closer, ran fingers through his chest hair.

His skin got hot and sweaty where her heavy arm and leg pressed against him. He tried to squirm out from under her.

She looked up. "What is it?"

"Nothing." He sank back into the pillow.

"Do you want me to leave?"

"No."

"Yes you do." She curled into a ball, sighed, rolled off the bed, and went into the living room.

"Your clothes are still wet," he called after her.

She plucked them from the floor, squeezed. "Just a little damp." She shrugged into her bra. "I'd better get going."

Morgan watched her dress through the bedroom door and was certain he was supposed to stop her. She was expecting some word from him, the big callback where he asked where she was off to. He'd pull her back into bed, drag her beneath the silky, intimate prison of the sheets. It's what she expected.

But he could not quite summon the energy. Appropriate words refused to form. He watched her button the blouse, zip jeans, slip her bare feet into squeaky leather hiking boots. And even when he heard his front door open and close, he couldn't quite make himself tell her to stop, couldn't think of a single thing that didn't sound trite and placating.

He heard her engine start over the patter of rain, heard the car fade down the lane.

Thank God.

He'd been unable to resist her fleshy immediacy. This sort of thing had always been his problem.

But in the sticky, hot, awkward after-tangle of limbs and linen, he could only believe he was repeating the same sort of behavior which had landed him in this shit-pie of a situation in the first place. He did not know Ginny Conrad very well. Sure, he knew her taste and her feel and the breathless, urgent whine that squeezed out of her just before orgasm. But he didn't know what she'd do. What was her temperament? For all Morgan knew, Ginny was a walking mouth ready to gossip away any hope he ever had of steady employment.

He swung his feet over the bed, stood with a low groan. A twinge in his lower back. Ginny had ridden him long and hard, almost shaking apart the bed frame. He was getting too old for this. And too fat. He reminded himself about joining a gym.

He grabbed his pants off the floor, and something tumbled out of the pocket, landed hard and sharp on the top of his bare foot. Cold and metal.

"Goddammit!" He hopped, gritted his teeth, rubbed the foot. "Son of a bitch." He looked at his foot, red and swelling fast. He had the kind of skin that bruised easily purple and ugly green.

He scanned the floor to see what had bashed him.

The gun.

It lay on the hardwood floor daring him to pick it up.

He didn't want to bend over the way his back felt, so he nudged it with a toe, metal heavy and cold. Shoved it slowly under the bed. It made a scraping noise on the wood, like a murdered tin man being dragged into the gutter. Good, leave it there. Morgan could climb under the bed for it some other time.

He stepped into his pants, foot still throbbing, back complaining. His head hurt too. Stress.

He stepped into his slippers and grabbed a green flannel shirt off the doorknob on his way to the kitchen. He found a bottle of aspirin. Empty.

"Goddammit." He shook his head at his own stupidity, putting the aspirin bottle back empty. He always did that sort of thing, milk jugs and pie pans. It made girlfriends crazy, probably why he hadn't lived with anyone in five years.

The phone rang.

Morgan glared at it, willed it to shut up. It rang again.

He picked it up. "Hello?"

"It's Jones." The old man's voice rattled on the other end like a bad stereo speaker.

Hell and damnation. He must've wanted his gun back. Or maybe there'd been trouble with Annie, the body discovered, police on their way to slap him in cuffs. Morgan went chill and damp under the armpits, felt dread swell in his belly. *Oh, God, that's it, isn't it?* It was all blowing up in his face.

"You look at them poems yet?" Jones asked.

"Uh..." What?

"I don't have formal education like you, but I want to make them good. You told me you was going to read them."

"Yes. But I've only just started." Lies. "I need more time to really go over them carefully— Mr. Jones, is everything, I mean, it's all okay, right? You're only calling about the poems?"

"I helped you with your little problem," Jones said. "Should be fine. Now, I think maybe I should come over there."

"Why?"

"We can talk about the poems."

"No."

"No? What do you fucking mean no?"

"I have to..." *Think, Jay.* "I have a function on campus. I was honestly just walking out the door."

"Oh, bullshit. I'm coming over there right now."

"Uh..."

"I'll see you in a few minutes." He hung up.

Morgan flew for the door, grabbed keys, jerked his coat off the back of a chair.

Outside, the rain still fell but only gently. Halfway to his car Morgan noticed he was still wearing slippers, water soaking through cold. He thought about going back for shoes. Screw it.

He jumped in his car, cranked it.

Fled.

Ginny drove home.

She felt confident she could make Morgan want her, could manipulate him with the right combination of tears and sex. Men were insecure, horny, ego-driven apes. Control the dick and you control the man. The tears pressed the guilt buttons.

Of course, too many tears at the wrong time could send a guy running. Owning a man was a delicate business.

She thumbed a Nine Inch Nails tape into her cassette player, pounded the steering wheel in time with the driving rhythm. She squirmed in the seat, wet clothes uncomfortable.

Maybe Morgan had hit a dry spell. His writing output had evidently slowed to nothing. Maybe the professor was all out of inspiration. But Ginny could fix that too. Like that woman who inspired Pollock in the Ed Harris movie.

Ginny rubbed lightly between her legs. Sore. Morgan had pounded her good. A slight tingle.

She hurried home, wanted to flip on her computer. She felt like writing.

nine

Harold Jenks discovered the graduate dorms were full and were going to stay that way. They wouldn't kick anybody out just so he could move in. Jenks had thrown a shit fit.

The deputy director of student housing showed up to hush him, and Jenks called the man a racist. When the director of student housing and the vice president of student affairs showed up, he'd called them racists too.

They finally agreed to find him housing off campus and to foot the bill. At first, they'd assigned Jenks an unfurnished apartment five miles from campus. Jenks had loudly pointed out he had no furniture and no car, so they located a furnished studio four blocks from campus. The vice president had even called security to come drive Jenks to his new digs.

Looking around his new place, Jenks nodded and smiled big.

These dumb rednecks were fucking pushovers. He threw his duffel on the bed. He shoved Red Zach's gym bag underneath. He went to the room's only window, leaned on the sill, and looked at the wet street below. The studio was warm and comfortable, over a garage in a quiet residential neighborhood.

Stealing Sherman Ellis's life was going even more smoothly than Jenks had planned.

Jenks had a rap sheet of minor crimes as long as his arm. That sort of reputation dogged a man, pulled his life down into the mud. Jenks had tried to right himself once, get out of the ghetto life of poverty and petty crime. But he found all doors closed to him. No one believed a thug would reform. Nobody wanted an employee you couldn't turn your back on.

So Harold Jenks decided he would simply cease to be Harold Jenks. Sherman Ellis had no family and no record. Jenks would drape himself in Ellis's innocence, wrap himself in Ellis's accomplishments, a cloak of safety and legitimacy.

There'd be problems, of course. He'd need to stay clean. If he got picked up even for jaywalking the whole scam would be shot to shit. He couldn't let himself be fingerprinted. He'd already vowed never to return to East St. Louis. Too many people knew him there.

But what worried him most were the classes, the teachers. Worried? Hell, he was terrified. Jenks knew he was smart. You had to be to survive on the streets. But he was smart enough to know the difference between intelligence and education. Jenks had barely made it out of high school.

But poetry? Shit, how hard could that be?

He pulled an N.W.A. CD out of his duffel and a Walkman. He thumbed the PLAY button and slipped on the headphones, bobbing his head with the rap music and slapping his thigh to the beat. But this time he really listened, took note how the rapper bit off the words. Jenks mouthed the syllables, moved his mouth over the vowel sounds. Yeah, this was his kind of poetry. He could do this, no problem.

And they'd give him a college *degree* for it? White people were crazy.

He shut off the Walkman, dropped it on the bed. He'd study more later. Right now he had more immediate problems.

He took his rapidly shrinking roll of cash from his jeans pocket, counted the wrinkled bills. Jenks had exactly sixty-one dollars to his name, and that wasn't going to do it. The minifridge was empty, and he strongly suspected he was going to need books and other supplies. Pencils and shit, notebooks.

He counted it again. Still sixty-one bucks. He checked his other pockets. Nothing.

And he hadn't set up the deal yet to move Red Zach's coke. Once he did that he'd be set for a while, but that wasn't helping him now. Jenks needed operating capital. Going straight would need to be put on hold just a little longer.

Okay. He knew what to do.

He stripped out of his clothes. His body was lean, hard, three knife scars about an inch long across his belly. He pulled a pair of plain black sweatpants out of his duffel and stepped into them. He put on the matching sweatshirt. Then the black knit ski mask. He rolled the mask up above his eyes until it just looked like a watch cap.

The Glock would be a problem. A nice bit of heat, 9mm. He checked the clip. It was full, so he smacked it into the pistol. Jenks liked the metallic *click* when the clip snapped into place.

But it wouldn't stay in the elastic band of the sweats. He took a half-used roll of duct tape from the duffel, ripped off a piece. He used it to tape the Glock across the small of his back. He danced around a little, hopped twice, shook his ass, but the Glock stayed put. Good.

Jenks looked at his watch. Shit. It was too early. He pulled the gun off his back and dropped it on the bed next to the Walkman.

The little twenty-four-hour convenience store he'd spotted three blocks away might still be busy, students filling up on RC Colas and MoonPies. He'd wait.

The convenience store was not the perfect target. It was too close to where he lived, but he didn't have a ride and you can't take a taxi to a holdup.

Also, it might not be much of a score. Last time he'd done a Quickie-Mart, he made off with only twenty-three dollars and a fistful of SlimJims.

But Jenks had to have some cash.

No matter how much Jenks had screamed and ranted and called everyone within earshot a racist, the lady at the financial aid office insisted that stipend checks were only—ONLY—disbursed on the last day of the month.

About two in the morning, Jenks figured it was time.

He taped the gun to his back again, and made sure nobody was watching when he left the garage apartment. Once, on his way to the convenience store, a set of headlights scared him into a row of low hedges.

At the convenience store, he watched through the window for ten minutes, nerving himself up and making sure the old guy behind the register was alone.

Then he pulled the Glock and went in fast.

The old man turned big eyes on Jenks in slow motion, mouth dropping open, blood draining from his face.

I can't kill this guy, Jenks thought. Black man kill a white dude in this dumbshit, redneck town and they'll level the place looking for him. Too many of these convenience stores had hidden cameras, and there was always the chance of some bystander seeing him no matter how careful Jenks was. But he'd need to put the fear of Jenks's 9mm into this guy. Let him know not to twitch. Bluff him.

"Don't move, motherfucker!" Jenks held the Glock sideways at arm's length. "Get in that register, old man. Get out that green stuff."

"What the hell, boy? You on the crack?"

"Don't give me no shit. Just the money."

"Get the hell out of here, boy. I work for a living."

Jenks waved the gun, shoved it in the man's face. Didn't this old fool know what was happening? "You want to die, motherfucker?" he screamed, deep-throated, saliva flying with each word. "I'm going to put a goddamn bullet in your brain, you dumb redneck." Back in East St. Louis, he'd be pulling this job with Spoon, and Spoon would have shot this dumb fuck by now.

Spoon had no patience for dumb white fucks.

"I mean it," Jenks yelled. "Gimmee that money." But he was losing his nerve, had already lost the edge of surprise he'd had when he'd exploded through the front door.

The old man's hands dipped under the counter, came back holding a pump shotgun, barrel sawed off short. He pumped a shell in slow and firm like he was shucking corn. Swung the barrel around to Jenks, who was already diving behind a display of two-liter Dr Pepper.

The shotgun blast shook the little store, riddled the Dr Pepper with double-ought pellets. Soda fizzed, foamed, sprayed sticky across the dirty tile floor and Jenks's back.

Jenks's cry was a strangled, animal bleat. He belly-crawled down the first aisle, a high-pitched shriek caught in the back of his throat. He heard the old man pump the shotgun again and crossed his arms over his head. *Oh, Lord, this fucker's crazy.*

The second blast shredded the candy racks. Butterfingers rained. The odor of chocolate and cordite swirled thick in the air.

"Show your ass, you son of a bitch." The old man fired twice more.

But Jenks was already running around the end of the aisle toward the rear of the store. He fired wildly back over his shoulder, the 9mm popping away at cigarettes and beef jerky.

Jenks looked up and could see the old man still behind the counter in the store's big, fish-eye mirror. The old dude was thumbing fresh shells into the shotgun.

Jenks ran for the door.

The old man pumped in a shell, swung the barrel in line with Jenks's chest. Jenks hit a muddy-slick patch of Dr Pepper just as the old man squeezed the trigger. Jenks's heels slid out from under him. He landed hard on his ass, bruised his tailbone.

The shotgun blast destroyed the newspaper display.

Jenks fast-crawled through the front doors, knocking them open with the top of his head. The doors swung closed behind him, and the old man's next shot obliterated the glass. Jenks ducked beneath the diamond glitter shower.

He stood and ran.

The old man was shouting something after him, but Jenks didn't try to hear. He pumped his arms and legs, ran a long way for a long time.

ten

It was Abba this time that rolled through the empty corridors of Albatross Hall's fifth floor. The treble-sharp, crisp disco-pop of "Super Trouper." Morgan followed the music to Valentine's office.

He was wet and unhappy. His feet were bricks of ice.

This late in the evening, he hadn't really expected the strange professor to be in his office. Morgan didn't exactly know what lured him up the stairs, up through the building's dead floors to seek the bizarre reclusive poet who haunted the vacant offices.

He approached the door, prepared to knock, but stopped when he heard voices. Several voices. Cheerful and occasionally boisterous voices all simmering on the other side of Valentine's door.

And the door opened.

A nice-looking woman in a deep blue cocktail dress almost ran into him, stopped short, delicate hand going to the plunging V of her neckline. "Oh. Sorry, didn't see you there." She was small, blond, handsome, makeup only slightly too heavy

It occurred to Morgan to say, "Uh..."

"I'm just looking for the little girls' room." She slipped past him. "Go ahead on in." And she glided down the hall.

Morgan stepped into the din.

Valentine's office was crowded with people. A few looked young enough to be students. He recognized at least three professors from his own department. One bumped into him and spilled beer on his sleeve.

It was Dirk Jakes.

"Morgan! Didn't expect to see you here, you old gypsy prof," Jakes said. "Sorry about the spill there, chief." Jakes dabbed at Morgan's sleeve with the tip of his tie.

Dirk Jakes was the loudest man Morgan had ever met. A blowhard, a self-promoter, and a merciless hack. He was squat, red-haired, red-nosed, and fit poorly into expensive dark suits. He puked out three pulpy crime novels a year and made Mickey Spillane look like William Faulkner. He taught fiction writing for the university.

"What is all this?" Morgan asked.

"A party. You've never seen a party before?"

"Why here?"

"Valentine's idea. All the stress builds up from the semester. Good to blow off steam."

"The semester's only a week old," Morgan said.

"You don't want the stress to build up," Jakes told him. "Gets you all tight in the bunghole."

"I see."

"You're not a tight in the bunghole type of guy, are you?" Jakes was clearly gearing up for a colossal drunk.

"I try not to be," Morgan said.

"That's swell, fabulous." Jakes nodded, pushed him on into the depths of the party. "The bar's over there someplace. Go loosen up your goddamn bunghole, for Pete's sake."

"Good idea." Morgan moved into the mass of partygoers, glad for an excuse to get away from Jakes. The party writhed around him, seemed to breathe in and out like a living thing.

He tried to spot Valentine but didn't see him.

Somebody grabbed his arm, and Morgan turned.

It was Dirk Jakes again.

"Listen, I forgot to tell you." Jakes wouldn't let go of his arm. "Don't mention to anyone that Valentine's back. Make like he's still in Prague, you get it?"

"I get it."

"Don't let the cat out of the bag, eh? The old man doesn't want the dean putting him on some goddamn bullshit committee or something, so he's lying low, *capische?*"

Morgan pried his arm loose. "I won't say a thing."

He made his way to the little fridge where he'd found a bottle of beer his last visit, but it was empty. A curtain on the back wall was pushed aside, and he saw that the wall had been knocked through into the next office. He ducked through, found another crowd of people on the other side. They stood around a keg of beer, a stack of yellow plastic cups on a sideboard.

Morgan took a cup, poured beer. Too foamy.

"You have to tilt the cup." The high-pitched voice belonged to a petite, raven-haired girl about twenty years old. "You have to tilt it. I know because I tend bar down at Peckerwood's, the sports bar across town. You know it?"

Morgan shook his head. "I'm new in town."

She took the cup out of Morgan's hand, dumped the foam, and tilted the cup. "See, like this." She poured the beer, smooth.

Morgan watched her pour. She was barely five feet tall, twig of a thing. Tight denim shorts, pink T-shirt a size too small. Flip-flops, toenails painted lime. She must've had boots around somewhere. He thought of his own freezing feet.

"You're a student here?" Morgan asked.

She shook her head, handed Morgan his cup. "I walk Professor Valentine's dogs."

"He has dogs?"

"Two Irish wolfhounds. Huge, but very gentle. I keep them for him ever since the problem with his house."

"I was looking for Valentine," Morgan said.

"I haven't seen him in a while." The girl's attention immediately whipped to a newcomer at the keg. "You have to tilt it or you'll get foam," she said.

Morgan drank half his beer and drifted back through the hole in the wall, where he found a couple of familiar faces, two more professors from his department.

They seemed to be in the middle of an argument, both very drunk.

"It's a ridiculous book and you know it, Pritcher. You Irish folk have been skating on Joyce for too long. *Finnegans Wake* is bullshit. Everyone knows it's bullshit. Joyce knew it was bullshit when he wrote it. Now get out of my face please, you ridiculous little tit."

Professor Louis Reams was a lanky, storklike man. Morgan had spoken casually with him a few times and seemed to remember he'd done his dissertation on the complex prosody of Sri Lankan poetry in translation. Morgan suspected Reams had an inferiority complex from having to explain all the time just exactly what his specialty was.

He towered over the much shorter Pritcher, jabbing a finger at his face as he spoke.

Professor Larry Pritcher looked uninterested, dismissed the

ranting Reams with a wave of his small, pale hand. Early in grad school, Pritcher had hitched himself to the James Joyce band-wagon and never looked back. He fully enjoyed the massive safety of James Joyce studies and relentlessly needled "fringe" scholar-ship as new wave, multicultural carnival acts.

"Put a cork in it, Reams," Pritcher said. "You're drunk."

"You have no concept of what it's like to follow an original thread of thought."

"This again."

"Fuck you with bells on." Reams gave him the *up yours* gesture.

Pritcher turned to Morgan. "Can you believe this guy? I'm just trying to have a goddamn drink."

Morgan blinked. He hadn't expected to be drawn into it. "Well..."

"Exactly," Pritcher said. "Nobody wants you here, Reams. You're bringing the party down."

Morgan noticed that the bulk of the party appeared to be press-ing on unhindered.

"The hell you say?" Reams scowled. "That true, Morgan? I'm somehow some kind of party pooper?"

"I don't think anyone wants to have an argument," Morgan said.

"So you *do* think I'm a party pooper."

"I never said—"

"Fine." Reams finished his beer in one angry gulp, threw the empty cup on the floor. "Screw you too, Morgan. Easy for you to judge. You're just passing through. I have to work here for Christ's sake."

Reams jostled his way through the crowd for the door, party-goers frowning after him.

"What a prick," Pritcher said.

"I think he took me wrong," Morgan said.

"He takes everything wrong. He's just wrongheaded altogether."

"Have you seen Valentine?" Morgan gulped beer, liked it, gulped some more.

"Not for a while." Pritcher cleared his throat, leaned in close to Morgan, spoke low in conspiracy tones. "Look, don't mention to anyone about Valentine's being back. He doesn't want—"

"I know," Morgan said. "Mum's the word."

Dirk Jakes surged out of the party crowd, landed on swaying legs in front of Pritcher and Morgan. "All the goddamn broads at this party must be dykes."

"Do tell," Pritcher said.

"Buncha damn lesbos," Jakes slurred. "You catch what I'm saying there, Morgo-man?" Jakes brayed laughter, yanked Morgan's sleeve.

Beer splashed over Morgan's cup. "Dammit. Again?"

"Jesus, sorry, Morgan." Jakes threw himself in reverse, stumbled back to have a look where he'd spilled the beer. "What the hell? Are those slippers?"

"Forget it," Morgan said. "You were telling us about the lesbians."

"Yeah. Every bitch here a damn rug-muncher."

"Striking out again, eh?" Pritcher's lips curled into a smug grin.

Morgan thought about the woman in the blue cocktail dress, the one who'd almost plowed into him on the way into the party. He craned his neck, scanned the party for her. Nowhere. Too bad.

"That bimbo at the keg was the worst." Jakes was still at it. "I know how to pour a fucking beer."

The party music segued into "Folsom Prison" by Johnny Cash.

Pritcher wrinkled up his whole face like somebody had taken a dump in his cup. "Country music? You must be joking. Who'd put that on?"

Jakes looked stunned. "Are you fucking kidding?"

"What would I kid about?" Pritcher asked.

Morgan wiggled his toes within the damp slippers. They were just getting dry when Jakes had splashed the beer on them. His feet were cold and wet and he was sick of Pritcher and especially Jakes.

"It's Johnny Cash, man." Jakes waved his cup in the air like that explained it. "Johnny fucking Cash."

"So?"

Jakes snorted. "You're an idiot."

"Okay, just forget it," Pritcher said. "I've had enough of these drunks, Morgan. I've got to get up early anyway."

"On a Saturday?" Morgan asked.

"I ride my bicycle in the mornings. Good night."

Morgan waved as he left.

"What a dink," Jakes said. "Can you imagine not liking Johnny Cash?"

Morgan didn't say anything.

"I'm going to find some pussy," Jakes said. "There must be some scratch at this party that isn't lesbo." And he was off to it again.

Morgan looked in his cup. He saw no beer and that made him unhappy. He threaded his way back to the keg.

The sports bar girl had moved on. Morgan elbowed a fat guy out of the way and refilled his cup. He wasn't sure when he might be able to make it around to the keg again, so he threw back the beer fast and filled up again. He took his fresh beer back into the crowd.

The noise and the beer and the party were crowding out thoughts Morgan didn't want to think. He was starting to feel good, a nice glow in his belly. He even forgot about his wet slippers.

A tap on his shoulder.

He turned and looked down into the soft eyes of the woman in the blue V-neck dress. She looked good.

"You're Morgan?" she shouted over the music.

He smiled, nodded.

"This way." She grabbed his elbow, pulled him along.

Morgan followed gladly.

She led him from the party, down the hall. She turned, walked, turned again, walked more, turned a few more times. The building didn't seem big enough for this. Surely they were going in circles. Morgan couldn't keep track, but he wasn't trying too hard.

And he didn't wonder too hard where he was going. It was good not to make such hard decisions for a change. He allowed himself a brief fantasy, like in *Penthouse Forum*. She'd take him to a secluded room, where she'd lift her skirt, tug aside her panties, and offer herself to him.

That didn't happen.

She pushed open a door and led him into a smoky room lit by candles. A man he didn't know sat deep in a cushy armchair. Valentine sat at the far end of a long, low sofa.

"Ah, good. It's Professor Morgan." Valentine puffed savagely on his bong. "Brad, this is Bill Morgan. Bill, Brad Eubanks. He's the custodian here."

"It's Jay, actually." Morgan shook the man's hand.

"How do," Brad said.

"I'm afraid I never got your name," Morgan said to the woman.

"Annette Grayson." She offered a slim hand.

Morgan shook. It was soft and cool. He let go reluctantly.

"We teach in the same department," she said. "I manage the Writing Lab and oversee Freshman Composition. I'm surprised we haven't run into each other before now."

"I'm sorry it's been so long."

She pointed at Morgan's beer cup. "You don't actually want that, do you?"

"Don't I?"

"Let me fix you something for a grown-up."

She produced a bottle of vodka from thin air. Where had that been, between the couch cushions? Tonic next and a lime. Morgan was still reeling from the sleight of hand, when Annette pushed the vodka tonic at him. He took it, drank. Made the whole thing disappear presto chango.

Valentine was on about something, but Morgan only considered the bottom of his empty cup.

"A refill?" Annette was already pouring.

She reads minds too. Good woman.

Valentine went on about the state of poetry and academia, all the time puffing at his bong like some kind of homemade life-support system. Morgan's cup never seemed to get empty. His face warmed, and he floated through the hazy conversation with eyelids heavy, head bobbing in eager drunken agreement with the random conversation.

The night didn't really end. It trailed off like an ellipsis.

eleven

When Morgan awoke the next morning on the couch, he was bitterly disappointed not to find Annette Grayson underneath him. After three or four vodka tonics he'd offered subtle hints, made it clear he was interested. After a few more drinks his suggestions became more overt.

Annette had only giggled, shook her head, gently pushed him back whenever he'd tried to lean in for a kiss.

Morgan couldn't remember when he'd lost track of the janitor or Valentine. At some point in the evening he'd simply found himself alone with the head of Composition and Rhetoric.

Morgan shifted on the couch. Something was digging mercilessly into his back. He arched, reached underneath. It was the empty vodka bottle.

He sat up. His head was appalled at the notion and began to

throb. His stomach gurgled, and Morgan belched a sick blend of beer, vodka, and lime. His feet felt slick and ripe within his slippers. *I must reek.*

He heaved himself to his feet, stumbled out of the room. In the hall, he leaned raggedly against a wall, battled a sudden wave of nausea. Nothing came up. He swallowed hard. Belched a few more times. He looked around the empty hall.

Lost again. The fifth floor of Albatross Hall was more confusing than the minotaur's maze. Morgan closed his eyes, hung his head as if in prayer. He listened.

The music. He'd come to count on it now. Classical this time.

He followed it to Valentine's office, found the old man in a frayed blue robe. He was brushing his teeth. Valentine spit into a glass, wiped his mouth on a sleeve.

Valentine looked at Morgan and frowned. "Good God, Bill. You're a wreck."

"I slept on your couch."

"Perfectly all right." Valentine ushered him in. "How about some coffee?"

"That would help. Thanks."

Valentine poured it into a mug that said *Tenure means never having to say you're sorry.*

Morgan closed his eyes as he sipped. The hot coffee hit his belly, and Morgan waited. When it didn't come back up, he drank some more. He started to feel a little better but not much.

Morgan cleared his throat. "Professor Valentine?"

"Yes?"

"Why do you live in Albatross Hall?"

"My house burned down."

"That explains it," Morgan said. "Are you rebuilding or hunting for a new one?"

"Neither. That's why I'm living here."

"I understand." Morgan didn't understand.

"My house burned down, let's see, I guess it would be about six years ago. I spent all the money on this lovely girl. Young, twenty or twenty-one, I think. A little wisp of a thing. In pigtails she passed for sixteen. A clever little poet too." Valentine sounded dangerously nostalgic. "We blew it all in Fiji. Then she left me for a Samoan pastry chef. You want a refill on that coffee?"

"No thanks," Morgan said. "I guess I'd better get going."

It took Morgan twenty minutes to find the stairway. He climbed down and found his way out of the building. The early morning was gray and damp. The sudden cold battered him, but helped wake him too. The world was wet. It would rain again soon.

Morgan stumbled along the sidewalk in the direction of—he hoped—his car. He didn't bother avoiding the puddles. When he got home, he'd throw the slippers away.

And then he saw Reams crouching low along the sidewalk behind some bushes. Reams looked wild, hair tousled, bags under his eyes. His nose and cheeks were red from the weather. He was wearing the same clothing as the night before at the party.

But then again, so was Morgan.

Reams had a thick, hardcover book in his clenched hands.

Morgan was fresh out of tact. "What the fuck are you doing, Reams?"

Reams leapt from the bushes, snagged Morgan by the wrists, and pulled him down into the foliage. Morgan landed in a tangled pile with Reams.

"Shut up, Morgan," Reams said. "You'll give away our position."

"Goddammit." Morgan rolled onto his side, pushed himself

onto an elbow, and shook his head. "For Christ's sake I'm covered in mud here." Morgan noticed the book in Reams's white-knuckled hands was a copy of *Finnegans Wake.*

Reams returned to his crouch. "Quiet. Here he comes."

Morgan squinted through the shrubs, looked down the sidewalk. A lone man on a frail bicycle, the thin wheels whirring in the quiet morning.

The rain began again.

"Reams." Morgan tapped the jittery man on the shoulder. "Uh . . . Reams?"

Reams swatted Morgan's hand away. "We'll show the little son of a bitch what Joyce is good for."

Morgan recognized the cyclist. It was Pritcher. He wore an obscene spandex outfit that bunched his nuts into a tight wad. *Certainly he doesn't realize how ridiculous he looks. He wouldn't leave the house if he knew he looked like that.*

Pritcher's ten-speed was humming along at a good clip when it passed between the big fountain and Reams's hiding place. Reams darted from his crouch, sprung himself at Pritcher's bicycle. He flung the copy of *Finnegans Wake.*

It sailed, the cover opening wide, pages flapping. The book spun end over end like some awkward, epileptic wounded bird in its final tailspin.

Morgan watched, his jaw dropping, stomach tightening.

Joyce's complex novel hit, a corner of the cover lodging in the spokes of the rear wheel. The simple machinery of the bicycle clenched, gears jamming, chain tangled. Pritcher screeched like a fruit bat and flew over the handlebars.

He sailed high and far, landing in a half splash, half crunch in the big stone fountain.

Morgan gulped. "Jesus, Reams, you killed him."

Pritcher lay still for a long time. The rain came harder. Morgan stood next to Reams, put his hand on the professor's shoulder. Both men prayed for Pritcher to move.

"You'd better go have a look, Morgan."

"To hell with that," Morgan said. "You go look. You're the one that killed him. What the hell were you thinking?"

"I don't know." Reams's voice sounded far away. "I was crazy. He just made me insane, I guess. I must've been out of my mind. You'll testify, right, Morgan? I wasn't in my right mind."

They still watched. Pritcher still didn't move.

"I'll have to take responsibility," Reams said. He stuck his chest out, lifted his chin. "I've killed a man, and I'm going to pay for that."

Pritcher's foot twitched. Loud cursing and splashing came from the fountain.

"He's fine!" Reams said. "Run!"

Reams elbowed Morgan aside, tore off through the bushes like he was on fire, a panicked stumbling and clawing. Morgan followed. They pushed their way through to the parking lot on the other side. Morgan's car was near.

"This way," Morgan shouted.

Morgan didn't bother to see if Reams followed. He ran for his car as fast as he could while digging into his front pocket for his keys. The keys were stuck, tangled in stray threads inside his pocket. Morgan ran awkwardly, tugging at the keys.

He reached the car door and jerked hard, tore the keys loose, half his pant leg ripping open down to the knees.

"Shit."

Morgan unlocked the door, climbed inside, cranked the engine.

Reams was on the other side, hitting the passenger window with the heel of his hand. "Let me in, man. Hurry."

Morgan flashed on an old black-and-white submarine movie. A sailor trapped on the other side of a sealed hatch, the compartment filling with seawater. He thought just for a moment about leaving him. Morgan popped the locks, let Reams in.

They drove fast, sideswiped a library book return box with a metallic *crinch*. Morgan flipped on the windshield wipers, found the road. Both men breathed hard.

Reams leaned back, sprawled in the passenger seat, rubbed at his eyes.

The windshield fogged over. Morgan wiped at it with a sleeve.

"I can't believe it," Reams said. "I thought I'd killed him. I could have fucked up my whole life. I'm up for tenure next year. You can't get tenure if you kill a guy."

"No. It's not like the old days," Morgan said.

"I really thought I'd broken his neck, Morgan. Do you know what that feels like? The thought that you've killed somebody?"

Morgan saw Annie Walsh's face in his mind, saw her naked, skin slack and cold in his bed. Remembered the weight of her wrapped in the plastic. He started to speak, to say something to Reams, but his voice caught. Another memory, the shallow grave in the peach orchard.

"I hope you never have to feel like that," Reams said.

twelve

Morgan dropped Reams off at his house then went home.

He was soaking wet. He peeled off the slippers and tossed them into the trash. He showered, thought about getting dressed, but crawled under the covers instead.

He didn't sleep well. Annie's corpse followed him through the world of dreams, called to him from beneath the ground. He knew somewhere a mother and father wondered why they hadn't heard from her. Friends would talk. Other professors would wonder why she wasn't attending class.

Morgan awoke sore, sweat slick on his forehead and under his arms. He tumbled out of bed, groaned, stood, stretched. He felt heavy and weak and unhappy. Maybe he'd try to write. Maybe a drink first. No, he needed another shower. He wanted to rinse off the nightmare sweat.

After the shower, he shuffled into the kitchen. He looked out the window and saw that the day was creeping into evening.

He made coffee, stood and watched it brew, then poured himself a mug, took it to his little desk. It was a mess, so he started cleaning and found an unfamiliar manila folder. He opened it.

It was Fred Jones's poetry.

"Hell."

Something caught his eye, so he kept reading. A good line here and there. He read two or three, came to one that might work with some edits. The old man had decent instincts, smooth with images. Nothing too didactic. The poems must have been in chronological order because they improved as he went along. He pulled out two near the bottom and began marking them with a green pen. As Morgan critiqued each poem, he came to a horrifying realization.

The old man was good.

His images were fresh and energetic, savagely raw and gritty without being overly gruesome. They didn't pander. His voice was rugged, straightforward, and American.

Morgan was sick with jealousy but couldn't pull himself away from the old man's work. Outside it grew full dark, the weather turning sour yet again. The wind kicked up. A little rain. Morgan switched on the tiny desk lamp and kept reading.

After another hour, the wind really started to howl, so he didn't hear when Jones walked into his house, stood over him at the desk, and put the gun to his forehead.

Morgan felt his sphincter twitch. He was going to die.

"You stupid goddamn punk." Jones shook the pistol at him. It was an automatic with a silencer. The old man dripped, the gun glistened wet. "You said you was going to take care of the girl, and here I find she's walking around breathing. For fuck's sake you know what kind of position I'm in? I can't have this dumb kid opening her yap."

The barrel of the gun was gigantic.

And this old man was about to blow his head off. Morgan's eyes fogged with tears, and he was ashamed to meet death so feebly. No one would come to his funeral, he thought. Not his ex-wife. He wasn't that close to anyone in the department. He would be buried alone and forgotten like Annie Walsh.

Part of Morgan knew it was what he deserved. He was a small, sad man living a miserable little life. But he wanted to keep on living that little life.

"She won't say anything," Morgan said. "I know her. She won't talk."

"Don't yank me off, you dumb egghead. She's a girl. Girls can't help blabbing their big fucking mouths all over creation."

"Don't kill me."

"Shut up. Sometimes you people just don't understand—"

He looked down at his poems spread across Morgan's desk, plucked one from the pile with wet, bony fingers. "You wrote on these?"

Morgan nodded.

Jones looked at the changes. "Better."

"Yes."

Jones pulled up a chair, scooted close to Morgan, and shifted the gun to his other hand. He pointed to one of the poems where Morgan had crossed out the word *is* three times. "What's wrong with that?"

"It's a be-verb," Morgan said. "They're weak."

"What do you mean?"

Morgan explained, and the old man understood.

"Are you going to kill me?" asked Morgan.

"No."

"What about Ginny Conrad?"

"You banging her?"

"Yes."

Jones scratched his head, exhaled. Tired. "That's okay, then, I guess. But I'm going to keep an eye on her."

"Thanks."

"What about these things?" Jones meant the poems.

"They're pretty good, Mr. Jones."

"Okay."

Morgan said, "How about twice a month? We'll talk about these and whatever new ones you bring."

"You want to help me?"

Morgan nodded. "I'd like to try."

"Okay," Jones said. "I'll bring doughnuts. What do you like? You like cream-filled?"

thirteen

Harold Jenks fidgeted in his desk, looked at the other grad students who looked back at him like he was a fucking Martian.

A black Martian.

The desks were arranged in a circle, so everyone could see everyone else. He fingered the paper in front of him. His first poem. Professor Morgan had looked annoyed when Jenks had finally shown after missing the first few classes. The professor told Jenks to hand in a poem right away if he wanted to fit back into the rotation. Jenks was catching on to the routine. Half the class handed in poems one week, the other half the next week. Everybody got photocopies of all the poems. It was his job to take the poems home, read them, then come back to class and say things to help the poem be better.

It had sounded easy.

Professor Morgan shuffled into class five minutes late, sat at his desk in the circle. "Okay," Morgan said. "Which poem will we look at first?"

Jenks's stomach clenched. He didn't want to be first.

"How about Belinda's?" Morgan said.

Belinda was a tiny blond girl who was so white she was almost invisible. Jenks shifted her poem to the top of his pile. He'd read the poem five times last night. Slowly. He had no fucking idea what it was about.

Belinda sat up straight, took the gum out of her mouth, and stuck it on the end of her finger. She extended the finger, the wad of gum glistening pink, held her poem with the other fingers.

She cleared her throat and read: "This poem is called 'Like Dust in the Wind.'"

Her eyes circled the room. She lowered her voice, soaked heavy with emotion. "My heart is a desert flower, blooming in season, sleeping through summer heat. Water it with your tears. Feed it kisses. Place petals on your dead eyes like pennies. Your breath is the hot desert wind, blowing only from the west."

Belinda bit her bottom lip, looked coyly around the circle again, and settled back into her seat and waited for the commentary to begin.

Jenks decided Belinda was one sad sorry bitch.

"Thank you, Belinda," Morgan said. "That was very moving." He scanned the faces in the room. "Who'd like to start us off?"

Half the class looked away. Jenks made a close inspection of his fingernails.

The kid next to Jenks cleared his throat. What was his name? Timothy Lancaster. Blue blazer, penny-loafer motherfucker.

Lancaster said, "The juxtaposition of the active and the static present an interesting tension in this poem, I think."

Jenks cocked an eye at him. *Say what?*

Morgan raised an eyebrow. "How do you figure?"

"It's a basic battle of the sexes theme," Lancaster said. "Although rather eloquently cast in nature terms. The blooming flower represents femininity, womanhood. Static and ready to receive a seed. Women have nesting instincts, roots. The wind represents the male. I think the speaker of this poem has issues with the lack of commitment males have in her life."

Belinda glowered.

Wait. What was homeboy saying, that the flower was like symbolic of some ripe cootchie? With his pencil, Jenks circled the words *desert flower* and wrote the word *vagina* next to it. Hold on. It said her heart was the flower. Jenks crossed out what he'd written. Square one.

"Look. First thing's first, okay?" It was Wayne DelPrego, the redneck dude who sat on the other side of Lancaster. "You can't say 'Dust in the Wind' in the title. People will think of the Kansas song."

They went on like this for about fifteen more minutes, Morgan nodding thoughtfully the whole time without saying anything significant. What the fuck? The guy was supposed to be the teacher. Was he going to explain this poem or not?

Not.

They went through two more poems. One was about a mother dying. The other one from a nerd guy with glasses thick as ashtrays. His poem seemed mostly to be about *Star Trek*. Most of the class hated it. They disrespected the nerd boy's poem, and he just sat there and took it. That seemed to be what the class was about. You read your poem, then let everyone talk you down.

Fuck that.

Whenever Morgan asked the students who'd like to comment on the poetry, the professor's eyes always landed on Jenks briefly before Jenks looked away. This wouldn't play for long. Sooner or later Jenks would be expected to speak up.

Another grad student read his poem. Jenks had tuned out. These people were all speaking some other language. His poem didn't sound anything like theirs.

"Mr. Ellis!"

Jenks blinked. The professor had to say Sherman Ellis's name twice. Jenks hadn't been listening. "Yo."

Morgan frowned. "Yes, yo to you too. We have just enough time left to workshop your poem."

Jenks cleared his throat and read:

> *If it weren't for family,*
> *Sister, father, brother, mother,*
> *How would I know when I was home?*
>
> *I thank God for my family*
> *Each one is like no other*
> *I take them in my heart wherever I may roam.*

Jenks was still working on his masterpiece, but he'd needed a poem quick. So he'd taken this one from a greeting card he'd seen in the grocery store. He looked at the professor for a reaction. Morgan had his nose all wrinkled up like he smelled dog shit. That couldn't be good.

"Well, isn't that warm and fuzzy," Morgan said.

"It is a bit saccharine," Lancaster said. "I'm not sure such an abundance of sentimentality concentrated in so few lines is the best strategy."

Jenks couldn't tell if he was being disrespected or not.

DelPrego yawned, ran a hand through his shaggy hair. "It's crap."

Oh, yeah. Jenks was being disrespected all right.

Part 2

fourteen

Deke Stubbs had the kind of scruples one would expect in a private eye.

Which is to say he didn't have any.

Stubbs leaned back in his office chair, heaved his thick, short legs upon the desk. He smiled his gray teeth, cradled the phone against his thick chunk of chin while popping open a warm Busch. He had a sucker on the line and smelled a payday. The sucker used to be a client.

But Stubbs needed a shave, a new suit, a muffler for his Dodge, last month's rent, and a blow job. And all that cost money.

"I know you paid me to take these photos of your wife," Stubbs said to the client. "But I was thinking your wife would pay more."

The guy squawked angry on the other end.

"I'm not trying to put the bite on nobody," Stubbs said. "I was just supposing out loud. That's all."

Stubbs sipped beer, listened to the client give him an earful. The guy called Stubbs every name in the book, made the usual threats. Stubbs didn't care. He took it all in, waited. He knew the guy would cough up if he wanted the divorce case settled his way. No matter how much the client paid Stubbs, he'd save money in the long run by showing his wife was doing the dirty with the family dentist. Same old story every time. The client was really yelling now. He didn't seem to want to let up.

"Listen," Stubbs said, "I don't like you talking to me like that, but I'm going to forgive you because I know this is a surprise. Maybe a little stressful. But normally I'd come over there and stick a long knife right into your fat belly. Maybe I will anyway. You ever stick a knife into somebody's belly? The blood pours out all warm and sticky. And when you twist the knife, the blood keeps coming. Sometimes the blade gets into the bowel. The bowel juice gets mixed in with the blood, smells something awful."

Silence on the other end.

Stubbs's office door creaked open. Stubbs looked at his watch. His 10 A.M. appointment was fifteen minutes early.

A man and a woman entered. Upper-middle-class. Professionals. Good citizens. About two years ago, Stubbs had decided he needed a better class of sucker, so he'd sprung for a big advertisement in the Yellow Pages. It was a great ad. He'd used words like *discreet*, *professionalism*, and *state-licensed*. The ad had brought in a whole new kind of clientele. Half of them turned around and walked out the moment they saw Stubbs. But the other half more than paid for the ad.

"I'll have to call you back," Stubbs said into the phone. "Think about what I said."

He hung up.

"We're the Walshes," the man said. "I'm Dave and this is my wife Eileen."

"Have a seat, folks." Stubbs waved a hand at the two rickety chairs across his desk.

They sat.

Stubbs said, "Now on the phone you mentioned something about your daughter." Stubbs pawed through his top desk drawer. He was out of Winstons. "Either of you folks have a cigarette?"

"We don't smoke," the woman said.

"Annie," Dave said. "She's missing."

The wife leaned forward, grabbed the edge of the desk. White knuckles. "It's been two weeks!"

Stubbs nodded, pulled a legal pad out of his top desk drawer. "I'm just going to take some notes, okay? You tell me all about it."

They talked. Stubbs listened.

The woman was obviously in charge. Dave would start a sentence, but Eileen would finish it. They were *desperate*. Annie had never gone *this* long without calling before.

Stubbs made concerned noises, wrote on his notepad.

When Eileen Walsh signaled she was done with her story, Stubbs set the notepad aside. He steepled his hands under his chin, looked deep into their eyes, and said, "I'm going to need some money up front."

It was two in the afternoon the next day when Stubbs left Tulsa traveling east toward Fumbee. His Dodge sounded good. He wore a shiny new black suit (on sale at Sears). His rent was paid current, and his dingus still tingled from Lola's all-night love fest. Stubbs made a mental note to buy her a dozen roses. No, make that carnations. Roses were too expensive.

He lit a fresh Winston, puffed hard and fast.

He unfolded the map, and found the little spec that indicated where he was going. Eastern Oklahoma University. The parents had given him some good stuff. A copy of her class schedule, apartment address, name of her roommate, plenty of good stuff. These were real parents, took an interest in the kid. Stubbs's mother never knew where he was half the time, and his father couldn't give a shit.

A bit harsh maybe, but it had taught Stubbs self-reliance. He could think on his feet, improvise. One lesson he'd learned over and over again was never trust anybody. Another lesson that had come in handy was never to give a sucker an even break. And maybe that meant he didn't have a long list of close friends, but it also meant he never risked having someone let him down. Sure, he'd come up hard and tough. But he'd learned.

And he'd turned out okay.

fifteen

Morgan had been grinning wide and goofy all morning since Annette Grayson had called him to meet for lunch. After two weeks of her coyly sidestepping invitations for dinner or drinks, it finally looked like he was going to make some headway. He went home before meeting her, put on his charcoal slacks, red silk shirt. He looked slick.

He searched under his bed for his belt and spotted the pistol Fred Jones had given him. He recoiled, the memory of it clenching his gut.

He stood. Never mind the belt.

Morgan had almost hypnotized himself into forgetting about Annie Walsh's cold body buried in the peach orchard just outside of town. But he couldn't quite forget the way her head tilted when she was listening or the way her eyes squeezed shut when she laughed.

Last week when Jones had been over to discuss his latest batch of poems, Morgan had almost snapped. He said he couldn't stand it anymore. Couldn't eat or sleep. He was going to the police. He'd tell everything, say he was out of his mind, that he'd panicked.

Jones had gripped Morgan's wrist with strong bony fingers, had spoken low, almost a growl. "You listen to me, Professor. Forget about it. It's handled. You get it? You didn't kill that kid. She zapped herself on pills. Why should you get tangled up in that? How's that fair?"

Morgan had listened, nodded, sluggishly followed the old man's lead. Sure, why should he suffer?

But now he couldn't help thinking about it again. About Annie.

Not now, dumbass. Annette's waiting.

He climbed into his Buick and was five minutes late arriving at someplace called The Sprout Shack.

He walked in, spotted her, and his smile fell into little chunks, bounced, and clattered around his ankles. Two other professors sat with Annette. He didn't know their names, but he'd seen them around Albatross Hall. This wasn't going to be the intimate lunch Morgan had in mind.

Annette spotted Morgan and waved him over. He sat opposite her, draped the cloth napkin over his lap, tried to smile again, and it came out like a tired grimace.

"Have you been sleeping okay?" Annette asked.

"Sure." He nodded at the two strange professors. "Hey. I'm Jay Morgan."

The two professors nodded back.

"Hello. Susan Criger." She was beefy, red-faced, hair knotted in a severe bun.

The other guy was bland, vanilla pudding complexion. Hair the color of old parchment. "Good to meet you, Dr. Morgan."

"I'm not a doctor," Morgan said. "I have an MFA."

"I'm glad you could all make it," Annette said. "I think you all know what we need to discuss."

"Evidently not." Morgan realized it had come out a bit caustic and tried to smile again to make up for it. But the muscles in his face wouldn't work. His smile was broken.

"It's Sherman Ellis." Annette toyed with her water glass, shook her head, and finally shrugged. "I don't know what to do with him or what to make of him. He's supposed to be tutoring undergrads in the Writing Lab, but, well to be blunt, he's useless. I had to explain to him what a gerund was."

The beefy woman nodded. "I suppose you've gotten the same speech from the dean we have. I was told to—and I quote—'use the kid gloves.'"

Morgan grabbed a menu, scanned it, and was horrified to find himself in a health food restaurant. "What is this? Curd? What the hell is curd?"

Annette ignored him. "I know the university is under a lot of pressure to reach out to minority students, but I'm worried about standards. I don't think—"

The waiter arrived, set plates in front of Annette and the other two professors.

"We went ahead and ordered," Annette told Morgan. "Hope you don't mind."

"No problem." Morgan looked at her plate. Annette seemed to have ordered some kind of shredded green Brillo pad surrounded by quivering blocks of pale goo.

The waiter looked at Morgan, his pen hovering over his order pad. "Sir?"

Morgan pointed at Annette's plate. "What's that?"

"Alfalfa sprouts and caraway-seed tofu cubes."

"I think I'm going to need a minute."

The waiter left. Morgan thought he might have been rolling his eyes.

"Look, it doesn't matter," the other professor said. He poked at a puddle of coarse gray gunk on his plate. "Dean Whittaker has the administration behind him. It's a public relations show now, and they don't want to have to tell anyone they flunked out an African-American student. They'll say we don't understand his ebonics or that he was culturally displaced and needed special consideration or Lord knows what. The fact that he doesn't know a Restoration drama from an episode of *Mama's Family* won't matter to anyone."

He stood, dropped his napkin in the chair. "I'm sorry, Dr. Grayson. I'm not sticking my neck out. It's not worth my job. Come on, Susan. I'll buy you a cheeseburger across the street." He nodded at Morgan. "Good to meet you."

Susan Criger stood, shook her head at Annette. "Sorry. Ethically, I'm on your side. You know how I feel about grade inflation, but now isn't the time for this sort of battle. Sorry." She followed the other professor to the register. They paid quickly and left the restaurant.

Annette sat back in her chair, crossed her arms. She looked at Morgan. "Well, what do you think?"

Morgan set the menu aside. "I think a cheeseburger sounds pretty good."

"Not about that!"

Morgan threw up his hands. "Well, what do you want me to say? I thought you asked me here—why *did* you ask me here?"

"I thought that was obvious."

"It's not. You and those other two seem to have a problem with Sherman Ellis."

"Doesn't he seem a bit odd to you? I mean, is he the caliber of student you're accustomed to?" She harpooned a tofu cube with her fork, sniffed it, popped it into her mouth. She frowned and shoved in a bale of sprouts on top of the tofu, crunched without enjoyment.

"Ellis is exactly as bad as all of my other poets," Morgan said. "Ellis only stands out in that he thinks rap and poetry are the same thing. But in terms of quality he's as bad as all of the other pinheads."

"You don't sound like you enjoy your job."

"You don't look like you're enjoying your lunch."

She stabbed another chunk of tofu, squinted at it, sighed. "I don't eat meat." She put the fork down. "But I could use some comfort food. I suppose you could talk me into a cheese pizza."

"I bet I could talk you into a pitcher of beer too."

Rico's New York Style Pizza was a pleasantly shabby place with red-and-white plastic tablecloths. The guy who owned it wasn't named Rico and had never been to New York. But the pizza was hot and the cheese thick.

Annette had eaten three slices and was on her fourth, the stringy cheese stretching from the slice to her teeth. She reeled in the cheese with a slurp and pushed it down with three serious gulps of cold beer.

"After my divorce I went on this health kick." Annette refilled her mug from the nearly empty pitcher. "I lost twelve pounds and firmed up my abs and lowered my cholesterol. The whole deal."

"Sounds terrible." Morgan sprinkled red pepper on his pizza.

"It is," she said. "I've been hard at it about three years. I sold his golf clubs and used the cash to buy this stationary bike. I do about two hours a night. I'll have to do three tonight after this pig fest."

But she didn't let up, dipped the crust into a stray puddle of sauce, and ate it.

"I started doing sit-ups a week ago," Morgan said. He'd also started walking a mile a day in the evenings and laying off the bottle. So far he hadn't seen the results, but he kept telling himself to be patient.

"Yeah, well it won't make you happy," she said. "I got myself into this routine. Exercise and vitamins and sprouts and yoga and I even did my apartment all in feng shui and I guess I've prolonged my life for twenty years; but I'm not *living*, if you see what I mean. I've locked myself into such a rigid routine it's like I'm some kind of robot. I mean I've exercised and dieted and exercised and believe me I've got one killer body under these frumpy teacher clothes, but what good is it? It's been so long since I've"—she shook her head—"Never mind. I'm running off at the mouth."

"No, do go on." Morgan grinned, flashed his blue eyes. "How long since you've what?"

Annette leaned back in the booth, half smiled at Morgan over her beer mug. "I know professors like you. You've probably got some free-spirit poetry spiel you toss around until some big-eyed grad student decides she wants to be your protégé."

Morgan flushed and turned off his eyes. She'd caught him trying to use the same look he used on young girls. Indeed, he had been about to make his standard pitch. Foolish. That wouldn't work on Annette. She was a mature, smart woman, not a blushing twenty-year-old.

"I'm divorced too," Morgan said. "But I threw myself into self-destruction instead of health, late nights, hit the booze hard, moved around job to job."

"How long's it been?"

"Seven years," Morgan said. "She tossed me out. I'm no good

on my own. I stay up too late, bad eating habits. I don't really take care of myself."

Was this it? Was this how adults talked to one another? It had been a long time.

"Listen," Morgan said, "I've been after you to have dinner with me for a while now. How about this Friday night?"

She scrunched her face, tapped her face with a thin finger. "I don't think so, Jay. I like you. Really. But I don't think you'd be good for me. I can't start living big overnight, and I don't think a week of sit-ups is going to change you. I think we better try being friends for a while."

"I understand." He felt a sulk coming on and didn't try to stop it.

"But listen, I meant what I said about Ellis. Something's going on."

"Uh-huh."

"I want you to talk to the dean," she said. "The more of us who protest the better. Whittaker needs to know the faculty won't sit still for every bullshit scheme the administration tries to put over."

"Uh-huh."

"Are you even paying attention to me? This is important."

"If you say so."

"Dammit!" Her nostrils flared. "I worked my ass off to get where I am. I'm not going to be a professor at some backwater diploma mill. I'm going to find out about this Ellis kid, and I'll do it alone if I have to." She slid out of the booth, dropped a twenty on the table. "That should cover my part of lunch."

She didn't quite storm out, but she didn't look back.

sixteen

I don't want to see any more rodents," Morgan said. "You understand?"

"Yes." Lancaster looked sheepish.

"No rats, no mice, no hamsters, no kind of furry animals at all, okay? I don't want to read any more poems in which furry animals are symbolic of anything at all. You get me?"

Lancaster gulped. "Yes, sir."

"I don't even want to see little animals symbolize themselves. I don't want to even see a person in your poem wearing fuzzy bedroom slippers that are even remotely reminiscent of anything animal-like at all."

Lancaster went red at the ears. He couldn't look at the rest of the class, head down.

Morgan had to come down on the kid hard. Sometimes these students got stuck in a rut and it just got worse and worse until somebody gave them a slap. "I hope I've been clear."

Lancaster nodded.

"I want to read a poem about people. They can be fucking or making soup or driving tractors or buying baseball cards on eBay or chewing tobacco or anything you damn well want. But I want people."

Lancaster said nothing, didn't budge. He'd been thoroughly squashed.

"Okay." Morgan shuffled his stack of papers to the last poem of the day. Hell. It was the Ellis kid's turn. Morgan had been dreading this. He looked at his watch. Maybe he could claim they were out of time, put off Ellis's poem until next class. No good. Still fifteen minutes left. Nothing to do but forge ahead.

"Sherman, read us your poem please."

Ellis actually stood. This was different. Morgan wondered for a second if Ellis was actually about to leave, run out of the class instead of read his poem. Morgan had seen it happen before. But Ellis wasn't going anywhere. He had a fierce look in his eyes, chest puffed out.

Ellis waved his fist in the air, slapped his chest with the other hand. "Okay, y'all, this is Sherman E in the house. I'm gonna need some help with this one. Everybody say YEAH!"

Everybody froze. The students looked at Morgan.

Then the poem:

> *I was cruising the hood in my red Mercedes,*
> *keeping it real with my homies and my ladies,*
> *nobody can touch my crew because all them cats are fraidies.*
> *Them St. Louis niggers ain't got no class,*
> *twitching on the crack bust a cap in my ass.*

Ellis recited his poem like he was angry, slapping his desk with the rhythm, saliva flying from his mouth, eyes white and wild.

> *They rocking and shaken and frying up some bacon,*
> *but if they think they know Sherman E then they sadly*
> *   mistaken.*
> *Gonna POP that COP*
> *Cocksucker motherfucker never make me STOP.*
> *Bleed the bitch out now shout now shout.*

At this point Ellis grabbed his own balls, hopped up and down.

> *On your knees on your knees, show you what it's 'bout.*
> *I'll pull you a stunt, smoke my blunt Sherman E don't*
> *Take shit from some cunt.*

Ellis looked at Morgan, waited for commentary.

The class sat in dead quiet. Dumbstruck. Morgan went pale, his lips squeezed tight and bloodred like wet paint.

Belinda paled, hugged herself in her seat.

Terrible. Morgan shook his head. *What the hell am I supposed to do with that?*

Lancaster tugged at his collar. "Well..." He looked at his copy of the poem, made useless scratches with his pen. "Well, yes. Okay then. I think it's very brave of Sherman to embrace certain clichés and stereotypes in an attempt to . . . uh . . . explore the dangers of..." He shook his head. "Look, I don't really know *what* Sherman was trying to do."

DelPrego's mouth hung open. "Jesus." He barked a hard laugh. "I mean...Jesus."

Morgan shuffled the stack of poems, stood slowly. He turned, walked out the door. The students waited a minute, looked at one another, but their professor didn't come back.

Ginny waited on Morgan's porch. She was there smiling coyly when he arrived home.

He froze when he saw her, looked around.

"I thought you'd call me," Ginny said. That's how it was supposed to work. She cast her spell, and the poet wouldn't be able to live without her. But he hadn't called.

"I didn't think you wanted me to." He unlocked the front door, and she followed him in.

"You hurt my feelings," she said.

"I didn't mean to."

"No, I was being dumb." She put her hand on his hip. Tentative. This would be the test. If he shrugged her off, then she was barking up the wrong tree. "Can we go in the bedroom?"

"Sure."

Gotcha.

He stood stiffly, let her unzip him, strip him clean. She unbuttoned her blouse, wriggled out of her too tight jeans, white breasts spilling over a red lace bra. She peeled off thong panties. They moved to the bed and didn't talk.

When she was on top of him, Morgan tilted his head back into the pillow, closed his eyes. Ginny ground into him, bit her lower lip hard. Even if Morgan never helped her writing career, she still liked this part. Liked it a lot.

seventeen

Harold Jenks slumped at the bar between his new classmates Timothy Lancaster III and Wayne DelPrego. They'd just started their fourth pitcher of beer.

When class had ended and Morgan had walked out, Jenks had just stood there with his balls in his hand. His first poem hadn't gone over so well, so he'd really tried to sell this one, put everything into it. Make it one righteous, kick-ass performance. But by the time he'd finished reading, he'd found himself in a roomful of truly terrified white people.

Most of the class had filed out, carefully not making eye contact. But Wayne DelPrego had approached him, shaking his head, a smart-ass grin crooked on his face.

"Christ Almighty," DelPrego said. "You've either got some jumbo, supersized testicles or you're high."

Jenks told DelPrego to fuck his mother.

"Take it easy, man," DelPrego said. "The poetry thing's a tough gig. Let me buy you a beer. Timothy and I get one after every workshop."

Jenks thought briefly about busting DelPrego in the mouth, but decided a beer would be more helpful. He looked at his watch. It wasn't even noon.

Time flew by at the bar, and Jenks found himself deep in meaningless conversation with Lancaster and DelPrego.

"Have you seen the statistics on college binge drinking?" Lancaster held his beer mug up for inspection, wiped a smudge clean with his napkin. "This is dangerously stereotypical behavior we're engaging in."

"Oh, yeah?" Jenks said. "Well, you just ended your sentence with a preposition." Dr. Grayson had just drilled him on prepositions yesterday in the Writing Lab. She was one hard-core bitch.

"Touché." Lancaster sipped beer, but it had gotten warm. He frowned, pushed the mug away.

"Shit," DelPrego said. "After Morgan's class, we need a few belts. That guy doesn't like anything."

"I hear that." Lancaster had told Jenks his poem amounted to little more than predictable rhyme and juvenile posturing. No imagery, little attention to the intricacies of language. Jenks wasn't totally sure he knew what that meant, but he was sure it wasn't good. But at least Lancaster hadn't walked out of class looking like he was about to puke.

This shit was going to be harder than he thought.

"Yes, well, he wasn't totally without a point," Lancaster said. He waved the bartender over. "Take this away," he said, indicating the beer mug. "Bring me a chardonnay please."

The big bartender scowled down at him. "This ain't exactly a chardonnay-type place."

Jenks chuckled. It was true. The place was pretty rough and backwoodsy. A long unpainted pine bar, mismatched stools, seats, and tables. DelPrego had told Jenks that the noise coming out of the jukebox was some shit called Vince Gill. But the place had pool tables and cold beer, and right now that was enough. DelPrego had convinced Jenks and Lancaster to enter the place on the grounds the drinks were cheap.

"You don't like my rhymes?" Jenks asked Lancaster.

"Just a second, Sherman." Lancaster turned back to the bartender. "Do you have any wine at all?"

The bartender bent behind the bar, came back up with a screwcap jug the size of a Volkswagen, half-full. "This. It's red."

"Dear God. No, I can't drink that. Just a glass of water with lemon."

The bartender rolled his eyes and walked away. It didn't look like he was in any hurry to bring Lancaster his water.

Jenks tapped Lancaster's shoulder. "I asked you a question."

Lancaster sighed. "Frankly, I didn't care for it. Perhaps I'm too traditional."

"Fuck you, man."

DelPrego snickered.

"Fuck you too," Jenks said.

"That's another thing," Lancaster said. "You don't seem to get the idea of the workshop. Perhaps they do it differently where you're from. But essentially, we're supposed to say whatever we think about the work. You're not supposed to take it personally. I mean it's about focusing on the work, not the person."

"Fuck you anyway."

"Like you can talk, Timothy," DelPrego said. "Professor Morgan didn't like your shit either. Or mine for that matter. He hates us, man."

Jenks slapped the bar with an open palm. "That's what I'm talking 'bout. That motherfucker can't be pleased about nothing. Why try? He ain't going to like it anyway."

"We just have to tune in to his aesthetic," Lancaster said.

"Right now I'm just going to tune in to this." DelPrego gulped beer.

"Okay," Jenks said. "You know all about it, then explain this shit to me."

"I'll try," Lancaster said. "Poetry is like, it's like..." He pinched his thumb and forefinger together like he was trying to pluck the definition of poetry out of midair. "Poetry is reminding you about truths you forgot you already knew. A poem doesn't tell us something, it shows us. It doesn't reflect an experience. A poem is its own experience."

"I don't understand one fucking thing you're saying."

"Let's all get some guns and go to Mexico," DelPrego said. "Let's get whores."

"Yes, that sounds constructive," Lancaster said.

"How would you cats like to earn a few extra dollars?" asked Jenks. He realized he was feeling a bit drunk himself but didn't care. He drained his mug.

"Who you want us to kill?" DelPrego said.

Jenks didn't laugh. "I'm serious. Can you boys be tough? Can we be tight?"

Lancaster sighed. "I think you're both already tight."

"Hey, I ain't so fucked up I don't know what I'm talking about. You guys got enough money? Is that it? You're so up to your asses in greenbacks that you don't need any more?"

"Is it something illegal?" asked DelPrego. "I mean, I don't care. I just want to know."

"Shit, I ain't saying nothing until I knew we're tight. This kinda shit get fucked up quick if it ain't handled by guys that don't have trust. Now, when I see we tight, I'll let you know. But I'm thinking we can be tight."

"Is there some sort of written exam for this?" Lancaster asked. "How does one go about becoming tight?"

"I'll tell you when it happens."

Jenks still wasn't sure about these two, but they seemed to be regular guys. They just wanted to find out how to get through school, how to get ahead, how to keep a roof over their heads and once in a while find some pussy. Lancaster was a little strange and maybe too smart for his own damn good, but he didn't talk down to Jenks. He didn't *patronize*. A word he got from Grayson.

Patronize.

"We want you sons a bitches out of here right now. Just about had enough of listening to your bullshit."

The three of them spun on their barstools, looked into the glassy eyes of two gigantic rednecks. They had full, thick beards, bellies hanging over big belt buckles. One wore a Sooners cap. The other had a buzz cut and a faded Marine Corps tattoo on his massive upper arm. They both held pool cues.

A fresh cigarette dangled from Sooner Cap's mouth. It bobbed up and down as he talked. "We don't want your kind in here. So get the hell out right now."

Jenks almost said something, but DelPrego opened his mouth first.

"Come on, guys. It's the twenty-first century," DelPrego said. "Don't tell me you've never seen a black person."

"We don't give a shit about blacks," Tattoo Man said. "It's him." He jabbed a finger at Lancaster. "We don't like faggots."

Lancaster's jaw dropped. "What?"

"Get out of our bar, faggot."

The blood drained from Lancaster's face. "But—I assure you—" he sputtered.

This was trouble. Jenks sized up the rednecks. Both of them tensed for it. Sooner Cap had on a pair of heavy work boots, but Tattoo Man wore only soft sneakers. Jenks scanned their jeans for gun-shaped bulges or knives, but they looked clean. He didn't like the way they held those pool cues.

DelPrego hopped off his stool, spoke to Sooner Cap. "He's not a faggot."

"Shut up, punk."

"He's no faggot, and I should know," DelPrego said. "Because I'm the faggot, and I just love to suck big cock."

Sooner Cap blinked, stepped back like he'd been struck.

"That's right." DelPrego licked his lips. "Man, I'd just love to have a big, sweaty pair of redneck balls on my chin right now. I get hot and horny just thinking about it."

Sooner Cap realized he was being had. "How about I smash you right in your smart-ass little mouth?"

Lancaster gulped. "For the love of God, Wayne, let it go."

Jenks tensed. Here it came.

DelPrego pointed. "Holy shit. What's that behind you?"

Sooner Cap said, "You don't think I'm going to fall for—"

DelPrego didn't wait to see if he fell for it or not. He brought the uppercut fast, popped Sooner Cap on the point of his chin. The redneck's head snapped back. He stumbled.

Tattoo Man swung the pool cue at Jenks, but Jenks ducked. The cue struck Lancaster in the face, swept him off the barstool like he was made of tissue. Lancaster yelled, blood spraying from his nose.

Jenks stomped hard with his heel on top of Tattoo Man's left tennis shoe. His heel struck the foot hard. Jenks heard and felt the man's bone snap. Tattoo Man screamed. Jenks double-punched him in the kidneys, and Tattoo Man bent, grabbed himself. Jenks swung hard, and his knuckles smacked just over Tattoo Man's ear.

Tattoo Man fell over into a little heap, didn't move.

Sooner Cap had DelPrego in a headlock. Jenks picked up Tattoo Man's pool cue, swung hard, and broke the wood over Sooner Cap's back. He let go of DelPrego, who turned and threw a quick punch into the redneck's massive gut. Sooner Cap *whuffed* air and went to one knee.

"That's enough!" the bartender barked. He held an aluminum baseball bat and banged it on the bar.

Sooner Cap started to get up. He was breathing hard. "You... fuckers."

"Come on!" Jenks grabbed Lancaster under one arm, started for the door.

DelPrego took Lancaster's other arm, burst out of the saloon and into the parking lot.

The redneck's curses followed them. "You little faggots. Come back here again and you're dead. You hear me? Dead!"

The three poets sat in a nearly deserted Wendy's. Jenks ate a double cheeseburger and a Biggie fries. DelPrego held a small Frosty to the side of his head where his ear had swollen.

Lancaster sat with his head tilted back, crumpled and bloody napkins on the table in front of him. He'd torn little strips of napkin and had jammed them into his nostrils to stanch the blood flow. Once in a while he'd moan quietly and rub his temples.

"Shit, boy, where'd you learn to fight like that?" Jenks asked DelPrego. "You almost got your fucking self killed."

"I watch a lot of *Rockford Files* reruns."

"TV. Shit, that figures."

"Do we qualify as tight now?" Lancaster asked, his stuffed nose making him hard to understand, the words coming out "Do be qualiby ad dight dow?"

Jenks laughed. "Almost."

"Sure we are," DelPrego said. "We're a hell of a team. The brother, the white guy, and the faggot."

He laughed and so did Jenks.

Lancaster groaned and very slowly lifted his middle finger.

eighteen

Morgan tried to roll over, but Ginny's slab of thigh held him in place. He didn't want to wake her. He lay still, staring at the ceiling, feeling empty and listless. The mad tumble with Ginny had been a good distraction after Annette had shrugged him off, but already Ginny's hot skin pressed against him in bed. Oppressive.

And it wasn't just Annette.

For a long time Morgan had been directionless. He'd realized it while working with the old man, Fred Jones. It was the first time he'd felt like a poet or a teacher in years. And he'd realized it again talking to Annette Grayson, telling her how he'd blown with the wind from one temporary job to another.

And then there was Annie Walsh. The dreams were getting worse. In the most recent, he could hear her clawing under the ground. His dream self tried to dig her out, pale hands ripping at the hard winter ground, digging without a shovel, fingernails hurt and bleeding.

Morgan shuddered.

Ginny's breathing changed, and Morgan suspected she was awake. They both pretended to sleep.

After half an hour, Morgan figured something had to give. He opened his mouth, drew breath to speak, didn't know what to say, and shut it again.

"What is it?" Ginny asked.

"I didn't know if you were awake yet."

"I'm awake."

Morgan still didn't know what to say.

Ginny said, "It's like we have a secret together. Don't you think that makes people close? It's kind of a prefabricated intimacy. And I need this once in a while, to be close and naked with somebody I can trust. Maybe a weird kind of trust but it's there, and I want you to feel it too."

"I feel it."

"It doesn't seem like you do. I can't handle boys my age. If they sleep with a girl once, they either think they own her or they want to throw her out like an empty beer can. I like that you're older. I want us to be friends. I read your poetry book."

"Which one? *A Shot of Bourbon for the Soul*?"

"The other one. The hat one."

"*In the Museum of Men's Hats*. That was my first one. It wasn't very good."

"I thought it was pretty good."

"Thanks."

"Are you working on anything now?"

Morgan squirmed, shifted away from her. "Not right now."

"Writer's block."

"No." It came out more harsh than he'd meant. "I just haven't decided on anything yet."

"I think you're stuck."

"What would you know about it?"

"I want you to be able to tell me."

"It's not anything for you to worry about."

"This is part of it," Ginny said. "I want us to tell each other things."

"I don't want to tell you."

A shrug. "Got to tell somebody. Do you have anyone to talk to?"

"I'm not a talker."

"That's bad."

"Yeah..." He didn't know what he wanted to say. He'd been closed up, closed off, didn't know how to say what was wrong. Maybe he didn't even know because he couldn't say it out loud. "What if I try, really try my best, and nothing comes?"

He'd never said that out loud before.

"We all get scared." She twirled his chest hair.

That was all she said. Morgan suddenly felt tired again. He moved closer to her, put his head on the pillow. He felt lighter. He drifted. Sleep.

When he awoke, Ginny was gone. Morgan didn't feel bad about it.

He walked around the cold house naked, looked into each room. He didn't know what he was looking for, but he felt he was looking for something. An invisible need drew him. He wandered to his desk, opened the bottom drawer. An old accordion folder.

His poetry.

Halfhearted attempts at least a year old. He winced at the

pages. Old themes and strategies mixed and matched and re-hashed. It was painful to read but he made himself. He wrapped up the folder, put his head in his hands, and closed his eyes. It was worse than he remembered. Even his grad students were showing brighter sparks of originality.

He lifted his head. Set his jaw. It was time. Too long he'd galumphed along, stagnant. What was it Keats had written? *Half in love with easeful death*. That was Morgan all over. He'd been walking around dead, and it had been easy, so Morgan let it go on.

No more.

He showered, dressed. He scooped up the poems quickly before he could change his mind. He jogged to his Buick, drove to campus.

In Albatross Hall he took the stairs up two at a time. On the fifth floor, he listened for the music. It wasn't there, but it didn't matter. He knew the way. He found Valentine's office, knocked once, barged inside. He was breathing hard, heart thumping into his throat.

Valentine sat on his couch, sipping a cup of tea. He arched his eyebrows at Morgan. There was a portable TV the size of a toaster on Valentine's lap.

"These are some of my poems." Morgan showed him the folder. "I'm—" He shook his head, cleared his throat. "I'm having some problems with my writing, and you're the single greatest living poet I know. I need your help."

"Don't be ridiculous," Valentine said. "*Wheel of Fortune* is on."

Dean Whittaker sat at his desk, shuffled papers, made stern phone calls to department heads. He went about the machinery of being dean, the dogged determination of an academic administrator. He crossed *T*'s, dotted *i*'s.

A knock.

Whittaker looked up. "Come in."

The door swung open, and Jay Morgan walked in. He flipped a two-fingered salute at the dean and sat in the chair across from him.

"Good. You got my message," Whittaker said. "I tried to find you in your office, but you're a hard man to track down."

"Sorry, I was consulting with a colleague."

The dean searched Morgan's face. There was something different about the man. His head was up. He was smiling. There was an easy look in his eyes. The dean thought he might smell alcohol.

"I wanted to talk to you about the Spring Reading. We usually have a few handpicked grad students read. I want you to make sure Sherman Ellis is one of them."

Morgan smiled big. "Sure. Let's give him an NEA grant too."

Whittaker frowned, shot radioactive heat rays out of his eyes at Morgan.

Morgan gulped. "You're serious."

Whittaker raised an eyebrow. He'd had nothing but complaints about this Ellis kid, and so he wasn't surprised at Morgan's lack of enthusiasm. He'd had to be tough with a few of the faculty to keep them in line on the subject.

"I take it he's doing well in your workshop."

"Not at all," Morgan said.

"Tough titty. Look, Morgan, we both know this is a public relations move. The university wants to show off their new African-American student. With or without you the administration wants Ellis. But if you don't want to be part of this, I completely understand."

Morgan stood. "I don't want to be part of it."

Whittaker cleared his throat, the rough sound of a surgical saw cutting into bone. "However..."

Morgan sat down again.

"I'd hate to think you weren't a team player." The dean shook his head like he was disappointed with a puppy that had shit on the carpet. "After all, when you go to your next job after this, you'll want to give me as a reference. They always check your last employer, and they always want to know if a professor is a team player."

Morgan felt sweat behind his ears. He wiped his forehead, swallowed hard. "I don't think you understand. Ellis read his last poem, and, well, he scared the crap out of everybody in the class. I mean, I just don't think it's the feel-good poetry you want for a public relations event."

"It's *exactly* what we want," Whittaker said. "Tell Ellis to let it all hang out. Let him be ethnic as hell. We'll show the regents we can be as multicultural as anyone."

"But—"

"There's another consideration," the dean said. "I'm getting a little concerned about Professor Valentine. He might be close to retirement. That would mean an open position for a tenure track professor." The dean could see he had Morgan's interest. The classic carrot and stick ploy. A brand-new job or a ruined career. "I'm sure you know what a lot of trouble it is to put together a search committee and go through a hiring process. It would sure be easier on everyone if there was a poet right here under our nose who fit the bill."

Morgan nodded slowly. "I want to be a team player, Dr. Whittaker. I'll get ahold of Ellis. I'll make it happen."

Whittaker sat back in his chair, an evil smile spread thin across his face. "I knew we could count on you, Morgan."

Morgan felt excited and frightened and a little sick as he left the dean's office. Sherman Ellis. Why in the hell did they want this gangster rap craziness as part of their annual poetry reading?

But Morgan wanted that job. God, how he wanted it. He tried not to think of Valentine. Hey, it was eat or be eaten. Morgan was tired of going from school to school. What if he couldn't get another position? He couldn't live on adjunct pay. Hell, he might actually have to resort to teaching high school. No, he wouldn't be able to stomach that. Teenagers scared the hell out of him.

Okay, he'd find Ellis. Tell him he was going to read some goddamn poetry and that was it. Morgan would write the poems himself if he had to. All Sherman Ellis would have to do was stand up there and read them without alienating every white person in the room.

nineteen

Jenks had set up the deal for early in the morning.

DelPrego had been strangely eager. Lancaster didn't want anything to do with it, but Jenks had insisted over and over again that Lancaster would only be required to sit in the car.

Jenks rode between Lancaster and DelPrego in DelPrego's fifteen-year-old pickup truck. The day was cold but clear, and they drove with the windows down, huddled close across the truck's bench seat. Jenks wore a heavy army surplus jacket, baggy, big pockets. He pulled his dark blue watch cap over his ears. Lancaster wore a long camel hair coat, slightly worn at the elbows. It had once been an expensive garment, but Lancaster confessed he'd picked it up at a thrift store in Tulsa. DelPrego's denim jacket was too light for the weather, but the cold never seemed to bother him.

They each sipped a large cup of convenience store coffee.

"I can't believe you talked me into this," Lancaster said. "A drug sale. This is nothing but a common drug sale. We're criminals."

"A thousand bucks to each of you just to ride along," Jenks said. "This guy's a professional dealer. He don't get it from me, he just gets it from somebody else."

"Where'd you get all that cocaine?" DelPrego asked.

"Just a fluke. This is my one deal." Jenks held his coffee cup with both hands, felt the warmth. "As soon as I get this money it's straight and narrow for me."

"Good," Lancaster said. "Otherwise, count me out."

"Me too," DelPrego said. "I'm flat-ass broke. They cut off my phone. I need cash so bad I'd sell coke to my grandmother."

"Okay then. One score and it's all done." Jenks pointed to the left. "Down that dirt road."

"How the hell you know where to go?" DelPrego turned the truck.

"I was out here yesterday to find the guy. He said come back today and he'd have the cash. That's why I needed you guys."

"But how did you know the first time?" DelPrego shot a glance at him.

"You keep your ears open and you hear things."

"I still don't like it," Lancaster said.

"We can stop the truck and let you out," Jenks said.

"I'm just saying I don't like it," Lancaster said. "I'm nervous that's all."

"Good. Keep you on your toes."

The land sloped up gently, and they saw the gray, weatherworn barn on a rise a half mile up. They drove toward it easy and slow. A little squat house a few dozen yards from the barn. One half-assed tornado would knock the place to kindling.

"This isn't where drug dealers live in the movies," DelPrego said.

Jenks wasn't listening. He pulled the .32 revolver and the 9mm Glock from two of his baggy pockets. "Here." He dropped the revolver into Lancaster's lap.

"What!" Lancaster jerked, looked down at the gun like Jenks had dumped hot coals on his crotch. "I don't want this thing."

"Shit." Jenks slammed a clip into the Glock. "What the fuck you think you're here for? To keep me company?"

"I don't want it." Lancaster looked sick. "You said all I had to do was sit in the car. Give it to Wayne."

"Don't bother." DelPrego reached under his seat, pulled out a double-barreled shotgun. "Twelve-gauge. Loaded with buckshot." The barrels had been hacked short. The whole gun was barely two feet long, stock and all.

Lancaster groaned.

"Good." Jenks stuck the Glock in his belt under the army jacket. "You guys hang back. That's all. If he sees I got backup, he'll be less likely to pull a funny. Now drive up within a hundred feet of that barn. Nice and slow."

They finished their coffee, tossed the cups out the window.

Moses Duncan puffed a cigarette, watched through the crack in the barn door as the truck approached. He wore a heavy corduroy jacket which hid the .38 revolver in his belt. The pistol was thirty years old and had been his daddy's. He'd kept it clean and well oiled over the years, just like Daddy had shown him.

The truck was getting closer, and he could see three men in the front seat. That damn coon had brought friends. Hell, he should have figured. Well, that was okay. He had friends too. Big John up in the loft with a shotgun. His pal Eddie in the house, watching from the front window. Eddie was the most goddamn bad shot Moses had ever seen, but he could make a hell of a lot of noise with his army-issue .45.

The coon had approached him yesterday about buying a butt-load of coke at a fraction of the street value, and Moses thought, hell, why not get it for free? The guy was clearly from out of town. Nobody would miss him, and he could feed his body to the pigs. And the coke would be all his. He wouldn't have to filter the profits back to his contacts down in Oklahoma City. He could get a new Harley. Fix the thermostat in the house. Fix himself up with some new threads. Twenty grand for a hundred thousand dollars' worth of coke was actually a damn fine deal, but Duncan couldn't raise twenty grand any more than he could hammer a tent peg through a block of ice with his pecker.

No, there just wasn't any honest way to do this deal, and frankly Duncan didn't bet on losing any sleep over it.

Nothing to do now but let the truck get close and park. If he could get the coon into the barn, they could bushwhack him good.

"Stop the truck," Jenks said.

DelPrego parked the truck a hundred feet from the barn and shifted into park. He left the engine running.

"Here's how it's going to happen," Jenks said. "You guys get out the truck, see. Stand there by the open doors and watch me go toward the guy with the money. Be looking around in case he's got some buddies. Lancaster, you can leave that .32 in your coat pocket. It's small enough. Keep your hand in there like you're staying warm. Keep hold of the gun, be ready to bring it out fast in case some shit happens. You hear?"

Lancaster shook his head. "I changed my mind." He looked a

little green, breath short. "Wayne? You changed your mind too, right? I want to go."

Jenks ignored Lancaster, nudged DelPrego. "You'll need to leave that scattergun on the seat, but the door will be open so you can grab it quick if you have to."

"Right."

"But your main job is to drive. Some kind of hell breaks loose, you come get me. I'll jump in the bed so you can drive off quick. Slow down a little, so I can jump in the back."

"You expect trouble."

"Just being careful. Lancaster, you got to spray bullets at whoever's causing the trouble. Keep me covered until I'm in the truck."

"God. Sherman, look, I don't want to shoot anybody, okay? I don't think I can. You said all I had to do was sit in the car."

"Sit in the car *with* the gun. You just got to make them duck. Give me a chance to get back."

"I have to pee."

"Chances are he'll give me the money and I'll give him the powder and that's that. So you two stay cool. Don't twitch out on me. Keep your eyes open."

DelPrego opened their car door, stepped out. Lancaster was frozen in his seat. Jenks slid out DelPrego's side, walked around, and stood in front of the pickup. DelPrego leaned on the driver's-side door, the butt of the shotgun on the seat within quick reach.

The barn door creaked open and Moses Duncan stepped out. He had a paper grocery sack under his arm. Jenks tried to eye him for weapons, but that corduroy jacket was so baggy, could have been twenty guns and a bazooka under there. Jenks waved, set the gym bag with the cocaine on the hood of DelPrego's truck.

"Hey there, boy," called Duncan. "You're on time. Good. I got your money right here."

"Let's trade," Jenks said.

"That's fine. Come on in the barn and we'll settle up."

Jenks shook his head. "Out here in the open."

"Hell, boy, I just want to get out of the wind." Duncan frowned, rubbed his nose with his thumb. "Besides, I don't know them two fellows you brought. Sort of makes a man nervous."

"Look, dude, this is simple," Jenks said. "You walk this way and I'll walk to you and we'll trade in the middle."

Duncan looked back into the barn, turned again to Jenks. "Yeah, okay."

They both started walking and met between DelPrego's pickup and the barn. Jenks dropped the bag at Duncan's feet.

Duncan smiled big. He was missing a molar toward the back. "Got your cash right here. Had to hit up a few folks to raise this kind of money, but I managed to scrape it together." Duncan unrolled the top of the grocery sack, started to reach inside.

"Just hand me the bag." Jenks grabbed it, started to pull it out of Duncan's hands.

For a split second Duncan resisted, his smile wavering. "No problem. Count it if you want." He released his grip and Jenks took the sack.

It had happened before that some slick criminal had hidden a gun in the money bag, gone in for greenbacks and came out with the heat. Jenks wasn't taking any chances. He opened the bag, peeked inside.

DelPrego's voice came strained and panicked from behind. "Sherman, look out!"

Duncan's hand was halfway out from under his jacket. Jenks saw the pistol and leapt forward, tossed the bag of money into Duncan's face, and grabbed at the gun. Duncan kicked him away, pulled the pistol, but Jenks was already swinging. He popped

Duncan solid on the nose, pressed it flat. Duncan grunted and his pistol flew, landed behind him.

Jenks went for his Glock, and behind him DelPrego's shotgun thundered.

Jenks looked up.

A lanky redneck in a blue plaid shirt fell through the open door of the barn's loft. He tumbled in B-movie slow motion, ragged arms flapping in the air. He did a long slow flip and landed on his back in the dirt.

Explosions from the front window of the house. Shots.

Bullets chewed up the ground around Jenks's feet, flew over his head, dotted the hood of DelPrego's truck with metallic *ptunks*. Jenks fled toward the pickup.

DelPrego was in the driver's seat and already screaming toward him.

Lancaster dropped the .32 onto the floor of the pickup. He squeezed himself as low and as small as possible. DelPrego slammed on the brakes too late, smacked Jenks in the upper thighs with the front bumper.

Jenks sprawled back, landed hard in the dust. "Fuck!"

Shots from the barn now. Duncan had recovered his pistol and was blasting wildly from the barn door. Most of the shots went high, but one shattered a headlight.

Jenks fired from his back, upside down over his head back at Duncan, didn't hit anything but sky. Jenks shifted, shot at the house, shattered the glass of the front window into glittering shards.

DelPrego stuck the sawed-off shotgun out the window, fired it one-handed. The buckshot pellets scorched the barn door, but a few ventilated Duncan's jacket under his left arm. Duncan's scream was high-pitched, like a frightened animal's. He ducked back into the barn, pushed the door closed.

Jenks groaned to his feet, hobbled around to the side of the pickup, and threw himself in the bed. He still had the gym bag in a tight grip. "Drive! Get the fuck out of here, man."

DelPrego drove twenty feet then slammed on the brakes again.

"What are you doing?" Lancaster's eyes were as big as dinner plates. Shots had erupted again from the house's front window. "Keep driving."

"I'm going for the money," DelPrego shouted. "Cover me."

DelPrego dashed from the truck, snatched the paper sack out of the dirt.

"Cover you? What?" Lancaster yelled after him.

Jenks raised his head from the back of the pickup, saw what DelPrego was doing. "Run, white boy. Move your ass." He pointed the Glock at the house, unloaded the rest of his clip, the pistol bucking in his hand. More glass rained.

DelPrego jumped back in the truck, tossed the sack into Lancaster's lap.

He slapped the truck in gear and fishtailed around, stomped the gas. He clipped Duncan's mailbox as he made the turn out of the driveway. The mailbox made a hollow pop and spun off into the hedges. He hauled ass down the narrow dirt road, the plume of dust behind him like some kind of freak sandstorm. Each bump and dip almost tossed Jenks out of the back. He only slowed down when they finally reached the highway.

DelPrego pointed the truck back toward town, chest heaving. Lancaster still shook.

In the bed, Jenks lay flat on his back, looked up unblinking at the cloudless blue sky stretching wide and forever. After a few minutes he climbed to one knee and knocked on the little window in back of the cab.

Lancaster slid it open.

"Check the money," Jenks said.

Lancaster opened the bag, pulled out a wad of newspaper cut to seem like bills. He dumped the whole bag onto the floor of the pickup at his feet. It was all newspaper.

"Oh, no," Lancaster said. "We were almost killed. Almost shot for shredded newspaper. I can't believe I let you two talk me into this."

Jenks wasn't listening. He was already trying to figure what his next move would be.

"Cheer up." DelPrego grinned big at Lancaster. "If it makes you feel any better, you can have my share."

Moses Duncan unbuttoned his jacket with trembling hands. His ribs blazed. He felt warm and wet under his shirt. He peeled the jacket off, explored his side with tentative fingers. It stung. He wiped the blood away, made himself look.

One of the shotgun pellets had only scraped him, a deep gash, plenty of blood.

Nervous laughter spilled out of him. He thought the shotgun had ended him, the hot stab of pain when the guy in the truck had squeezed one off. He ripped off his T-shirt, bunched it against the wound.

He looked outside, saw Big John flat on his back.

"Hell."

He took two halting steps toward the house, saw the shattered glass of the front window. He tried to shout "Eddie" but it came out hoarse and choked. He was shivering now, breath coming in short, aching gasps. He gathered his voice. "Eddie!"

Nothing.

twenty

Deke Stubbs sat across from the bored police sergeant, trying not to look as impatient as he felt. The sergeant was on the phone and didn't seem in any kind of hurry to get back to the P.I.

Stubbs craned his neck, looked around the station. It was a pretty rinky-dink, tinstar operation. They probably handled minor crime, drunk college kids, traffic tickets, the usual. The sergeant wore his khaki shirt with the top two buttons open. A big straw hat pushed back on his head, and a police revolver slung low on his hip like a gunfighter's. He probably had a lasso in his pickup.

Stubbs didn't think he was going to get much from the local law, but he thought he might as well work the case by the numbers. The Walshes had called the cops when they hadn't heard from their daughter in four days. According to Eileen Walsh the cops were "impotent yahoos." Probably true. In any case, he was obligated to stop in and see if there'd been any developments.

The sergeant hung up the phone. His eyes focused on Stubbs again, and he frowned. "Oh, yeah. Now what can we do you for, Mr. Stunk?" His voice had a deep twang.

"It's Stubbs." He stuck a cigarette between his lips. "I told you already, Sarge. I'm following up on a missing college kid. Annie Walsh. Her parents called you and made a report."

"Don't light that. No smoking in county buildings."

Stubbs stuck the cigarette behind his ear. He looked at the cop's name tag. "Listen, Sergeant Hightower, maybe this is a bother for you, but the parents are really worried. How about you just check the files?"

Hightower nodded, smacked his teeth, and ran a thumb over the stubble on his chin. "Well, let me tell you something, Stubbs. Better yet, let me *show* you something." He stood slowly, shuffled to a file cabinet behind his desk. He opened the top drawer, pulled out a thick file, and put it in front of Stubbs as he sat down again.

"That's just this last eighteen months or so," Hightower said. "All parents who've called about missing kids. Nearly four hundred on file. Half these parents phone all panicked if the kids miss responding to one e-mail. And the kids, hell, they get a taste of freedom and that's all she wrote. You think they always tell their folks when they run off with a boyfriend or a girlfriend or join some cult or even just load up a van full of beer with some fraternity buddies and head to Mexico? Shit no. Most of them turn up a week or a month later and can't believe anybody was looking for them. And one more thing. Once the little spoiled brats leave the county, it ain't *our* problem no more. We'll forward the report to the State Police if someone requests it, but it almost never gets that far."

"What about the ones dead or kidnapped?"

Hightower sighed. "It happens, but not often and not recently."

"Annie Walsh has been missing two weeks."

"Hell, she could be in Colorado skiing."

"Or she could be dead."

"True enough," Hightower said. "But until we get a body or some other kind of evidence it just ain't a priority."

Stubbs grinned and stood. "Thanks, Sarge. It's cops like you that keep guys like me in business."

Hightower frowned, watched the private investigator shake his head as he left the police station.

Stubbs drove in ever-widening circles around the little college town. He wasn't sight-seeing or getting the lay of the land although maybe that was a good idea. He simply thought better while driving. He hung one arm out the open window of the Dodge, let the cold blast him sharp in the face. It felt good.

He wasn't thinking about how to go about his investigation. That was no problem. He just needed to find a thread, some kind of trail, then he'd keep following it until it led to Annie Walsh. Someone had seen or talked to the girl. Stubbs just needed to find out who.

How far could he string the Walshes along? Stubbs got paid by the day, and this wouldn't be the first time he took a more or less straightforward case and stretched it out like he was searching for the Lindbergh baby. He figured he could feed the Walshes little tidbits of information every two or three days, who he'd interviewed, where he'd been. From their end it would look like he was doing a lot of work.

Okay, so what was the first stop? He checked his notepad, read the address for Annie's apartment. Maybe the roommate would be home. A good place to start.

*   *   *

The girl was a stick figure, sickly pale, glasses thick. Lips fat and dark red. She looked at Stubbs through the door crack and over the chain. "Yeah?"

"I'm Deke Stubbs. Sorry to bother you. I'm a private investigator. Annie's parents hired me to look for her. Can we talk?"

She unchained the door and opened it a bit wider, leaned against the door frame, looking up at Stubbs without any particular expectations.

Stubbs checked his notepad. "You're Tiffany?"

"Just Tiff."

"Sure. You mind if I come in?"

She thought about it a little too long, but then stepped aside. Stubbs walked in, looked the place over. Secondhand furniture, a futon couch, prints of classic paintings cheaply framed. The living room turned into the dining room with a small kitchen on the side.

"When was the last time you saw Annie?" he asked.

"I've already been through this with Annie's mom," she said. "All I know is she's not here and rent's due in a week."

"Yeah, that's a drag, but it would help. Really."

"It was right after the start of school, about two weeks ago. Maybe a bit more, but I didn't think much about it when I didn't see her for a while."

"Why's that?"

"I didn't say this to Annie's mom, but in my opinion the girl was pretty much a slut. I'm sorry if that's offensive."

"I'm not offended."

"When a girl has a different boyfriend one right after another, she's a slut. So I hardly ever saw her sometimes. She'd stop in to check mail or change clothes or whatever, but she'd sleep out a lot of nights."

"Do you have names for any of these guys?"

"It wasn't any of my business, and I didn't care and I didn't *want* to know. Sometimes older men would come pick her up. You know what I mean by older."

"It doesn't sound like you liked her."

"She was just a roommate."

"Can I look in her room?"

Tiff shrugged. "It's through there."

She led him past a bathroom down a short hall, opened a door. A tiny bedroom. Clothes piled on the bed and behind the door. No pictures on the wall. Spartan.

Stubbs opened dresser drawers, pushed the clothes around. Nothing.

"What are you looking for?" Tiff acted like somebody who didn't want to seem interested but was.

"I don't know." Stubbs looked under the bed. "Anything helpful."

"She didn't have a lot of stuff," Tiff said. "All the furniture is mine."

Stubbs circled to the other side of the bed. He'd tuned the girl out. He sat on the bed, ran his hands between the mattress and box spring. His fingers hit something.

"Can I get a glass of water?" He rubbed his throat. "Dust."

"Sure." She left.

Stubbs pulled out the book. It was a journal, fake-leather bound, lined blank pages like they had in most bookstores. He thumbed through it quickly. It was half journal and half poetry notebook. Some of the entries had dates. Many didn't. He closed it and shoved it in his jacket pocket.

Tiff returned and gave him the water.

He gulped, smacked his lips. "Thanks." He handed the glass back to her. "I guess that's all. Nothing here."

"Sorry."

"Just routine. Had to give it a try." He took a business card out of his wallet. "My number's on here. Give me a ring if you hear from Annie or find out anything useful. Her folks are worried."

"Okay."

He gave her a final wave as he left the duplex. He slouched into the Dodge and pointed it toward a TGI Friday's he'd seen on the way into town. He'd have a beer and go through the journal.

A thread, that was all he needed. The little start of a trail to follow.

twenty-one

Jenks, DelPrego, and Lancaster stood around the hood of DelPrego's pickup in dreary silence. Jenks quietly puffed a Philly Blunt. They were parked in front of Jenks's garage apartment. The neighborhood was still, most everyone at work or school.

DelPrego fingered one of the ragged bullet holes in the hood. "They shot my truck."

They lapsed back into silence. Lancaster shifted from one foot to another.

Jenks sucked deep on the cigar, held the smoke in his lungs, then let it out in a long gray stream. He looked at DelPrego. "You ran me over, you dumbass."

"Yeah." DelPrego's grin was a bit forced. "Sorry about that."

"This is pointless," Lancaster said abruptly. "Sherman, if you're smart you'll flush that stuff down the toilet and never think about it again."

Jenks nodded, puffed, scratched his chin, and considered the gym bag still in the bed of the pickup. Lancaster was right, but Jenks just couldn't bring himself to do it. A hundred grand of coke. There had to be a way he could turn a buck on the stuff. He might have to go to Tulsa to make some kind of deal or maybe OK City.

"I want to go home." Lancaster looked pointedly at DelPrego.

DelPrego asked Jenks, "You need a ride anyplace? I'm going to take him."

Jenks continued to stare straight ahead. "Go ahead. See you in class."

DelPrego and Lancaster climbed into the pickup. DelPrego leaned out his window. His wide grin was genuine this time. "Cheer up, Sherm. We'll think of something."

That boy always thinks some shit is funny. Jenks fought down his own grin.

DelPrego backed out of the driveway, Jenks still staring at his shoes and absently smoking the cigar. The truck was already two blocks away and turning the corner when Jenks's head snapped up. He ran after the truck, waved his arms. "Wait!"

They didn't hear, kept driving.

The gym bag was still in the back of the pickup. Shit. Jenks flicked the stub of the cigar into the street. Anyway, he'd call Wayne. Tell him to bring the bag in, hide it in back of a closet or something and get it from him later.

He climbed the stairs to his apartment, unlocked the door, and went in.

Quick, strong hands grabbed him. A punch in the gut. Jenks coughed air, doubled over. The hands shoved him to the floor, and he landed hard.

"What the fuck!" Jenks looked up. Red Zach towered over him.

Jenks felt his stomach heave. "Oh, shit."

"You're damn right, oh shit. I should bust a cap in your black ass right here."

Zach wore a lime-green suit with a black shirt. Two of his bruisers flanked him, thick-necked sons of bitches with shaved heads and dark glasses. Spoon Oliver sat on the bed. He sported two swollen eyes and a split lip. Zach's boys had worked him over good.

"I want my goddamn coke," Zach said. "Or you're one dead nigger. You're already in for two broken legs."

"Zach—"

"Shut the fuck up." Zach kicked Jenks hard in the ribs.

Jenks glanced at Spoon, but Spoon wouldn't meet his eyes.

"Your boy ain't going to help you," Zach said. "He gave you up quick. We had to pop him a few times, but he was only too happy to talk. He told us all about Sherman Ellis and your damn-fool fucked-up idea to come here and pose like a college boy." Zach laughed without humor, a grim chuckle. He shook his head. "Like you could make these folks think you was college educated."

Zach squatted next to Jenks, gathered a fistful of Jenks's shirt. He pulled Jenks close and spit in his face. Jenks winced like it was acid. Saliva ran down the side of his nose.

"Anything I can't hold with, it's an uppity nigger thinks he's better than the rest of the folks from the hood." Zach let go of Jenks. "You're nothing. You hear that? You stick with me and let me guide you, you could have been something. But now you're nothing."

Zach stood, straightened his jacket. He pulled a fat, silver revolver from his belt and thumbed back the hammer, pointed it at Jenks's head. "I want my coke, you dumb shit."

"I can call—" Shit. Jenks remembered Wayne DelPrego's phone had been cut off. "I can get it. Damn, Zach, you know I wouldn't—"

"Shut your fucking mouth, nigger."

"I'm just saying, you got to let me explain about—"

Zach lifted his foot and stomped his heel across Jenks's mouth, mashed his lips against his teeth. Blood smeared down Jenks's chin. One of his lower teeth was loose.

"Save the bullshit. You're close to being a dead motherfucker, Harold Jenks. Now save your life and get my fucking cocaine." Zach pressed the barrel of the pistol against Jenks's head. "Or am I saying something too hard for you to understand? I think I'm saying some pretty simple shit here, but let me know if I'm going too fast for you."

"I hear you," Jenks said. His lips throbbed. "But it's not here."

"We know that, motherfucker. We already looked."

"I can get it."

And he would. You didn't cross Red Zach. It was like a law of nature. The tides, the rotation of the Earth, the flow of time and Red Zach. Jenks had been crazy to try. Now he was looking at a pair of broken legs if he was lucky. A one-way trip to the bottom of a lake if he wasn't.

"If you just wait an hour," Jenks said, "I can bring you the stuff."

Zach kicked him in the side of the head. Jenks went flat to the floor, bells going off in his head, his ear buzzing hot where the heel of Zach's shoe had dug in.

"How fucking stupid you think I am?" Zach said. "You think I'm going to let you cut out again? You know how much trouble I had already tracking you down to this shithole, redneck town? I got a car around back. We'll take you. Keep an eye on you the whole way."

*   *   *

Red Zach's stretch limo eased to a stop in front of Wayne DelPrego's shabby trailer. The pickup was parked out front. Jenks had half hoped DelPrego would be gone. No such luck.

"I'll go in and get it," Jenks said.

"I'll send one of my boys to keep you company," Zach said. He nudged one of the bruisers, who got out of the limo.

Jenks got out too. He walked ahead, the bruiser right on his heels. "Yo. What's your name?" Jenks asked.

"My name is Mr. Stomp-your-punk-ass if you trying anything," said the gangster. "Just keep walking."

As they passed the pickup, Jenks glanced into the bed. No gym bag.

Jenks climbed the three metal steps and knocked on the trailer door, the bruiser crowding him close from behind. Nobody answered. Jenks knocked again. He was sweating now, feeling a little dizzy. *Come on Wayne, you dumb shit. These motherfuckers are going to bag my ass. Be home.*

"Try the knob." The bruiser shoved his shoulder.

"Okay, man. Take it easy."

Jenks turned the knob, pushed. The door swung inward. The bruiser shoved again, and they both entered the trailer. Jenks thought about calling Wayne's name but didn't. The trailer smelled like burnt coffee. It was a cramped single-wide, the kitchen/dining room to the right, a narrow hall leading left.

"Where's the coke?" the bruiser asked.

"We have to look for it."

"Best get looking then." The bruiser cracked his knuckles.

"Cool it, okay? Let me look around."

"I'll come with."

They walked down the hall, and Jenks looked in two of the open doors, a dingy bathroom with a wad of dirty towels on the floor and a small bedroom full of junk. The door at the end of the hall was closed.

The bruiser crossed his arms behind Jenks; he was becoming bored with the situation. "Last door."

"Uh-huh." Jenks opened it, walked into the trailer's master bedroom.

He turned and stood there, looking back through the door at the bruiser. He didn't move.

"Well?" The bruiser looked at Jenks expectantly.

Jenks looked back at him, face blank.

"You just going to stand there, nigger?"

"I need you to help me move the bed. The stuff is in the floor underneath."

"Move it your own damn self."

"Don't be like that. Help me move this."

The bruiser sighed, walked into the bedroom. "I don't get paid to be no—"

The golf club smacked into the side of the bruiser's head with a sickening crunch. The bruiser stumbled forward, frantic, high-pitched screams jumping out of his throat. He tried to go into his jacket for his gun.

DelPrego leapt from his hiding spot beside his dresser, swung the club again in a long, overhand arc, brought it down with a loud *thwack* on top of the bruiser's skull. The bruiser's eyes rolled back. He pitched forward, landed facefirst, and didn't move.

DelPrego's eyes were wild and jittery. "Jesus Christ, Jesus Christ." He knelt next to the bruiser and dropped the club, threw open the unconscious man's jacket. An enormous automatic pistol hung from a shoulder holster. DelPrego drew it from the holster, held it up to his eyes. It said Desert Eagle .357 on the side. "Oh shit shit shit."

Jenks said, "Goddamn. You whacked him good. I bet he's dead."

"Shit shit shit shit. I saw you guys coming, looked like trouble." DelPrego's eyes bounced between the dead man and the gun in his own hand. "I thought you needed help—this guy—I was just trying to *help!*"

DelPrego was wired, freaked out. Jenks shook him by the shoulder. "Wayne, listen to me. This guy's just the tip of the motherfucking iceberg. You got a back door?"

DelPrego stood, grabbed his denim jacket off the bed. "This way."

"Wait!" Jenks grabbed DelPrego's arm. "Where's the coke?"

"It ain't here."

"What!"

"I stashed it." DelPrego jerked his arm away from Jenks. "Come on."

He led Jenks back to the kitchen. On the way, Jenks glanced out the window. Zach's other bruiser was out of the limo and coming toward the trailer.

"We got to hurry."

DelPrego threw open the back door and jumped. No steps. Jenks followed, tumbled on the grass, but jumped up again quick. The backyard led to trees.

"Come on," yelled DelPrego. He ran for the trees.

The other bruiser came around the far end of the trailer, gun drawn. He spotted Jenks.

Jenks followed DelPrego into the trees. Thick underbrush, limbs, and vines grabbing at Jenks's arms and face.

"You're dead, Jenks." Shots tore through the trees, whipped overhead.

Jenks plunged after DelPrego farther into the bush. Jenks had thought this merely a stand of trees. He'd expected to come through them, emerge on the other side in another neighborhood, but this was deep, dark, no-shit jungle. He prayed DelPrego knew where he was going.

"Jenks!" More shots. But both shots and shouts were more distant now. Zach's thug wasn't following them into the woods.

Jenks didn't slow down. He pumped his legs, dodged low-hanging branches trying to keep up with DelPrego. He'd never seen a white boy run so fast.

twenty-two

Maybe we should take a break," Fred Jones said. "You seem distracted."

"I'm sorry." Morgan shuffled the stack of poems, set them aside. "I'm worried about one of my students. He wasn't in class." Neither Sherman Ellis nor Wayne DelPrego had shown for yesterday's workshop. When Morgan had asked Timothy Lancaster about it, the young man simply looked nervous and denied knowing anything. And Lancaster sported a wicked bruise across the bridge of his nose.

Morgan hadn't asked.

The university poetry reading was only a week away. He needed to get in touch with Ellis. Soon.

"Here." Fred Jones handed a cellophane-wrapped cigar to Morgan. "It's a Macanudo. Smoke it."

"I don't smoke, but thanks," Morgan said.

"No, smoke it for me." The old man folded his gnarled hands on the table in front of him. He had a long face, weary and slack with age. "Please," he said again quietly. "The doctor don't let me smoke 'em no more, but I like the smell. I ain't smelled one in months and I'm going loopy."

"Okay." Morgan unwrapped it, stuck it in his mouth.

"You've got to bite the end first," Jones said. "Or just nip a piece off with this. Just enough to draw air." He pulled a penknife out of his baggy trousers, handed it to Morgan.

Morgan sliced off the end like he was cutting a carrot and stuck the cigar in his mouth. "I don't think I have any matches."

"I figured." Jones slid a gold lighter across the table. Expensive and old.

Morgan lit the cigar, puffed. The smoke went to his nose, hit the back of his throat hot and rough. He coughed.

"Don't suck it in your lungs. Just puff slow and easy. It'll last a while if you don't suck it too fast."

"Okay." Morgan puffed again, blew out a cloud of blue-gray smoke.

Jones closed his eyes, ran a hand over his freckled, bald head. He breathed deep. "Boy, that takes me back."

Morgan was getting the hang of it, not inhaling too deep. "Let me know if I can take a few shots of bourbon for you or run some call girls in here."

The old man chuckled.

"This could be a poem," Morgan said.

"You write it."

Morgan was already juggling the syntax in his head, listing words that might go in the poem. *Surrogate* seemed too formal. The tone would have to be nostalgic, sweetly sad. He looked around for a pen, found one, and scratched a note to himself.

"Bob doesn't smoke for you?" Morgan meant the ever-hungry giant who chauffeured Jones and ran his errands.

"Asthma," Jones said.

Morgan flicked the ashes into a half-empty coffee cup. "Why poetry, Mr. Jones?"

"Because I don't paint."

Fair enough. "I've noticed a sort of submerged theme in your work. It's reoccurs quite often."

"What do you mean?"

"Easier to show you. Once I point it out, I'm sure you'll see." He pulled two of Jones's poems from the stack, turned them around, and slid them side by side in front of the old man. "Read these and think about them thematically."

Jones didn't read them. "What the hell you talking about? Two completely different poems. This one's about an arsonist and this other one is a man who kills people with piano wire."

"Geeze, these things are so violent."

"So what?"

Morgan shrugged. "In any case, those are just the vehicles," Morgan said. He kept the cigar in the side of his mouth as he talked. He was beginning to like it. "Let me show you something." He stood, scanned the bookshelf in his living room, and came back to the table with *The Collected Works of Wallace Stevens*. "Listen." He read a poem:

> *"Anecdote of the Jar"*
>
> *I placed a jar in Tennessee,*
> *And round it was upon a hill.*
> *It made the slovenly wilderness*
> *Surround that hill.*

The wilderness rose up to it,
And sprawled around, no longer wild.
The jar was round upon the ground
And tall and of a port in air.

It took dominion everywhere.
The jar was gray and bare.
It did not give of bird or bush,
Like nothing else in Tennessee.

"What's going on in the poem?" Morgan waited, puffed the cigar.

Jones turned the book toward him. He read again silently, his lips moving. "This jar is changing everything just by being there. It's making itself the center of the world."

"But is it really?"

"What do you mean?"

"Is it really doing anything? It's just sitting there, right?"

Jones thought for a long time. Morgan didn't mind. He was enjoying the cigar. He thought a cold beer would go well with the smoke, but it was still before noon and Morgan had recently set some new rules for himself.

He was getting his shit together.

Jones leaned back in his chair, rubbed his chin. "You know what I think?"

"What do you think?"

"I think it's both," the old man said. "I think it's doing nothing and everything at the same time. I think it's only perception that makes it seem like it's changing everything. Then again, maybe perception is all we got, right? So changing perception is like changing reality."

Morgan took the cigar out of his mouth, looked at Jones.

Jones scanned the poem again. "Jesus. That's a pretty fucking good poem. Once you figure it out."

"Yes."

"Got any more like this?"

"You can borrow the book."

"Thanks."

Morgan said, "That's pretty smart, Mr. Jones. Not a lot of people get it right off."

"Thanks, but I'd trade being smart for being able to smoke that cigar."

The phone rang. Morgan set the cigar across the top of the coffee cup, excused himself, and picked it up in the kitchen.

"Morgan, is that you?" Louis Reams's voice was edgy and hushed.

"It's me." Morgan hadn't spoken to the professor since the bicycle incident.

"Have you seen Pritcher? The big faker is walking around campus wearing this ridiculous neck brace. He's been asking a lot of very pointed questions too."

"I think you need to consider that he might really have been seriously hurt," Morgan said.

"Ha. I know better. He's out to get me. Yes, I admit it was a lapse in judgment, a bit juvenile."

"A bit."

"But now he sees his chance. If he can prove I did it, he'll have me by the balls. That's just what he wants, the son of a bitch. Morgan, you didn't mention what happened to anybody did you?"

"No."

"I need you to keep it under your hat. You wouldn't tell would you? That would be playing right into his hands."

"I said I hadn't mentioned it."

"You won't will you?"

"I'll keep quiet."

"Good man." Reams sounded relieved. "I knew I could count on you. I'm going to pay you back."

"That's okay."

"Really. I want to show my appreciation."

"Reams, I don't want you to pay me back."

Reams didn't hear. "I know a fellow down at San Gabriel College in Houston. They're going to need a one-year poet next fall."

Now Morgan was listening. He'd sent out at least thirty applications for next fall and had turned up nothing. Securing a job for next year would take a big load off his mind. And he wouldn't have to track down Ellis for the ridiculous poetry reading. Wouldn't have to be under Whittaker's thumb.

"I'm listening," Morgan said.

"Not now," Reams said. "Got to go. Got to keep an eye out for Pritcher. Can't stay in one spot too long."

"Reams—"

He'd already hung up.

Morgan returned to the table. "Sorry."

"You'll let it go out." Jones pointed at the cigar.

"Right." He stuck it back in his mouth, resuscitated the glowing tip with sharp puffs.

"You know what that jar poem made me think of?"

Morgan kept puffing but arched his eyebrows.

"When I was ten years old, my father took me camping way back in the Catskills," Jones said. "It wasn't like it is now. You could find a forest, go back in there for days."

"Did you fish?"

"No. Just hiking. I liked to build campfires, cook over the wood coals. For some reason a hot dog tastes better in the woods. You get away from the city and you can really see the stars."

"I like to fish," Morgan said. "Supposed to be some good trout streams over the line into Arkansas."

"I'm in the middle of a fucking story here."

"Sorry. Go ahead."

"Anyway I'm hiking pretty far. Dad and me had been hiking all day and it was starting to get dark and we're way gone into the woods, deeper than we've ever been before. I'm thinking maybe we're walking in a spot where nobody's ever been before. Maybe we're the first people ever. You ever think that when you were a kid?"

"Yes."

"So I'm thinking maybe Indians had been here, but other than that we were the first. I guess even at ten I thought maybe that wasn't true, but a ten-year-old can think anything. That's the genius of being ten. Anything can be true. And it's a split second—literally the next second—after I think this that I take one more step and see a beer bottle, a Pabst."

Morgan started to laugh, shut himself up.

The old man shook his head. "The whole forest arranged itself around that beer bottle, my whole life. Everything I thought. Like that jar on a hill in Tennessee. Seems dumb, I guess. But I was mad about that bottle for a long time. Not because of littering. I don't give a shit about that. Because it took away what it felt like to be ten."

Morgan puffed the cigar. The old man closed his eyes and smelled it.

"Maybe I talk too much," Jones said.

"No. I know what you mean."

"What about you?" Jones scooted forward in his chair. "Something's gnawing on you. I can tell."

"I'm supposed to get one of my students to do a poetry reading in a week, but I think he's skipped out on me."

"Kids." Jones waved his hands like that covered the whole subject.

"What about you, Mr. Jones? Ever read your poems in front of people?"

Jones said, "You ever drop your britches and wave your pecker at a passing bus?"

twenty-three

Moses Duncan drove his pal Eddie home from the county hospital. They'd told the doctor that the broken window which caused the dozens of cuts on Eddie's face had been shattered by a hard-thrown baseball. Eddie's entire face was wrapped in gauze like a mummy's, only slits for his eyes and nostrils. His lips had been badly lacerated, so he didn't have a mouth hole.

"Mmmmph. Mmm mmmph," Eddie said.

"Don't you sweat it, Eddie." Duncan gripped the steering wheel tight. He still burned with hatred, the image of Big John's body sprawled in the dust branded on his mind's eye. His side stung too from the slight buckshot wound. "We'll get that coon and his buddies too. We'll go home and get the shotguns and we'll find that son of a bitch."

"Mmmph."

"You leave that to me," Duncan said. "Not many black guys around here. Hell, we'll just cruise up and down every street until we find him if we have to. Don't worry. We'll get him."

"Mmmmph umph mmmmph."

"Damn straight." Duncan wondered how he understood Eddie so well. "You know I think I'd of been a good dentist. I could probably understand folks even with my hands in their mouths."

"Mmmph Ummm Mmmph."

Duncan frowned. "No need to get nasty, Eddie. Just ain't called for."

"Mmph."

"Okay, then."

Red Zach sat in the back of his limo. He was pissed. Why couldn't it just be easy for once?

Spoon sat across from him, one of Zach's big goons uncomfortably close. Spoon looked drained, broken, and scared. He kept his eyes on the floor of the car.

Okay, Zach had to get in character, so he could play hard-ass with Spoon. Not for the first time, Zach supposed he needed to train some middle-management personnel, a couple of good men to do all this bruiser work. Zach could lounge on the beach in Antigua and hear all about it via cell phone or e-mail. The key to an operation like this was to get it on autopilot as much as possible. Zach wanted to put as much distance as possible between himself and the dirty work.

But until then, if he wanted shit done right, he'd have to do it himself.

"Your boy Harold killed one of mine in that trailer," Zach said. "You don't think I can just let that go, do you?"

Spoon shook his head.

"Where's he going now?"

"I don't know, Red. Shit, he don't tell me nothing."

"That's what you said the first time," Zach said. "Once we helped you remember, you told us about Harold coming to Oklahoma."

Spoon's hand went to his split lip. "I don't know, man. You got to believe me."

Zach smiled. "Okay, I believe you." He nodded to the goon.

Moving fast, the goon looped the length of piano wire over Spoon's neck, yanked. Spoon's eyes bulged. His tongue popped from his mouth. His whole face bunched tight like the last bit of toothpaste being squeezed from the tube.

Zach flipped open his cell phone and thumbed the speed-dial. "This is Red. I need all the boys down here right now."

Spoon kicked. The goon hanging tight. Blood from Spoon's throat.

Zach wasn't paying attention anymore. "Don't waste my time asking why. Get the fuck down here and make sure everyone's packing heat. We going to make an example."

Spoon went slack, eyes wide. The body slumped to the car floor.

Zach folded the cell phone closed, looked at the body and the goon and the blood. "Goddammit. You got blood on the seat. Shit."

The goon hung his head, looked sheepish.

Deke Stubbs had found a lot of names and a lot of secrets in Annie Walsh's journal. Two names stood out. Moses Duncan and Timothy Lancaster. Annie had tried to be subtle in some of her journal entries, but it was obvious that Duncan was her connection. A good possibility.

Duncan wasn't in the phone book, but Lancaster was. His apartment was close.

The two beers Stubbs had swilled at Friday's put him in the mood for more. He stopped at a Quickie-Mart and bought a six-pack of Busch and a copy of *Hustler*. He drank one in the parking lot and flipped through the jack-off magazine. He was getting crazy horny again. Something happened to Stubbs when he saw skin. It made him desperate crazy. Maybe that's why he was always forking over big bucks to get his rocks off.

He threw the magazine into the backseat before it made him too crazy. He flipped through Annie Walsh's journal instead.

Apparently, Annie had boinked this Lancaster kid a month back as some sort of experiment. The journal said that Lancaster "intrigued" her.

A place to start. A thread.

Stubbs pulled out of the parking lot, tossed the empty beer can into the backseat. He opened another, slurped, held the can between his legs, and pointed the Dodge toward Lancaster's apartment.

He was in no particular hurry. He was getting paid by the day.

twenty-four

Jenks scooted close to the little campfire DelPrego had built. They were deep in the strange woods, glowing eyes watching from the shadows. Jenks gritted his teeth against the wind that whistled through the branches.

"We can't stay out here." For the first time, DelPrego showed he was aware of the cold. "This fire ain't enough. I can't feel my damn fingers." He blew on them, held them toward the fire. The wind stung his ears.

Jenks didn't say anything. He was cold too, but didn't know where to go. He couldn't go back to his garage apartment, that was for damn sure.

"Let's get my truck," DelPrego said. "We could sneak back slow. Check it out. If we can get to the truck, we can go anywhere."

"Shit on that idea. You don't know Red Zach. I'd rather freeze than have my own balls fed to me."

A long silence before DelPrego spoke. "What's going on?"

Jenks looked at the fire, didn't say anything.

"Sherman." DelPrego raised his voice. "Who's Jenks? He called you Jenks."

"Never mind."

"Fuck that. Talk to me. I killed—" DelPrego's voice caught. He swallowed hard. "I bashed a man's skull in with a golf club. I thought I was doing it to save a friend." His voice shook, tight, nerves raw. "Now you goddamn tell me what's going on right fucking now."

Jenks opened his mouth, shut it again. He needed to gather himself.

"I'll tell you, but you got to let me tell it all."

"Fine."

"You got to listen," Jenks said. "You got to let me get it all out, try to understand where I'm coming from."

"I said fine."

Jenks let it all spill out, Spoon and the alley and Sherman Ellis. He told him about his crazy idea to steal Ellis's life, slip into Eastern Oklahoma University, and write poetry. It had been his way out, his way to shed the ghetto and the drug trade and all the gangster bullshit. And he realized he was telling the story for himself too, trying to downplay his part in Ellis's death. He needed to believe, even more than he needed to convince DelPrego, that what he had done was forgivable. Or at least understandable.

And by the end of Jenks's story, the truth had shifted, taken on a new shade. He told DelPrego that his old life, his old patterns, the old ways had such deep hooks in him, that only a crazy plan could get him free. Sherman Ellis had lost his life, but Jenks could resurrect it again, make it work for good. Sherman Ellis's death could save Harold Jenks.

Jenks's story trickled out. He looked at DelPrego, but couldn't see his expression in the dark. The fire had dwindled, the coals casting them in a dim, hellish orange. The silence stretched.

"Wayne?"

"Don't talk to me."

"I had to do what I had to—"

"Stop talking right now."

Jenks started to bark at DelPrego. *Fuck you, man. You don't know what I had to live with.* He clapped his mouth shut, saw the bulk clenched in DelPrego's fist glinting orange and metallic in the light of the coals. It was the big automatic DelPrego had taken off Zach's boy. The complexion of Jenks's situation shifted uneasily. He was aware of the woods again. It would be a long time before a body was found out here. DelPrego wasn't quite pointing the pistol at him, but Jenks kept his mouth shut.

"I'm going to tell you something," DelPrego said at last. "I don't know anything about your life. Maybe we had to kill that guy in the trailer or be killed ourselves."

DelPrego's voice tightened. "But you can't steal education, man. It's up here." He tapped his head with the pistol barrel. "You can steal a car or a radio or a big-ass bag full of drugs, but you can't steal an education."

"I'm not hurting anybody."

"Fuck you." DelPrego stood, sudden, violent, knocking sticks into the fire and spreading the coals. Sparks. "You're hurting me, man. Me. I worked my ass off for my college education. I pulled third shift as a security guard at a rendering plant, stayed up all night wired on coffee reading Milton and Shakespearean sonnets and smelling hog stink just so I could pay rent and buy books. My senior year, I slept more nights in the library than I did in my bed."

He exhaled raggedly, sat down again hard. "Maybe my life wasn't dangerous. Maybe my neighborhood wasn't as tough, but I earned my education." He tapped the side of his head again. "Everything in here belongs to me."

DelPrego stood, shook the gun at Jenks. "This fucking thing is your way." He turned, tossed the pistol into the woods.

Jenks felt hot in the face. DelPrego made him mad and guilty. "That's right. You didn't come from my neighborhood. You *don't* know what it's like."

"I'll bet Sherman Ellis did."

The words hit Jenks like a punch in the gut. DelPrego had said what Jenks secretly already knew deep in his heart. Sherman Ellis had earned his way. Sherman Ellis had worked for it. Jenks had tried to sneak in the back door.

Jenks wiped at his eyes. "Fucking campfire. Too much smoke."

The fire's orange glow faded.

"What's your name?"

Jenks looked up. "W-w-what?" He was freezing.

"Your real name."

"Harold Jenks."

"Okay."

Jenks said, "I know it won't work, so don't worry about me. Shit, you should see how the professors look at me. They know something ain't right. I can't do it, so don't worry. I'm not stealing anything." He sniffed, wiped his nose on his sleeve. "Only class I'm keeping up in is the poetry workshop, and that's only because I'm as bad as everybody else."

DelPrego laughed sudden and hard, the tension draining. "Shit. Professor Morgan. What would he say?" More laughter.

Jenks laughed too, wiped his eyes again. When the laughter spent itself, he asked, "You still mad?"

DelPrego said, "Mostly I'm cold."

"Me too. Let's get the fuck out of here."

"Where?"

Jenks stood, stomped his feet. They felt like lead bricks. "Anyplace indoors."

DelPrego snapped his fingers. "I know, follow me. The back of the campus is only about a mile this way." He headed off into the underbrush.

Jenks followed, shoving his way through the branches. He was so cold he could barely move. They made their way slowly.

"Wayne?"

"Yeah?"

"Where's the gym bag?" Jenks hesitated to raise this question, but he had to know.

"I stashed it. Someplace safe."

"Where?"

"Someplace safe."

So that's how it is, thought Jenks. *Okay. I won't press it for now.*

They found an open window and climbed in. Jenks was so happy to be in the relative warmth of the classroom he didn't bother asking DelPrego why they'd broken into Albatross Hall. At least it was unlikely Red Zach would find them there.

"Come on." DelPrego led him out of the classroom and down the hall to the stairwell.

They climbed.

The fifth floor looked deserted. Dark.

"What are we doing here?" Jenks asked.

"Quiet." DelPrego froze, listened. "You hear that?"

Jenks listened too. "Music."

"Yeah."

"What is it?"

"Wagner," DelPrego said.

DelPrego walked faster, Jenks right behind him. They took a few turns and ended at a door. The music came from the other side. DelPrego twisted the knob, pushed the door open slowly.

DelPrego looked in. "Professor Valentine?"

The old man jerked his head around. "Wayne. Hello. A bit late to be out and about isn't it?"

Valentine was reading an enormous leather-bound Bible. He was stark naked except for a black beret with the words SEA WORLD, ORLANDO, stitched in yellow.

"I thought you were still away," DelPrego said.

"A long story." Valentine's eyes shifted from DelPrego to Jenks. "Who's your friend?"

DelPrego hesitated. "Sherman Ellis."

Jenks wondered about DelPrego. He hadn't told his real name. DelPrego wasn't going to rat him out. Not yet anyway.

Valentine leapt up, setting the Bible aside. He walked to Jenks, hand outstretched, his old-man genitalia swinging between his legs like a Ziploc bag of shriveled fruit.

"Good to meet you, Ellis."

Jenks shook his hand. Not eagerly. "You're naked."

"Yes."

"Could you not be, please?"

Valentine chuckled, crossed the room, grabbed a robe, put it on.

"I didn't know you'd be here," DelPrego said. "We were sort of looking for a place to hide out."

"How long do you want to stay?"

"Until the heat's off," DelPrego said.

"On the lam, eh? I understand," Valentine said. "But mum's the word. Nobody knows I'm here."

And that suited them just fine.

Part 3

twenty-five

Deke Stubbs knocked on Timothy Lancaster's door. He smelled like a six-pack of Busch. He swallowed a belch.

Lancaster opened the door a crack, eyed the detective. Lancaster looked a little annoyed and also worried. A nervous bookworm type, custom-made to cave under pressure. Stubbs liked it when they were worried. He could lean on them good and stiff and get them to talk. He hadn't had to do that with Annie Walsh's mousy roommate, but he wouldn't mind with this guy.

They stared at each other a long second.

Finally Lancaster said, "Yes?" The word slipped meekly through the crack in the door like an apology.

"Lancaster?"

Another long pause from the kid. "Yes."

"Can I ask you some questions?"

The pause was really long this time. "About what?"

"About Annie Walsh," Stubbs said. "And about drugs." Stubbs threw the part in about drugs at the last second. Sure. Shake the kid up. He looked nervous already, so why not push the envelope?

The kid paled. "Are you the police?"

"Drug Enforcement Administration." Stubbs flipped his wallet open and closed again at light-speed before shoving it back into his jacket. "I think you better let me in."

Lancaster stepped back, eyes steady on Stubbs.

Stubbs closed the door behind him, looked around the apartment. The kid had about a thousand books stacked along the walls. He read the title of one at eye level, "*The Spanish Tragedy.*"

Lancaster didn't say anything.

"We had a Spanish tragedy ourselves a few months ago. Buncha wetbacks coming across near Juarez, and we knew some of them were mules, carting a wad of smack across the river. So we figured what the heck, shoot 'em all and let God sort 'em out." Stubbs mimed sighting a rifle. "We picked 'em off as they hit the American side. That's how we handle drug dealers in the DEA."

Lancaster looked like he was about to puke or faint.

"Listen, kid. I think you know why I'm here. I need you to talk and I need you to talk right now and real loud about what you know."

"About what?"

"Everything. All of it." This wasn't the approach Stubbs had in mind when he came to talk to Lancaster, but it was obvious the kid was right on the edge. If Stubbs could just nudge him over, he might spill his guts big-time. There was some shit going on here and it was all tangled together, drugs and Annie Walsh and this kid Lancaster. A lot of dumb shits thought detective work was all fingerprints and looking at cigar ash under a magnifying glass like

Sherlock fucking Holmes. Bullshit. It was asking the right questions and squeezing out useful answers.

Lancaster started to shrug and talk and stammer all at the same time.

"Hey, take it easy," Stubbs said. "I'm here to save your ass if you cooperate. You got any beer?"

Lancaster raised an eyebrow. "Uh . . . I have a Grolsch in the refrigerator."

"And that's beer?"

Lancaster nodded.

"Bring it."

Lancaster went to the kitchen, came back with a big green bottle, and handed it to Stubbs. His hands shook.

Stubbs tried to open the bottle. But the cap wouldn't twist.

"Sorry," Lancaster said. He went to the kitchen again and came back with a church key. He popped open the beer for Stubbs.

Stubbs drank. "This some foreign shit?"

"From Denmark."

Stubbs took another slug. "Not bad."

"I haven't seen Annie Walsh in weeks," Lancaster said.

Good. The kid was ready to talk. The suspense was eating him alive.

"To hell with Walsh, kid," Stubbs said. "Talk to me about the drugs."

"I really don't know anything about that." Lancaster's voice was weaker than dishwater. He wouldn't meet Stubbs's eyes.

"Talk, kid."

"I-I don't know anything."

"Talk, you little shit. I'll put you in jail and you'll get butt-raped by a nigger the size of Mike Tyson."

"I don't know—"

"Talk!"

"Please, I—"

"You little prick." Stubbs shook the beer bottle at him. It foamed, dripped on the carpet. "I'll shove this bottle up your ass and break it off. You don't fuck with the Drug Enforcement Agency." He put his nose an inch from Lancaster's, yelled, beer spit flying.

Lancaster backed up, eyes wide. Terror.

"Come back here." Stubbs grabbed Lancaster's arm at the elbow, dug into a pressure point with his thumb.

Lancaster winced, tried to twist away. Stubbs held him one-handed.

The detective finished the beer, tossed the bottle onto the floor. It rolled up against a stack of books. "This way." Stubbs pulled Lancaster into the kitchen.

"Hey."

"Shut up."

Stubbs shoved the kid up against the kitchen cabinets. "Stay put."

Lancaster obeyed.

The kitchen was dim and yellow, paint chipping on the cabinets. The linoleum needed a good scrub.

Stubbs opened the refrigerator, took out another Grolsch, opened it. He smacked his lips, stood examining Lancaster's open refrigerator. "Holy shit, kid. How do you live?" There were two more beers, a jar of pickle brine, a soy sauce packet, and a defeated length of sagging celery.

He closed the refrigerator again, gulped the beer as he opened random kitchen cabinets.

"Don't you need a warrant or something?" Lancaster asked.

Stubbs tapped his chest with a fat finger. Hard. "You a lawyer, kid?"

"What department did you say you were with?"

"Drug Enforcement Agency, so don't yank me off, okay?"

Lancaster said, "When you first came in you said you were with the Drug Enforcement *Administration*. Not Agency."

Stubbs froze. "What?"

"I think you'd better go," Lancaster said. He was wary, but the tables were slowly turning. "Or maybe I should call the local authorities, and we could all discuss this together." Lancaster was testing the waters. He had a piece of something and was pushing it now.

"Now hold on, kid. Wait a minute." Stubbs was losing control of the situation, scrambling to get the upper hand again was making it worse. "Dammit, I'm with the Drug Enforcement— The DEA goddammit!"

Lancaster lifted the phone off the hook. It was an old rotary dial model on the kitchen wall. "Let's get a few deputies over here."

"Kid, don't—"

"I'm sure impersonating an officer of the law is some kind of serious offense," Lancaster said. He had a full smug going. He didn't believe in Stubbs anymore.

"Kid, I swear, you're making a mistake."

Lancaster dialed.

Stubbs grabbed the phone with two meaty hands and ripped it off the wall. Dropped it on the floor and kicked it. Lancaster was already running. He pushed past Stubbs, through the living room, making for the front door.

Stubbs ran after him, dove at the kid's legs, and tangled him up. Both on the floor. Lancaster tried to kick Stubbs away, the heel of his shoe digging sharply into the top of Stubbs's head. Stubbs yanked his legs, climbed on top of them so he couldn't kick, punched Lancaster hard once in the gut.

Lancaster *whuffed* air. His eyes bulged.

Stubbs shifted up, sat on Lancaster's chest. Stubbs was huffing hard at the sudden exertion. Slick beer sweat under his arms and on his forehead. He felt the distant tug of nausea.

"Drugs," Stubbs barked.

"It wasn't me. I-It was Ellis." Lancaster gulped air. Tears streaming from the sides of his eyes.

Stubbs slapped him loud across the face. "Who the fuck's Ellis?"

"Sherman Ellis. A student in my class with Professor Morgan. He had a whole bag of cocaine. I only even looked at it once."

A whole bag of coke? *How much?* Stubbs wondered.

"Please, I can't breathe." Lancaster writhed beneath Stubbs's mass.

Stubbs took Lancaster's throat in his hands. "You'll get worse than that. How much coke? Did the Ellis kid say?"

"Like a hundred thousand bucks' worth. Maybe more. I don't know. He was going to dump it off for twenty and give me and Wayne a thousand just to go with him."

"Wayne?"

"Another student."

A hundred thousand in coke. Stubbs knew some contacts in OK City. He could maybe unload the stuff for fifty or sixty easy. He felt his hands close on Lancaster's throat. Stubbs's own breath came hot with beer stink. His heart hammered in his head.

Lancaster gagged, pulled at Stubbs's thick fingers.

Stubbs could make a lot more on the coke than he could tracking down Annie for the Walshes. This was just the kind of opportunity he always kept an eye peeled for. His hands tightened again on Lancaster.

But this kid. This damn-smart-ass, know-it-all kid. He couldn't let him call the cops. They'd pull his license and slap a charge on him for sure. He couldn't let the kid talk. No way.

Lancaster bucked, scratched at Stubbs's hands, turned blue, mouth working noiselessly.

Always some smart-ass college punk making life hard for Stubbs.

But who had the drugs? This Ellis kid? Annie's journal had mentioned something about a drug connection. He'd ask Lancaster. He'd make the kid talk. He needed more information.

"Kid?"

But Timothy Lancaster lay stone-still, eyes open to the dull, cracked ceiling.

Stubbs drove fast, hands shaking and knuckle white on the steering wheel. Lancaster's last bottle of Grolsch nestled cold between his legs. He paged through Annie Walsh's journal on the seat next to him. He flipped to the last entry, read it.

Tonight I see Professor Morgan.

Not much help, but it was the last entry. This Morgan guy might've been the last person to see her. He flipped back through the journal. A car honked loud. Stubbs had slipped over into the other lane. He jerked the wheel back, kept thumbing in the journal.

He was breathing heavy, still seeing Lancaster's face. Damn, snotty, know-it-all kid. He gulped beer. Wiped his forehead with his sleeve. The window was down, cold air blowing, but Stubbs felt hot. Around his neck. His ears. Sweat.

Jay Morgan.

Okay, Professor Egghead. Let's see what you have for old Deke.

twenty-six

Morgan tried to get Ellis on the phone, but the kid was nowhere, hadn't shown for class. The dean would probably go ape-shit. Whittaker wanted Ellis.

Okay, screw it. He'd try calling again later, perhaps call some of Ellis's other professors. Maybe they knew where he was keeping himself. In the meantime, Morgan could get some work done.

He spread a blank sheet of lined paper on his desk, stared at it. Today he would write one good poem. Only one. He looked at the paper. It was still blank. He'd cleared his day, no tutoring, no grading. Nothing. Only the poem.

He got up, went into the kitchen, and put on a pot of coffee. He watched it brew. He looked over his shoulder at the relentlessly blank sheet of paper on his desk.

Poetry was hard.

He watched the pot fill, then poured a mug, walked slowly back to his desk, sipping. He eased back into the chair. Morgan had not one idea in his empty head, not even the seed of an idea rattling in his hollow, freshly swept cranium.

He thought fleetingly about smoking the cigar for the old man. The idea danced just over the horizon of his imagination.

He picked up his pen. He made the point of his pen touch the paper. It left a black dot. Soon he'd make the pen move. It would be the start of a word. He felt it coming, the word forming. Potential energy built in his thumb and forefinger. Here came the first word. The poem was beginning.

The phone rang.

"Cocksuckers!"

Morgan threw down the pen, grabbed the phone. "What?"

"Hey now, Morgan. Get up on the wrong side of the bed?"

"I was working, Reams."

"Listen, how about you come over this afternoon and help me with a project? I'm building a gazebo. Just got back from Sears with quite an impressive assortment of tools. The lumber's piled high as an elephant's eye."

"I wouldn't know what to do."

"How hard can it be?" Reams said. "Hammer nails, saw wood, nothing to it."

"I told you I was working."

"So you did. What on?"

"Trying to write a poem."

"Is that all? Dash it out quick, then head over to my place. The sun's out and the beer is in the cooler. Be a good change of pace. Work with your hands for a change."

"I can't."

"You'll love it," Reams said. "We'll let our pants sag low until our butt cracks are showing. Sweat and everything like real handymen."

Morgan sighed. "I appreciate the call, Reams, but really I need to get in some writing."

"Well, okay then." A pout in Reams's voice. "Maybe next time." He hung up.

Morgan looked at his piece of paper. There was a jagged ink mark where his hand had jerked at the sound of the telephone. He crumpled the paper and tossed it over his shoulder. He spread a fresh sheet. This time he got a word out. *The.* He looked at it, shook his head, crossed it out, and replaced it with *A.* He crossed that out and wrote *The* again.

Good. This was progress. He began writing in earnest. Sweat broke out across his forehead. It came properly now, a line or two at a time. He crossed out a line, replaced it, switched lines around.

Finally Morgan had four good lines. The first stanza. He felt exhausted. He looked at the clock. Eighty-two minutes. Not bad. His coffee had cooled. He took his mug into the kitchen, dumped it into the sink, and poured a fresh cup.

Back at his desk.

The next stanza was crucial. He needed a good transition. He wanted the poem to make a turn in thought, but it needed to be subtle. His pen stalled again. He should never have gotten up for coffee. His rhythm had broken and he'd lost momentum. He frowned at the paper, tried to conjure the mood again.

A knock at the door.

"Goddammit!"

He looked out the front door's peephole. Ginny Conrad stood on his porch. She'd done something with her hair. It was pulled back, highlighted with garish burgundy streaks. She wore only a light jacket. Reams was right. It was a nice day, sun brilliant in the wide sky. Perhaps winter was fading at last.

She knocked again, and he opened the door.

"I was writing," Morgan told her. He wanted to preempt any ideas she might have about shucking her clothes and crawling into his bed.

She seemed not to hear, pushing her way in. "I thought we could have lunch."

"Lunch." Morgan tasted the word, rolled it around on his tongue. His concentration had broken anyway, and a bite would be good.

They ate at the same pizza joint Morgan had gone to with Annette Grayson. This time the meal was more relaxed. He wasn't on the make. No pressure. They talked of unimportant things and laughed.

Once, a silence between them stretched, and Ginny leaned slightly across the table and asked, "Do you wonder what it might be like if I were a little older and you were a little younger?"

"No, not really," Morgan said.

A grin tickled the corners of Ginny's mouth. "Neither do I."

"Good. Better this way."

"Better what way?" Ginny asked.

"Like this," Morgan said, but he really didn't know what he meant.

"I guess," Ginny said. "I don't know what I want."

"I don't know either."

"What?" Ginny asked. "You mean you don't know what I want or you don't know what you want?"

"I don't know."

And that about summed it up.

* * *

Back at the house, Ginny already had her blouse off before Morgan could decide to protest or not. He didn't want her. He felt guilty about not writing, and he was full of pizza.

He was, however, beginning to develop some sort of friendly feeling toward her, like for a distant niece or a cat. But he didn't want to sleep with her again, not now. It just wasn't in him. Even when she stripped completely, running her stiff fingers down between her furry folds, he couldn't quite imagine taking her in broad daylight after a heavy meal. It had been different during the driving rainstorm. Or maybe it was different now. Maybe everything was changing. Maybe *he'd* changed.

The phone rang.

She'd already slipped into his bed. "Let it ring."

"It might be important." He grabbed the phone. "Hello?"

"Is this Jay Morgan?" A woman's voice.

"Yes."

"This is Nurse Benneton at County General Hospital. We have a Louis Reams here. He's been injured, and he listed you as a contact name. Can you possibly come down and pick him up?"

"He listed me?"

"Yes, sir. Can you come down in the next twenty minutes or so?"

"But why would he list me?"

A pause. "Sir?"

"I don't want to pick him up."

Another pause. "He really shouldn't drive himself."

"How bad is he? What happened?"

"I'm afraid I can't release patient—"

"But you called me to pick him up, right? Doesn't that entitle me to know what happened?"

Ginny came to the bedroom doorway, holding a sheet over her but failing to cover up any of the important parts. She mouthed the words "what's wrong?"

Morgan waved her quiet. To the nurse he said, "Never mind. I'll be down as soon as I can." He hung up.

Ginny asked, "What is it?"

"I have to pick up a friend from the hospital," Morgan said. "Sorry, but I have to go."

"Is he hurt bad?"

"I'm sure he's okay," Morgan said.

"I'll wait here for you," Ginny said.

Morgan sighed. "Sure." He closed the door behind him.

Reams sat in the passenger seat of Morgan's car with his left hand in the air and his head down between his knees. A thick white bandage was tightly wrapped around his middle finger. Reams breathlessly related the story.

He'd been sawing wood with a particularly wicked little saw which had neatly sliced off the top half inch of the finger. Blood had spurted, and Reams had run in circles for a bit before calling an ambulance.

Morgan said Reams could probably have wrapped the finger in a towel and driven himself to the hospital.

"Too light-headed," Reams had explained. "I saw stars. I never believed that about seeing stars before, but I do now. I felt I was spiraling down into a long black hole, slipping right out of the daylight, swimming toward a long cottony sleep."

It sounded like something Reams had read in a Raymond Chandler novel.

Morgan turned onto Reams's road. "I'm taking you home. You need to stop anywhere first, get a prescription or anything?"

Reams shook a little bottle of pills in the other hand. "These will get me by for a day or two. Doctor had some samples. For pain." Reams still had his head between his legs.

"Jesus, will you sit up?" Morgan said.

"I need to sit like this. Isn't this what you're supposed to do?"

"That's for airline crashes. That's crash position you're in."

Reams said, "I thought I was supposed to let the blood flow to my head, or out of my head, or something."

"I'll have you home in a few minutes and you can stick your head in a bucket if you want."

"Dammit all, Morgan, have a heart why don't you? I've been mortally wounded."

"It's just your finger."

"I think I sliced an artery," Reams said. "If I'd passed out before I made it to the phone, I most likely would have bled to death."

Morgan doubted that.

"I'm feeling a little ill even now. I've had a shock to the system. That's how these seemingly little injuries can sometimes be serious. They shock the system."

"Don't puke in my car," Morgan said.

Morgan parked in Reams's driveway. Sluggishly, Reams climbed out, still holding his hand over his head. It looked like he was flipping the bird to the whole neighborhood. He fished his keys out of his pocket with the other hand.

"Thanks, Morgan. I didn't know who else to call, but I knew you said you'd be home all day."

"Go take one of your pills," Morgan said.

"Right." Reams closed the car door, took two steps toward his house, and stopped. He swayed. A pause. Reams tumbled, wilted facefirst into the front lawn.

Morgan watched for a few seconds, but Reams didn't get back up.

"Hell." Morgan shut off the car, climbed out, and picked Reams up from the grass. "You okay?"

"Hmm? What?" Reams rubbed his head. "See, I told you. I

asked the doctor for a transfusion, but he wouldn't do it. Damn quack."

"Uh-huh." Morgan dragged Reams to the front door, took his keys, and unlocked it. They went in. Morgan draped Reams on the sofa.

"Thanks, Morgan. I really owe you even more now."

"No, you don't."

"Yes, really. First that craziness with Pritcher and now this. I think you ought to come down to Houston with me. I know I can put in a word with that guy I know, get you a job lined up for fall."

"I'll think about it."

"Good." Reams squirmed on the sofa, arranged it so his hand was elevated above his head. "What's it like?"

Morgan sat in an uncomfortable wooden chair across from Reams. "What's what like?"

"The gypsy prof gig, moving around all the time?"

Morgan thought about it. "I used to like it, or thought I did. Changing scenery all the time helped me not think about other things. But I think I'm getting tired of it. I think maybe I need some roots. It's time to start putting my energies back into my work, you know? Hard to accomplish anything when you're always worried about your next paycheck."

But Reams didn't hear. He snored lightly, middle finger over his head, blazing white to the world.

twenty-seven

While waiting for Morgan to return, Ginny Conrad went through all the professor's cabinets, closets, and drawers. She realized, even as she was doing it, that her actions were the result of a minor, quirky character flaw. She hated to be left out of anything, hated the thought that something was going on and she wasn't in on it.

Once, when she was eleven years old, she'd painted a Magic Marker moustache on herself and taken her father's Dodge. She'd picked up two friends and went to see an R-rated movie in which there was rumored to be nudity. The policeman who brought her home warned her father he'd better keep an eye on her.

The incident had only strengthened her resolve to get away with things. She made up her own rules as she went along, and damn the consequences.

Screwing Professor Jay Morgan was a thrill. He was older (a teacher!) and a writer. He hung out with dangerous criminals! Helping Professor Morgan stash the body of the dead girl had been one of the most exciting things she'd ever done. She'd been so horny in the peach orchard, she'd been unable to keep her hands off him.

But Morgan had been a bit of a dud since. He seemed timid, almost frightened, that he was going to be caught or that something would go wrong. Oh, the sex was halfway good, but she could get sex anywhere. And rummaging Morgan's closets was dullsville. Pale blue Hanes boxer shorts, a half-used tube of BENGAY, and a clip-on tie from Sears were the highlights.

She thought about putting her clothes on, leaving a note for Morgan.

No, she'd wait. One more roll in the hay before cutting him loose.

Deke Stubbs screeched into the parking space in front of the convenience store. He shut off the engine, went in, hands shaking as he pulled crumpled bills from his pants pocket. He bought another six-pack of beer and a pack of cigarettes.

The girl behind the counter looked scared of him. Stubbs caught his reflection in the fish-eye mirror behind the girl. He looked distorted and evil, eyes red, skin waxen and moist. *I'm a villain*, thought Stubbs, *like in a creepy foreign film or a Stephen King novel*. Stubbs didn't watch foreign films or read much beyond the sports page, but he knew he'd crossed some line and couldn't get back.

On his way out to the car he ripped a phone book out of a booth. He sat in the front seat, flipped through the residential listings until he found Jay Morgan's address.

He popped a beer, gulped half, lit a cigarette, and sucked it slowly. He let out a long gray breath.

There was nothing to do now but see this through. He nodded to himself, pleased with the grim finality of his decision. Yeah, he'd have to go all the way. The Lancaster kid wasn't coming back, and it wasn't like Stubbs planned to turn himself in and say he was sorry. Rage and craziness had killed the kid. Stubbs would have to get his shit together from there on out. It was all or nothing.

Tracking down the cocaine was his first priority. He'd look for Annie Walsh still, and he'd send the parents a bill of course. But following Annie's trail might lead him to the drugs. He was way too deep into this shit not to get some kind of payoff.

Stubbs finished the cigarette, started the engine, and pointed the car toward Morgan's house. No more kid gloves. He'd find out what Morgan knew about this the hard way or the easy way. It didn't matter.

Stubbs was committed.

He found Morgan's house and parked across from it on the street. He watched for ten minutes, but didn't see anybody in the windows. He drank one more beer while he thumbed through the *Hustler* again.

When he finished the beer, he crushed the can and tossed it into the backseat. He opened the glove compartment and pulled out his .45 automatic. No spare clip or extra bullets. He hardly used the thing. But now it was a sign he meant business. All the way. He shoved it into his coat pocket and climbed out of the car.

The sudden cool air on his sweaty face was a shock. He woke up a little bit. Breathed deep. His chest burned with beer and too much smoking. He belched, tasted acid.

He spit and started up the short walkway to the house.

He knocked, waited. Nobody.

This might even be better if the guy wasn't home. He could break in through the back maybe and poke around.

He knocked again. This time he heard movement. Somebody was coming to the door. One hand fell into his coat pocket, clutched the grip of the automatic. He heard locks turning.

The door opened a crack. A girl on the other side, hair tousled. Broad shoulders and a nice face. A hand holding up a bedsheet to her neck. Soft, round breasts floated underneath. They swung interestingly as the girl shifted her weight from one foot to the other and tried to get a better hold on the sheet. "Yes?" She looked through the crack at Stubbs.

"I'm looking for Morgan."

"He's not here. Can I take a message or something?"

"Who are you?"

A little frown from the girl, and Stubbs guessed what she might be thinking. She was young. Shouldn't answer the door naked, honey. Not even in a sheet. Stubbs's private-eye instinct kicked in, and he ran the possible scenarios through his brain. Maybe Morgan was married, had a little thing going with a student on the side. Anyway, she didn't like being asked who she was.

"I'm just a friend of his," she said. "He's letting me stay here for a while."

"Uh-huh."

Stubbs pushed his way in. She didn't know what to do, stepped aside for him. He looked around, gave the place the once-over. Not a lot of personal stuff, like maybe Morgan hadn't lived there too long. "I need to see him. Maybe I'll wait."

The girl didn't like that. "He didn't say anything about when he might be back. Better maybe if you just left a message."

"Where did he go?" Stubbs was still looking around the house, craned his neck to see back into the kitchen. He didn't look at her. He bent over the coffee table, spread the magazines around and looked at the titles. "*Paris Review.* What's that? From France?"

"No, it's— Look, I don't think you should wait," she said. "He might not be back for a while."

Now Stubbs turned his gaze on her, red-eyed, dark bags underneath. "Oh yeah?"

The girl realized her mistake. "I mean he *might* be back any minute. Just that you shouldn't wait. In case he's a little late." She trembled now. She was talking herself into being scared. "But he might come through the door any minute."

"I asked who you were."

"Ginny."

Stubbs stepped toward her, and she eased away from him, the sheet dragging on the floor. Stubbs stepped on it. She tugged gently, and Stubbs grinned. He breathed loudly through his mouth. Licked his lips.

"Please." She tugged at the sheet again. Her voice was calm, but her hand shook worse where the sheet was bunched in her fist. "I'm stuck. You're on the sheet."

"Yeah." Stubbs liked the soft, half-seen curves of her under the sheet. Big tits, round hips. He liked it when they were afraid.

He stepped on the sheet with his other foot. It pulled tight, and Ginny gasped, used both hands to pull back and keep herself covered. "Don't." She meant to shout it, but it came out plaintive. She couldn't find breath, couldn't raise her voice. A cold, paralyzing chill ran through her. "Don't," she said again, and she could only stare at him, feebly holding on to the sheet.

He moved close, grabbed the sheet in his free hand, and yanked it away. He still had the other hand in his gun pocket.

A scream rose up but caught in Ginny's throat. She only made a sick, strangled bleating sound. She felt like lead, sank back against the wall. Stubbs crowded her, breathed his stink on her neck.

"So I think you're ready to talk to me now, right?"

Stubbs touched her hip and she jumped.

"Yeah, you're ready. I want to know about Annie Walsh."

So that's it, thought Ginny. *He knows. He found out about the peach orchard.* Ginny's mouth fell open, and she sucked for air. She closed her eyes tight and shook her head. She couldn't breathe. The leaden feeling on her chest worsened, knees turning to cold jelly.

"And the cocaine. All of it. I know all about it so tell me. Start talking."

Stubbs slapped her on the hip, not hard, but enough to make a loud smack.

That snapped her out of it. A hoarse scream. Eyes wide. Startled, even amid the terror, at the sudden slap. She pushed past Stubbs, started to run for the door. He grabbed her hair, yanked her back. She yelled again, high-pitched and panicked.

Stubbs grabbed her by the upper arm, fingers sinking in soft flesh. He let go of the .45 in his pocket, used the hand to slap her face. Hard. Tears in her eyes. She kicked, twisted, pulled away.

Two more slaps. Bells in her ears, flashes of light drowning her vision. Ginny shook her head, and her sight came back. She was on the floor, curling into a ball.

Stubbs stood over her, straddling. "Little slut." But Stubbs wasn't talking to her, only muttering to himself. He tugged his belt loose, unbuttoned his pants.

Ginny shook her head. No. Please. But the words wouldn't come. The weight was back on her chest, no breath. The horror of the world pinned her naked to the cold floor, the unreal thought that this was actually happening to her. She watched Stubbs reach for her, her tears turning him into a blurry apparition.

Morgan froze when he saw his front door halfway open. The house was quiet, dark.

"Hello?"

Nothing.

He ran in, paused in the living room at the crumpled sheet on the floor. He picked it up, looked at it, looked around the room, dropped it again. "Ginny?"

Dread sprang up in his gut. "Ginny!"

He ran to the kitchen and back, then into the bedroom. When he tried the bathroom door it was locked. He knocked, tried the knob again.

No reply.

He banged with his fist. "Ginny! You in there?"

Morgan backed up three steps then threw his shoulder into the door. It made a cracking sound but didn't give. Pain lanced through his shoulder.

"Fucking shit." He rubbed the sore spot, gritted his teeth.

He backed up for another go at the door when he heard the voice. Weak, tentative.

He put his ear against the wood. "Ginny? Open up. It's me."

"Professor?"

"It's me, Ginny."

Shuffling on the other side, scratching. "Professor?" Dazed.

"It's Professor Morgan."

He heard the lock work. He pushed at the door. It opened an inch then stopped. He looked in. Ginny leaned against it naked.

"Ginny, now, come on. Back up and let me in. I'm going to help, just back up a bit, okay?"

Her head flopped. She reached, draped her arms around the toilet bowl, pulled herself out of the way.

Morgan went in, knelt next to her. "It's okay. I'm here." He took her in his arms, eased her down onto the tile. Her faced turned to his.

Morgan's eyes grew wide. He stifled a gasp. Both her eyes were swollen and purple. Dried blood from her nose and the corners of her mouth.

"Professor..."

"I'm here. It'll be okay." *Dear God.* Morgan's eyes misted. He forced his voice not to choke. "I've got you."

"I think I need some...a doctor."

"Yes. I'll take care of it."

Ginny struggled to talk. Only half her mouth seemed to work. "I screamed, and he...he went away. I screamed and screamed."

"Don't talk, Ginny. Take it easy."

"He said he knew about the...drugs..." She tried to pick her head up, neck limp, eyes unfocused.

"Take it easy. Just be still."

Morgan ran to the bedside phone. He had to dial three times with shaking hands before he got the 911 operator.

The paramedics seemed to take forever but finally found them in the bathroom, Morgan cradling Ginny's head in his lap.

By the time Morgan got to the hospital, they'd already taken Ginny back for X rays.

He paced.

Finally, a nurse came and told him that Ginny might have a concussion. The nurse was short with him. Cold.

She thinks I did that to her. Morgan felt sick in the pit of his belly. This must happen all the time. Violent parents, abusive spouses.

He fell down the stairs. She ran into a doorknob. Isn't that how it is in TV movies?

Morgan went to the men's room, splashed water on his cheeks and in his eyes. The memory of Ginny's swollen face was still too vivid, the bruises on her upper arms, the deep red welts on her legs and backside.

He went back to the nurses' station, tried to appear benign. "Will I be able to see her soon?"

"It will be a while yet." The nurse was tight-lipped, didn't look at him. Shuffled papers into charts as she spoke. "I'll notify you if she wants visitors."

Morgan noted the *if.*

He sat at the end of a line of hard, molded plastic chairs. The sick and injured passed before him, two hours dragging his eyelids down into a doze.

"Mr. Morgan."

His head jerked up, eyes focusing on the nurse.

She said, "You can go back and see her, but she's still a little groggy. The doctor gave her a mild sedative."

"Thank you."

He followed the nurse back, and she pointed behind a plastic curtain. Ginny lay on the other side, curled on an examination table. A stool nearby. Morgan sat, reached to stroke her hair but pulled his hand back. She'd been bandaged, put in a hospital gown, a light blue blanket pulled up to her shoulders.

Her eyes flickered open. "Professor?"

"Yes."

"I'm sorry." Her voice flat, eyes dark.

Morgan couldn't imagine what she was sorry about. "How are you?" The dumbest question in the world.

She told him, her voice small, each word precise like she was reading the ingredients to a complex recipe. They'd x-rayed her skull, nothing busted. No concussion. One cracked rib. Two stitches below her left ear. One tooth knocked loose. An orthodontist would have to be called in, but no complications were expected.

"What happened?"

She shook her head.

"You don't have to talk. Rest."

"He was looking for you," Ginny said.

"Who?"

"I don't know. He was crazy, asking about drugs and Annie."

A chill crept over Morgan. "What else?"

"I thought he'd ask about the peach orchard, but he never did. He thought we had some drugs, I think. Maybe hidden. I couldn't figure out what he wanted. I'd have told him anything, but I just couldn't understand what he wanted to know."

Tears welled in Ginny's eyes, spilled down her cheeks, but her voice was flat. She was detached, huddled somewhere far away. Morgan felt crushed listening to the young girl. She must've thought the world her giant playground when they buried Annie in the orchard. Maybe she didn't think of Annie as a person then, only an elaborate prop in the big-budget movie of her life. Now Ginny's relationship with the world had dramatically changed. Her life was no longer a bright plaything. It was hard and real and had knocked the light of youth from her face. Maybe she'd never get it back.

Now she would only be scared all the time. Like him.

"Did he ... did he make you ..." The words eluded him. No will to speak them.

"He tried to," she said. "He couldn't get hard. He already had his belt in his hand, so he used it to whip me. When he bent down I kicked him in the ... down there."

Morgan felt a ghost pang in his balls, winced.

"I got away and locked myself in the bathroom," she said. "He tried to get in, but I kept screaming. He must've worried about the noise and the neighbors and went away."

Morgan couldn't look at her, couldn't stand it. He wished he'd never come to Oklahoma, wished he hadn't been a teacher, that he didn't have to see this young girl have the love of life beat out of her. He taught poetry. What the hell was that? What the fuck good did poetry do anybody?

He said, "I'll take you home. You can stay with me for a while."

"No."

He opened his mouth to object, shut it again.

"I had the nurse call my parents," Ginny said. "They'll be here soon. Don't worry. I won't tell them anything."

"Oh, I didn't think— Okay."

"You've got to be careful."

He blinked. Did she mean about her parents?

She said, "It's not me he's after, Professor. He wants you. I just happened to be there."

He nodded, bit his lower lip. Of course. He hadn't thought beyond what to do with Ginny. The guy had something to do with Annie and drugs. It was all too much. Morgan didn't want to go back to his house. Didn't want to wait there for the guy to return.

"Professor, I think I need to sleep now."

"Do you want me to wait until—"

"My parents will be here soon."

"Okay." Morgan swallowed a lump in his throat. "I'm sorry, Ginny. This shouldn't have happened."

But she was already asleep.

twenty-eight

Morgan left the hospital numb and scared. He drove his car, automatically heading back to his little house. Halfway there he thought, *I can't stay at home. That guy'll come back.*

He turned the car around, headed for the Best Western at the edge of town. Halfway to the motel he turned around again. He hadn't any luggage, not even a toothbrush. He'd have to risk his house for twenty minutes, long enough to grab some clothes and his toilet kit.

His thoughts tumbled, wouldn't line up straight. He couldn't hide out at the Best Western the rest of the semester. Another thought. If the guy knew where he lived, he'd probably be able to track Morgan to his campus office. A night at a motel wouldn't solve anything.

Fuck it.

One night at a time. That was all he could manage.

He parked in front of his house and ran up to the porch. The front door still stood open. He looked in, crept around the house, searching for intruders. Empty.

He ran to the bedroom, yanked a gym bag out of the closet. Two shirts, three pairs of boxer shorts, a fistful of socks. Into the bathroom next. He couldn't find his leather toilet bag, so he swept his toothbrush and razor off the sink and into the gym bag. He already wore his coat. What else? He always forgot something.

"Professor Morgan?"

Morgan froze. The voice was male and deep, came from the front porch.

"Hello? Professor Morgan?"

Morgan made himself calm down. A killer wouldn't call out. He'd just barge in. Still...

"It's Sergeant Hightower from the police, Professor Morgan."

Morgan realized he was holding his breath. He let it out. He walked slowly into the living room, clutching the gym bag to his chest. "Yes?"

Sergeant Hightower wore his straw hat back on his head. Big country-boy smile. Heavy brown jacket over a khaki uniform. Gun slung low. "Morgan, right?"

"Yes."

Hightower still stood on the porch, leaned into the living room without actually stepping over the threshold. "I just came from the hospital."

"Yes?"

Hightower pulled a pen and notepad from his jacket pocket. He flipped open the notepad. "I just need to ask a few questions." He gestured into the house. "Uh...you mind?"

"Please come in." *Go away.*

Hightower eased into the living room. He looked infuriatingly comfortable with himself. He looked the place over, took off his hat, and dropped it on the sofa. His pen hovered over the notepad. "How do you know Miss Conrad, sir?"

"She's a student."

He nodded. "So you have her in a class then."

"No. She is a student in the department, but not actually in one of my classes."

Hightower raised an eyebrow. "Oh." He wrote in his little notebook.

What are you writing? Stop that.

"Were you tutoring her?" asked Hightower.

"No."

Hightower smiled again, wide and self-satisfied. "This isn't like *Twenty Questions*, Professor Morgan. You're allowed to volunteer anything that might speed this along."

"We were friends. She was interested in writing."

"Uh-huh." He scribbled in the notebook again.

Son of a bitch.

Hightower scratched his chin with his thumb, squinted at Morgan. "Taking a trip, Professor?"

"No." He looked down at the gym bag. "I mean yes. But not until tomorrow. I was just packing."

"Where you going?"

Good question. "I'm going to Houston. There's a conference. I'm attending with another professor."

"Right." The information went into Hightower's notebook. "Do you know anyone who might want to hurt Miss Conrad?"

"Of course not."

"Anyone gunning for you?" Hightower asked.

"Don't be ridiculous."

Hightower shrugged. "Something don't jibe. Nothing stolen, not a burglary. If it's a rapist, he didn't rape."

"I talked to Ginny," Morgan said. "She told me she kicked him in the balls and locked herself in the bathroom."

"Maybe. But she don't live here. You do."

"So the rapist happened to see her come in. Then he saw me leave and figured . . . hell, I don't know."

"Sure, sure." Hightower nodded. "I wouldn't worry about it, Professor." That goddamn smug grin again. "Us country cops are slow, but once we get our teeth into something we don't let go. This don't seem like a normal rape attempt, but we'll figure it."

"And what is it exactly you figure?"

A shrug. Morgan couldn't quite understand the cop. It was almost like he was lazily working the Sunday crossword puzzle rather than trying to solve a violent crime. "Can't quite put my finger on it."

"Maybe you'd better talk to Ginny," Morgan said. Anything to get the cop on his way. Morgan couldn't stand talking to him much longer.

"Yeah, well, I talked to her already." He shook his head, *tsked*. "Her story's about like yours. Too many gaps. But I figure she's maybe still in shock. I'll talk to her again when she comes around."

Morgan cleared his throat. "Is there anything else?"

Hightower shook his head. "Nope." He flipped his notebook closed, shoved it back into his jacket. "When you coming back from Houston?"

"Monday."

"Right." He put his hat back on and gave Morgan a two-fingered salute. "We'll be in touch."

Five seconds after Hightower left, Morgan collapsed onto his sofa. His sweaty shirt clung to him. His hands shook, knees like water. Had the cop seen how nervous he was? *God, I need a drink.*

Not yet.

He locked up, got in his car, and drove to Professor Reams's house.

Morgan woke up late the next morning on Reams's couch. He felt sore, unhappy, desperate. His life was out of control, and the only solution he could come up with was to run away and hide in Houston for the weekend. At least it would give him time to think.

Reams had been childishly overjoyed that Morgan had decided to make the conference. All Morgan had wanted to do was escape into sleep, but in his dreams, he saw Ginny's battered face. It became Annie's, all the guilt and bad decisions mixed up together. He'd woken in the middle of the night, his pillow damp with sweat, a feeling of deep anxiety over him like a heavy blanket. He'd finally drifted off again about 4 A.M.

Morgan heaved himself off the sofa, rubbed his back. He called out to Reams but didn't get an answer. He found a note near the coffeepot. Reams had gone out to gas up the car.

Morgan showered, dressed.

He drank coffee and stared a long time at the phone. He wanted to call Ginny. But not to check on her, and that made him feel guilty. He wanted to get his story straight with her, didn't want Hightower to find little details to pick at. Morgan was already a wreck. He couldn't take another go around with the hick cop.

Okay, forget it. He drank coffee. Ginny was smart. She wouldn't get him or herself into trouble. All Morgan needed to do was lie low for a day or two while he figured things out. And he'd been laying off the booze, trying to get healthy. The first thing Morgan wanted to do in Houston was hop off the wagon long enough for a stiff drink.

A car horn blared outside. Five seconds later, Reams stuck his head in the door. "Let's go, buddy. Train's leaving the station." His finger was still wrapped, but he wasn't sickly anymore. Reams had the energy of a kid on his way to summer camp.

"Okay." Morgan dumped his coffee in the sink, grabbed his gym bag.

On the way out to the car, Reams said, "I had to put the Volvo in the shop. Transmission trouble. But I got us this for the drive."

Morgan stopped on the passenger side of the brand-new Mercedes. It looked nice, long and black, tinted windows. Expensive.

He opened the back door, and the sharp stench of bourbon slapped him in the face. Dirk Jakes stuck his head out. "Hey there, Morgo-man. Ready for a road trip?"

Morgan's jaw dropped. "What the hell's he doing here?"

"It's his car," Reams said.

Jakes held up a hip flask, swirled it around. "How about a little eye-opener, Morgan?"

It was actually tempting. "No thanks." He tossed his gym bag into the backseat next to Jakes. Jakes opened his yap to say something, but Morgan shut the door on him. To Reams he said, "You didn't tell me he was coming."

"Oh, take it easy."

Morgan shook his head. Reams's steadfast enthusiasm for the trip was not contagious. Morgan second-guessed his own decision to hide out in Houston at the academic conference.

Morgan climbed into the front passenger seat and Reams got behind the wheel. Reams went through a complex series of checks: headlights, windshield wipers, turn signals. He turned on the heat and set the thermostat. He was especially concerned with getting the volume exactly right on the radio.

"For Christ's sake," Jakes yelled from the backseat. "It ain't the goddamn space shuttle. Just start driving."

Morgan fastened his seat belt.

"Wagons ho, gentlemen." Reams put the Mercedes into gear and headed for the highway.

Jakes leaned forward between Morgan and Reams. "Remember, guys. What happens on the road stays on the road."

"Exactly," Reams said. "Just a trio of stout lads out for a good time."

"What actually do you think you're going to do?" asked Morgan.

Jakes said, "First thing is we brace ourselves with a few drinkypoos, then we round up some tail."

Reams didn't look so gung ho anymore. "Uh...maybe that's not the best idea, Dirk."

"Oh, put a sock in it, you sissy." Jakes grabbed the crotch of his pants. "Damn, I got to take a piss. Pull into that Chevron, will you?"

"We've only been on the road three minutes," Reams said.

"Dammit, Reams, I'm not going to let you fuck up a perfectly good road trip with your bullshit rules and schedules. Now pull into that gas station so I can tap a kidney."

Morgan sank low in his seat. It was going to be a long drive.

Deke Stubbs let the Mercedes get a head start, then followed. An expensive car. Maybe it was the drug dealer making the buy. Maybe this Morgan character had the cocaine after all. Maybe they had some kind of racket going. The kid had said a hundred thousand dollars' worth. Hell, maybe more.

Stubbs was red-eyed, queasy, tired. He'd had a very, very bad couple of days, but it would all pay off when he found the drugs and the money. He could turn things around pretty quick then.

What he really needed was sleep. But not now. Not yet. He had to see where Morgan was going in that big black Mercedes. He leaned over, popped open the glove box, and found the half-empty bottle of caffeine pills. They came in handy when Stubbs was on all-night stakeouts.

He rubbed his balls. They still ached. That bitch had kicked him good, but he'd fixed her.

He popped two of the caffeine pills, washed them down with his last beer. Okay, Professor Morgan, you lead. Deke Stubbs is on your ass like shit on a shoe.

twenty-nine

On a hard-packed dirt road under a gray sky just north of Fumbee, Red Zach cursed an underling on his tiny cell phone. Zach wanted answers and he wanted them yesterday.

"I asked you who was in charge of this one-horse shithole," Zach yelled. "I got to know who to deal with."

Red Zach had been around long enough to know the score. You don't go deep-sixing motherfuckers on somebody else's turf without permission, and you don't go poking your nose into the local drug economy without paying respects to the chief. It was like a franchise thing. He could kill Jenks. That was okay. Jenks was one of his boys run amok. But shit was getting out of hand, and he needed to speak to the local boss, whoever the fuck that was.

"I told you," Zach yelled into the cell phone. "If Jenks is going to unload my merchandise around here, I got to know where he's going."

"Okay, boss," said the voice on the other end. "But Fumbee, Oklahoma, ain't even on the damn map. It's in some kinda fucking no-man's-land between Tulsa and Fayetteville. I don't think it's anybody's turf."

"I don't want to hear that shit," Zach said. "You call back with a name." He slapped the phone shut and looked at his boys down from St. Louis.

When Red Zach had called for reinforcements, he'd asked for a dozen of the meanest, bad-ass motherfuckers available. It had been a long time since he'd gathered this much muscle together in one place, but he was dog-determined to finish this shit quick.

He hadn't been this pissed in a long damn time, and it was all because of Harold Jenks. He'd looked out for the boy, brought him along, gave him all the breaks. Zach had plans to make something out of him. But Jenks stabbed him in the back. Nobody but nobody fucked with Red Zach. The fact it was somebody he trusted made it double-worse.

Zach looked at the razor-thin man directly across from him. Maurice Arnold. He was a light-skinned black man, shaved head, bright, straight teeth, alert brown eyes. He wore a simple gray suit and a muted red tie. He looked like somebody's tax attorney, but Zach knew Maurice was the baddest, cruelest motherfucker this side of the Mississippi. He'd led the pack of reinforcements down from St. Louis. He was the guy Zach called whenever he wanted to turn a problem into a violent, screaming, smoking mess. Maurice didn't just make problems go away. He made them sorry they'd ever decided to be problems.

"Maurice, I want Jenks and any motherfuckers with him to pay the price. You catch my drift?"

Maurice sat with his hands folded in his lap. He nodded politely. "I understand, sir. Leave them to me."

"I got a man watching that redneck's trailer, but they ain't been back," Zach said.

Zach's cell phone rang, and he flipped it open. "Talk."

"I got a name for you, boss."

"Let's hear it."

"Moses Duncan."

"Affiliated?"

"Nope. Freelance. Buys out of Tulsa for resale around Fumbee, especially the campus, but he don't answer to nobody."

"We'll see about that," Zach said. "Where is he?"

The voice on the other end gave him directions. "A farm outside town."

"Right. Anything else?"

"He's a white guy."

"You think I give a shit?" Zach said. "What, you think I'm a racist?"

"No, boss."

"Damn straight. I'll own his shit if he's black, white, green, or polka-dot. I'm an equal opportunity motherfucker."

The fifth floor of Albatross Hall was pissing off Harold Jenks.

He'd been going stir-crazy stuck up there with DelPrego and the whacked-out old professor, so he'd risked sneaking across campus to the student union for a milk shake and a newspaper.

Jenks had gone through the local section and the police blotter, but apparently nobody had found the dead body at DelPrego's trailer. Jenks didn't know if that was good news or not.

At least the milk shake had been good.

But upon climbing back up to the fifth floor of Albatross Hall, he'd found himself completely turned around. He'd listened for the music like DelPrego had instructed, but all was quiet. Jenks had concluded some crack-head architect son of a bitch was having a big laugh somewhere. Jenks was all turned around.

He stood, scratched his head, cursed again.

Then he heard it.

Slow footsteps and metal dragging. A peculiar rhythm. Step, step, drag. Step, step, drag. Jenks froze. What the hell was that? He strained to listen, tried to determine from which direction it was coming. *That shit's creeping me out.* It reminded him of this Frankenstein movie he'd seen as a kid. It had scared the shit out of him. No matter where the people ran, the Frankenstein kept coming. And he dragged one foot behind him, made that scraping noise.

Except this dragging was harsh and metallic.

So Jenks stood there, waited for the metal robot Frankenstein of Albatross Hall to come eat his lunch.

It was the custodian.

Jenks exhaled relief. What was that janitor dude's name again? Valentine had introduced them. Brad Eubanks. Valentine seemed to have some kind of arrangement with the man. Jenks didn't pretend to understand completely, but he thought the relationship between the old professor and the custodian might somehow be symbiotic.

Symbiotic. Where the hell had he picked up that word? Jenks's face twisted with a wry smile. Maybe college was rubbing off.

Eubanks saw him from the other end of the hall, waved him over. "Hey, now." A deep country accent, voice harsh with the twang. "Come gimmee a hand with this, young feller." Eubanks was dragging a long, thick metal pipe. Gleaming brass.

"What is that?" Jenks called.

"Fireman's pole. Come help."

Jenks jogged down to him, grabbed the other end of the twenty-foot pole. It was heavier than he'd thought. He grunted, tucked it up under his arm. "What's this for?"

Eubanks's laughter segued into a wheezing grunt. "A little project for the professor."

They waddled down the hall. Jenks started to sweat. He asked, "What's his deal anyway?"

"Valentine?"

"Uh-huh."

"He's crazy," Eubanks said. "Oh, not in a bad way. Not dangerous-like. I think he just likes it on campus. I think he's unhappy with the rest of the world. Here on campus he's an important genius."

"How's that?"

"Pulitzer Prize."

"Oh." Jenks had heard of that one.

"Personally, I can't see it," Eubanks said. "I borrowed some of his poetry books, ones he'd wrote hisself. Do you know them poems he wrote don't even *rhyme*?"

Jenks started to say something, bit his tongue.

"I mean, hell now, I may not be college educated, but I know poems should rhyme. Any first-grader knows that."

The custodian kept yakking about it. But the more Eubanks talked, the more Jenks didn't want to listen, the more he felt the distance.

thirty

The black Mercedes devoured the miles, State Highway 75 leading them over the line and into Dallas, where they picked up Interstate 45 south. Night fell. They'd run through Jakes's CD collection: Stones, John Prine, Willie Nelson, Freakwater, Steely Dan, the sound track to *Footloose*, and *Tony Orlando's Greatest Hits*. At Reams's insistence, they'd taken only one short break from the music to listen to *All Things Considered* on NPR.

Jakes had a little routine. He'd doze in the backseat awhile, start awake, launch into a story about some girl he'd fucked in college, take a slug from his flask (refilled periodically from a bottle in the trunk), then drop off to sleep again.

Morgan drove now, had the cruise control set to eighty-five.

Reams couldn't leave the dome light alone. "Why won't this infernal thing shut off?" He reached above his head, thumbed the switch without success, clicked his tongue.

"Leave it alone," Morgan said.

"It's bothering me."

"You've been screwing with it for an hour. Forget it."

Reams reached around the wheel, fussed with the switches on the steering column. The wipers came on.

Morgan slapped his hand. "Knock it off. I'm trying to drive."

"I know the button's over there somewhere for the interior lights," Reams said. "Try that switch over by that dial wheel thingy."

"No. I've tried them all already. Just leave it. And don't mess with the speakers or the radio. The balance is fine. The bass is fine. The treble is fine. Everything is fine. The heat is fine. Your seat is fine."

Jakes stirred in the backseat.

"Great." Morgan forced himself to unclench his teeth.

Jakes sat up, fumbled off the cap of his flask, and took a big slug. He belched, wiped his mouth on his sleeve. He rubbed his eyes with a knuckle, took another short drink.

Morgan and Reams braced themselves.

Jakes cleared his throat. "Did I ever tell you guys about this red-haired chick I knew at UCLA? Man she had tits—"

"White as snow with nipples like dark raspberries," Morgan and Reams said together.

Jakes blinked. "Yeah."

"You told us," Reams said. "This is the third time."

"She was the best one. I looked her name up on the Internet and got her phone number. Sometimes I think about giving her a call." He finished the flask, upended it again like he couldn't believe it was empty. "But I don't call. It's been maybe twelve years."

Jakes hiccuped. "Jesus, I don't feel so good."

"Lay off the bourbon," Morgan said.

"It's empty." Jakes tossed the flask onto the floor of the back-seat. It clanged harshly. "What the hell is this?" He bent, looked. "Some kind of drill thing and a hammer. What is this shit, Reams?"

Reams twisted, looked over his shoulder. "Blast. I meant to take all that back to Sears when I was out gassing the car. The tools for the gazebo."

"You're cluttering up my brand-new Kraut car with this shit."

"Sorry."

Jakes threw his head back with sloppy laughter. Loud. "Hey, Morgo, you hear about Bob Vila? Almost chopped himself in half."

"I heard," Morgan said.

Jakes squinted at the ceiling. "Why the hell's the dome light on?"

Morgan muttered.

"We can't figure how to turn it off," Reams said.

"It's one of them fucking buttons on the steering column," Jakes said.

"We tried them," Morgan said.

Jakes snorted. "Well, try them again, dammit. It's a brand-new car. I know the buttons work."

"They don't."

"Hell." He grabbed the hammer from the floor. "I'll fix it." He flicked his wrist, and the claw part of the hammer shattered the dome light with a loud pop. Glass rained, peppered Morgan and Reams. Reams covered his eyes, turned away.

Morgan jumped. "Shit!" He jerked the wheel, spilled into the next lane, nearly smacking a Honda Civic. It blared its horn, flashed its lights.

Morgan pulled back into his lane, heart thumping. "Christ, Jakes!"

"It's out."

"Idiot." Morgan gulped breath, held it, let it trickle out slowly.

"I don't think that was necessary," Reams told Jakes. "I could have taken the bulb out."

A lapse into angry silence.

But it was good to have the light out. Morgan could see better now. The road was nearly deserted, only a single set of headlights several car lengths behind, and the Honda, which had elected to speed up and put some distance between itself and the carload of morons.

Morgan included himself as one of the morons. How could he have thought a road trip with these two was a good idea? God was punishing him.

"Guys." It was Jakes.

Nobody spoke.

"Guys, I think I'm going to be sick."

Great. Morgan wondered if he should pull over. This stretch of road was very, very dark. *I don't want to die in Texas.*

"Try taking deep breaths," suggested Reams.

"Fuck the breaths, I'm...Jesus, I don't feel good."

"Take it easy," Morgan said. "We'll find someplace. Maybe drink some water. We'll stop and get some water."

"Oh, shit." Jakes groaned. "My stomach. Rough seas."

"Hang on," Morgan said. "Just take it easy."

Morgan prayed for an exit. Let Jakes puke all over an Amoco station.

"Jesus, here it comes. Oh, shit." He bent over, gagged, coughed. His gut heaved, and he spewed liquid, sprayed a good portion of the backseat.

"Not on the tools!" Reams yelled.

Too late. Jakes heaved again, coated the tools with gunk. The smell filled the car, acidic and boozy. Morgan almost puked too when it hit his nose. "Oh, my God." He hit the window buttons, lowered all four of them. At eighty-five miles per hour, the wind washed through the car quickly.

A blue sign ahead. Morgan squinted at it, crossed his fingers. It was a rest area.

"Yes!" Morgan mashed the accelerator.

Jakes lay in the fetal position, a thick strand of scummy saliva draped from his lower lip to the edge of the seat.

Reams said, "He doesn't look well at all."

Morgan flew down the off-ramp, skidded into a parking space near the rest rooms. The rest area was deserted except for the headlights that had been following. The other car pulled into the rest area too, parked on the far side. Shut off the lights.

Morgan shut off the Mercedes, flung the door open, and leapt out. He took a dozen quick steps before gulping clean, cold air.

"I think he's passed out," Reams called from the car.

Good, thought Morgan. *Let's dump him in the bushes and leave.*

Morgan walked into the men's room, unzipped at the first urinal. He finished, washed his hands.

Reams walked in, grabbed two fistfuls of paper towels, and left again without saying anything.

Morgan splashed water on his face. He looked at himself in the mirror. Bags under his eyes. He started laughing. Shook his head and laughed more. He looked at himself like a stranger. *Poor dumb bastard.* He was still chuckling when he left the rest room.

He stood in the lit doorway of the rest room, hands in pockets. He let the cold wash over him. Winter had started to ease these last few days, but at two in the morning, it was sharply cold. Damp. Refreshing, but it would get cold soon if he stood outside for very long.

Reams approached with an armload of something wrapped in newspaper. He frowned, eyes hard, his enthusiasm for the trip apparently spent.

"What's that?" Morgan asked.

"The drill, the saw, and the chisels," Reams said. "How am I supposed to return these goddamn things when they're covered in Jakes's vomit? It's revolting."

"Throw them away," Morgan said.

"They were expensive," Reams said. "Keep an eye on that idiot, will you? I left the doors open to air out, and I don't want him stumbling off. I'm going to try to clean these."

Morgan eyed the saw. "Please be careful."

"Give me some credit."

"Reams," Morgan said. "Be careful."

Reams frowned, walked past with the armload of pukey tools.

Morgan stood, looked at the night, heard the night sounds, the occasional car on the interstate. He rocked heel to toe with hands in pockets, the night air cloying on his face, damp on his ears, the back of his neck. His thin ponytail hung loose and limp. The cold air stung his throat and lungs.

He checked the Mercedes. Jakes hadn't budged. Morgan cast about for something else to look at.

Across the lot sat the car that had followed them into the rest area. Strange, thought Morgan. The driver hadn't got out to use the rest room. Morgan thought he could just see the outline of the driver's body behind the wheel. He watched for a moment. There. The red-orange pinpoint of a cigarette flaring in the front seat. The guy had pulled off to have a smoke.

The bright glow of the cigarette went out. It came back a second later, hovered in the implacable darkness a moment, then faded.

Morgan's gut grew heavy. Worry crawled up his spine, found a home in his brain. He hadn't thought about Ginny's attacker for hours. The endless string of minor annoyances perpetrated by his traveling companions had distracted him.

Ginny said he was after me, Morgan thought. *This dangerous fucking freak wants something from me, and I don't even know what. Something to do with Annie?* Morgan's eyes shifted nervously. Jakes's Mercedes and the other car were the only ones in the rest area.

Morgan kept his eyes on the strange car, reached behind him, and knocked on the men's room door, which was propped open. "Let's speed it up, okay, Reams? I want to get back on the road."

"Just a moment."

Morgan heard the water running, the tools clanking in the sink.

"I'll be in the car." Morgan fast-walked back to the Mercedes, took the keys out of his coat pocket with trembling hands. *It's just cold. That's all.*

He climbed in, cranked it. He kept glancing in the rearview mirror at the other car. No movement. Not even the glow of the cigarette. The back door was still open, but the dome light wasn't on since Jakes had smashed it. The car was still thick with the reek of vomit.

Reams returned and startled Morgan. Morgan had been watching the rearview mirror and hadn't seen the professor coming. Reams shoved Jakes's head back into the car. He dumped the tools onto the floor of the backseat, then slammed the door. He climbed into the front next to Morgan.

Reams's hand was wrapped in multiple layers of rest room paper towels. A little red spot forming where the blood seeped through.

"What happened?" Morgan asked.

"Nothing."

"Did you cut yourself again?"

"Never mind," Reams said. "Just drive."

Morgan backed the Mercedes out of the space, then took the on-ramp back to the interstate. He kept one eye on the other car in the mirror. It didn't turn its lights on, didn't follow. Morgan drove ten minutes. The interstate was long and dark and quiet. No other cars.

Maybe he was being paranoid. It was natural he'd be nervous, overcautious. He eased into the driver's seat, relaxed his grip on the wheel. Reams was quiet, Jakes passed out. Maybe the rest of the trip south would pass in relative peace.

He glanced at the mirror again, and his breath caught.

Distantly, a pair of headlights, two dots of light hugging the road behind.

This is a major interstate, Morgan told himself. *Even at this hour there'll be lots of people traveling. That doesn't have to be the car from the rest area.*

But deep in the pit of Morgan's belly, he knew it was.

Deke Stubbs kept his distance.

He figured the professor had almost made him back at the rest stop, but now he wasn't sure. He'd stay well behind them for a while. Creep up slowly with the daylight, mix in with the other cars as the morning traffic increased. No problem.

Stubbs unzipped himself and pulled out his pecker, he leaned, reached, grabbed an empty beer can off the passenger-side floor. He brought it to his pecker and pissed. He'd already filled two other cans. It sure would have been nice to use the pisser back at that rest stop, but Stubbs couldn't risk Morgan getting a look at him. Stubbs might want to get closer later on, and he wouldn't want the guy to recognize him.

Stubbs rolled down his window, tossed out the nearly full can, rolled his window back up.

The detective was tired and half-hungover and sick of driving. How far were these sons of bitches going? He thought about popping another couple of caffeine pills, but his stomach was already burning.

When he sold the drugs, maybe he'd set himself up in some other line of work. Being a private detective sucked.

thirty-one

The Houston Santa Anna Sheraton was nice, expensive, full-service, four stars. Morgan had been to several regional conferences where he'd stayed at whatever budget motel had been near the campus.

But the Thirteenth Annual International Interdisciplinary Conference of the Humanities & Fine Arts was something special. Scholars and writers from all fifty states and twenty-two countries stampeded like hypercaffeinated lemmings to the host city, where they delivered mind-numbingly complex papers on obscure subjects in their desperate bids to rack up points toward tenure. Morgan had been to more than one panel where the panelists outnumbered the audience.

Morgan had never stayed at a hotel nicer than the Holiday Inn Express. So he stood next to the Mercedes in the valet roundabout with his bag in his hand and waited for somebody to tell him what to do. Reams rummaged the trunk for his own bags.

The parking valet's red uniform reminded Morgan of a cartoon. The valet hovered, waited for somebody to hand him a set of keys.

The back door of the Mercedes swung open. Jake's empty bourbon bottle fell out, clanked alarmingly on the cement but didn't break. It rolled underneath the car.

Jakes stumbled out. "Jesus Christ." He rubbed his eyes, belched. He looked like death in a sports jacket, skin slick and ashen, hair matted, eyes dark.

Then Jakes took charge.

He dipped into his pocket, came out with a wad of ten-dollar bills big enough to choke a bison. "Morgan, give Junior the keys."

Morgan handed the keys to the valet.

Jakes gave the kid twenty bucks. "Don't park it next to any shit-mobiles." He peeled off two more bills and gave them to the valet. "Some kind of stench in the car. See what you can do."

"Yes, sir." He hopped into the driver's seat and drove away.

"Let's go, fellas," Jakes said. "Chop-chop."

A brace of bellboys leapt into action. They'd been unclear if Morgan and Reams were worth fawning over, but clearly Jakes was a man used to first-class service. They scooped up the luggage in a heartbeat. One took Morgan's bag away from him like Morgan had no business touching it.

The professors followed the luggage into the lobby. Jakes identified the bell captain and waved him over.

"I'm going to need a cold six-pack waiting in the room," Jakes said. "Also a plate of scrambled eggs, toast, and whatever fruit is fresh. I don't know the room number yet, but you'll find that out. Name's Dirk Jakes." He shoved a wad of cash at the bell captain.

"Very good, Mr. Jakes. What kind of beer?"

"Does the bar have Red Stripe?"

"I'm sorry, no."

"Find some."

"Yes, sir." The bell captain sped away with his orders.

Morgan could only stand with his hands in his pockets and wonder where his bag had been taken.

It was only 7 A.M., and the desk clerk was sorry to inform Jakes that check-in wasn't for several hours.

Jakes gave the man hell.

Nine minutes later Morgan stood in the room he was sharing with Reams. The luggage had been waiting for them. Jakes had his own room down the hall.

"I'm going to the conference rooms to check in, get my badge, and all that," Reams said.

"Uh-huh."

After Reams left, Morgan stripped down to his boxers and crawled into bed. His head hit the pillow, and he was out.

Morgan dreamed.

It was the updated version of a recurring dream he'd had in high school. In the high school version he drove his father's Pontiac. The steering was noodle loose, his arm muscles wouldn't work. The Pontiac was barely in control, all over the road, the fifteen-year-old Morgan paralyzed with cold-sweat fear. Not for his life. He feared what his old man would do to him when he wrecked the car. The brakes wouldn't work.

Inevitably, he'd be heading for a tree, a mailbox, another car, and his eyes would pop open right before impact. He'd awake with a strangled cry caught in his throat, heart pounding out of his chest.

The new version of the dream was similar but more terrifying.

He was behind the wheel of the Mercedes, trying to turn it around, so he could get back to Fumbee.

But when he tried to pull off the highway, the car refused to obey. He couldn't control the steering, kept missing the exits. Jakes yelled unintelligibly from the backseat. Reams wouldn't help.

Finally, Morgan wrenched the wheel. The Mercedes spun into an unreal blur. He pulled out of the spin, headed back the wrong way on the dark interstate.

He headed straight for a pair of headlights. Strangely, Morgan had control of the car now. He beeped his horn, flashed the high beams. The oncoming headlights remained on course, arrow-straight and fast. Morgan wouldn't budge either, but this time he had control of the car. He was committed to the deadly collision.

The headlights grew enormous in the windshield.

Reams grabbed his arm. "Morgan. Morgan."

Morgan wouldn't swerve, hands clenched to the wheel, teeth grinding. The engines roared, the monstrous headlights only a dozen feet away.

Reams screamed, "Morgan!"

"Morgan." Reams kicked the side of Morgan's bed. "Come on, now. It's noon. Let's grab a bite and catch the first session."

Morgan sat up in bed. He felt cold and not much rested.

Reams had showered, slipped into a pair of khakis and a navy polo shirt. A badge hung from the collar. It had his name and the name of the conference on it.

"I checked you in as well." Reams held up Morgan's badge then dropped it on the dresser. "It's 150 bucks for the whole weekend." Reams waited, looked expectantly at Morgan.

"I'll pay you back. Thanks."

Reams smiled relief. "Oh, I knew you would. We're supposed to meet Jakes in twenty minutes. Better snap to it."

"Right."

In the shower, Morgan leaned heavily against the tiles, let the hot water pelt him. Memory of the dream was already fading, but the sick feeling of worry stayed. And he hadn't forgotten about the man at the rest area or the headlights that dogged him until dawn. After sunrise, traffic had picked up, and he couldn't tell if he was being followed or not.

He tried to explain to himself rationally that he was being paranoid—a bit timid and pathetic, in fact. But the worry clung to him. He thought about Ginny's bruised face. He thought about the old man and Sherman Ellis and the upcoming poetry reading. He thought about the whole long, bad list of things he didn't want to think about. Annie and the peach orchard.

For the hundredth time, Morgan thought, *It's time to come clean. Time to explain it all to the police, tell them I panicked.* It was all a series of bad mistakes.

But could he do that now? He hadn't detected any sign of sympathy or understanding in Officer Hightower. The cop had seemed only smug, like he resented Morgan for some reason. And how would it look now to go to the police, when Hightower had been right there in his living room? That had been the time. It would have been so easy. *Look here, Officer Hightower, here's the whole story.*

And Ginny. If he went to the police now, he'd have to drag her into it, and she'd suffered enough. Worse, she might turn on him, blame him for everything.

The hot water ran out and Morgan shut off the shower. He dried himself, dressed in jeans and a green-and-yellow Hawaiian shirt with hula girls on surfboards. The conference was in the hotel, so he wouldn't need his jacket.

In the elevator on the way down, Reams said, "I've narrowed it down to two panels that start at the one o'clock session. Either one sounds interesting."

"You pick," Morgan said.

"No, no. Wait and hear the choices." Reams thumbed through the program. "We can either see *Homosexual Transmogrification in Androgynous Eighties Techno-Pop* or we can go to *Pimple and Blemish Imagery in Victorian Fiction.*"

The elevator opened and saved Morgan from deciding. They stepped out into the lobby. It writhed with activity. Conference-goers with dangling clip-on badges swarmed the place. It was like a tweed bomb had exploded in the Sheraton.

"This way," Reams said. "Jakes said he'd meet us in the lounge."

The lounge was crammed with scholars bracing themselves for the upcoming sessions. Jakes perched at the bar, chatted up a busty woman with her coppery hair piled in a tight bun. Morgan and Reams stood behind him.

"So I go out to the mailbox one day, and there's this check for 132,000 bucks," Jakes told her. "I didn't know what the hell it was for, so I called my agent. Turns out they'd sold the Asian rights to my last three novels. That's when I ran out and got the Mercedes."

The woman looked bored. She wore a pair of old-fashioned, black-framed glasses, which reminded Morgan of Ginny. Morgan thought he should maybe call her, but discarded the idea again. Her parents would be with her.

"So what do you do?" Jakes asked her.

"I compile bibliographies for Restoration drama criticism," she said.

Jakes broke into barking laughter, wiped his chin where he'd dribbled some beer. "Jesus, is there any money in that?"

"Not much." She stood, put money on the bar. "I have to get

ready for my panel." Not a lot of warmth in her voice. She left, and Morgan took her stool.

Jakes looked like a new man, hair combed, close shave. He wore an expensive checkered sports coat and creased trousers with cuffs. He ordered another beer. "Lots of tail at these conferences." He winked, sipped his beer.

"Right."

"I got a program for you." Reams handed it to Jakes.

"Thanks." Jakes threw it on the floor.

The bartender came over, indicated that the lounge was too crowded just to lounge. Reams ordered a draft beer. Morgan desperately wanted a giant, double vodka martini but ordered coffee instead.

"Big cocktail reception tonight," Jakes said. "Good place to snag some snatch."

"Let's talk about which panels to see," Reams suggested.

Jakes frowned. "Stuff that idea."

Morgan stood, tossed money on the bar for the coffee. He couldn't stand it, not if these two were going to start in again. "I'll catch up with you guys later. I'm not feeling so well."

Reams looked hurt, opened his mouth to say something, but Morgan was already making his escape. He eased his way through the bar crowd and headed for the elevators. He felt a tap on his shoulder.

If it were Reams, he'd tell the man as firmly as possible that he was not going to attend a panel on Victorian zits. He turned.

And looked into the smiling eyes of Annette Grayson.

"What are you doing here?" she asked. "Did you come to see my presentation?"

thirty-two

Morgan confessed he didn't know Grayson was going to be there. He told her that Reams had badgered him into attending.

Annette Grayson seemed glad to see him. Her eyes glittered, and Morgan soaked her in. He'd forgotten how pleasant she was to look at. Smile big, radiating, reaching her eyes, and lifting her whole face. Her hair was golden silk, loose about her shoulders. Skin tan and glowing. Annette Grayson was the brightest thing in the lobby of the Sheraton, and the sight of her hit Morgan in the gut. Took the wind from his lungs.

"Let me get you a drink," Morgan said.

"I can't," she said. "My old roommate from Bennington is giving a paper in a few minutes, and I'd promised I'd go."

"Later then?"

She bit her thumbnail, looked at Morgan, squinting her eyes. "Well…"

Morgan smiled. "What happens on the road, stays on the road. Besides, I feel I owe you an apology drink."

"Maybe you do," she said. "After dinner. Call my room." She told him the number.

"Okay."

She turned, headed through the crowd. She glanced back once, smiled over her shoulder, and was gone.

Morgan felt light. On some level, he knew his problems hadn't gone away. But they all seemed distant. Annette's scent still hung in the air where he stood. It wasn't a heavy perfume, not sickly sweet. More like a body splash. He sniffed the air. Citrus.

He chewed up the rest of the afternoon. Anticipation. Fluttering stomach. The look in Annette's eyes had promised something. Morgan wasn't sure what. Maybe another chance.

He ate dinner with Reams. The professor had launched into a tedious summary of the panels he'd attended. It went on all through dinner, but Morgan was in better spirits and tolerated Reams fairly well, even managed to contribute a few comments that made him seem interested. They'd gone to a steakhouse about a block from the hotel. A good porterhouse.

Once or twice Morgan's brain tried to remind him about Ginny and the headlights that had followed him to Houston and all the stone-hard troubles that awaited him beyond the out-of-focus, fuzzy-soft unreality of the conference. He beat the bad thoughts down, kicked them into the corner. Not tonight. Tonight he was having a drink with Annette Grayson.

Morgan shook loose of Reams back at the hotel, told him he wanted to go back up to the room for a while.

"You sure?" Reams asked. "I was going to that cocktail reception. The one Jakes was talking about."

"I might catch up later," Morgan said.

Morgan took the elevator up, let himself in the room with the plastic swipe-card. He went to the phone, grabbed it, put it down again. Too soon. He felt nervous about calling her and liked it. He hadn't felt nervous about a woman in a long time.

He went to the window and pushed the curtains back. It was just getting dark, and Houston was flickering to life.

He picked up the phone and dialed Annette.

One ring. "Hello?" Her voice was warm milk.

"It's Jay."

"Give me an hour," she said. "Down in the lounge."

"Okay."

He hung up and jumped in the shower. He got out and dressed, a clean blue shirt. He ironed a pair of tan slacks. He thought about cologne and wondered if it would be too much. All he had was Old Spice. He was embarrassed but liked the smell.

He combed his hair four times. There wasn't too much to comb. He tied his little ponytail fresh and tight.

He went down the elevator, stepped into the lobby. He looked at his watch. Twenty minutes early. He clasped his hands behind his back and strolled the hotel.

A little shop. He went in.

Gifts. Cigarettes, toothpaste, aspirin, postcards of glorious Texas. Morgan spotted a wood-and-glass cabinet behind the counter. He looked through the glass at cigars. He was feeling sporty and whimsical and called over the smarmy cashier.

The cashier lifted an eyebrow, the rest of his vanilla pudding face sagging with disinterest. "Sir?"

"I'm looking for a type of cigar." He tried to remember what

Fred Jones had given him the day they broke out the Wallace Stevens. "It's Mac something."

"Macanudo?" The cashier said the word through his nose.

"That's it. I'll take three."

"They're twelve dollars each, sir. Do you still want them?"

"Of course." Little bastard. "I said I'll take three." He handed over his Visa card.

Was it Morgan's clothes? Something about the way he carried himself that suggested he couldn't—or wouldn't—shell out for a good cigar?

The little man rang him up and Morgan left the shop. He took the cigars out of the bag and smelled one. Nice. It was as long as the one the old man had given him, but thinner. He looked at the band. Same kind. Same rich, earthy smell. He put one in his mouth without lighting it. He didn't have any matches. He thought about going back to the shop but decided against it. The cashier's inexplicably superior attitude was strangely unnerving. That happened to Morgan sometimes. A waiter or barber or movie usher or some other underling would be rude to him, and Morgan would be intimidated because he couldn't figure out if he'd done or said something wrong.

It was only much later in such situations that Morgan always wished he'd had a sharp comeback. Or a quick slap with a dueling glove. Or maybe if he'd just spit on their shoes. He was getting tired of letting life roll over him.

He went straight to the lounge and ordered a vodka martini. He drank it in three gulps and ordered another. Only then did he glance around for Annette. She hadn't arrived yet.

That little prick at the gift shop had spoiled his mood. He half thought it would be a good idea to take Dirk Jakes back with him to rip the guy a new asshole. Jakes would do it too, just for laughs.

And then Morgan was mad because a guy like Jakes could handle himself in those situations and Morgan couldn't. He finished the martini and ordered another one. The voice in his head told him to slow down, but it wasn't very convincing.

"What in the world's wrong with you?"

Morgan spun on his stool, looked into Annette's soft eyes. They cast their warm light on him. He realized his face had been frozen in a deep scowl. He sat up straight, forced his jaw muscles to unclench. He cleared his throat.

"You don't want to sit at the bar," he said. "There's a table over there."

"That's fine."

He bought her a white wine and took it to the corner table. Soft light. Quiet. The lounge was pleasantly deserted, most of the conferencegoers at the big reception.

Morgan asked if she were enjoying the conference.

She said she was.

And had her friend's panel gone well?

It had.

Thus concluded Morgan's cache of small talk. He was bone dry. The martinis took over.

"So what's wrong with me, huh?" Morgan asked it with a smile.

"There's nothing wrong with you."

"Then what's wrong with you?"

She laughed. "Nothing. There's nothing wrong with anybody."

"Afraid of me?"

"Not of you. That things won't work out like we want. That life will backfire."

"What's the solution?"

"Stick your head out of your hole once in a while," she said. "If it's clear, run out, grab a chunk of life, chew it up quick, and get back into your hole. A little at a time when the coast is clear."

"At Valentine's party, and when we had pizza, that was you coming out of the hole for a little look-see?" Morgan threw back his drink, waved at the bartender for another.

"That's right," Annette said. "I had a two-day hangover after Valentine's party, and I had to ride the stationary bicycle three hours to work off the pizza. Imagine living life that big all the time. Imagine the toll. It's like looking at God. You can't look directly at Him. You have to avert your eyes or look at a burning bush or something."

"What about Dirk Jakes?" Morgan asked. "Seems like he's going full blast all the time."

"He's an anomaly." She shrugged. "Or maybe a prophet. Cautionary example."

Morgan said, "This isn't your first glass of wine, is it?"

"I'm out of my hole for a look-see," she said. "I split a bottle of Chablis with my friend."

When the bartender brought the martini, Annette sent him back for more wine.

"What happened to you?" Morgan wasn't laughing now. He thought Annette's worldview sad and gray.

"I looked at life too directly the first time around. Good husband, good life, good everything, then I got the rug yanked. I'm lighter on my feet now. It won't happen again."

Morgan thought he understood, knew what it was like to have your guard up all the time.

The drinks came. Annette drank hers in two gulps. "Let's go upstairs and screw."

"Okay," Morgan said.

They leaned against each other in the elevator, her fingers light on his back. His heart fluttered, pumped hot blood to all the appropriate areas. His head swam. They went to her room.

Morgan had seen this before. There was something erotic and

hypnotic about hotel lounges and hotel rooms. Maybe it was being away from home. Maybe it was the little soaps and shower caps and one-use shampoo bottles and everything that hinted how temporary it all was. You didn't even have to make the bed.

Or maybe it was the ultracold air-conditioning. Annette's tan, smooth skin broke out in gooseflesh when Morgan slipped her dress off her shoulders. It shrunk to the floor around her ankles. The bra was easy to unsnap. He took a nipple into his warm mouth, and she threw her head back, moaned, grabbed the back of his head, twirled his ponytail in her fingers.

They stumbled to the bed, and her hands went to his belt. She unfastened him. Soon both were naked. He entered her quickly, and her ankles locked behind his back. He found a rhythm, sped up. She thrust back against his hips, grunting, panting, all the pent-up frustration heaving out with each slam of him against her.

She screamed her orgasm. He shook, released, went limp on top of her.

The whole thing had taken about ninety seconds.

"I think you'd better go," she said.

"What?"

"It's just . . . I feel embarrassed." She scooted out from under him and ran into the bathroom and slammed the door.

Morgan crawled off the bed, schlong dangling wet. He was dazed, bewildered. He gathered up his clothes, cradled them. He noticed absently he still wore his socks.

Annette came back wearing a white robe. "It's not right. We work together."

"But—"

"We got carried away." She pushed his shoulder gently, herded him toward the door.

"Let me get dressed!"

She paused, let him get into his boxers and trousers, then opened the door. She pushed him out. He opened his mouth but couldn't get a word out.

"I'm sorry," Annette said. "But we let the moment overcome our good judgment."

And the door was closed.

He put his shirt on, started down the hall, mouth still hanging open. Stunned.

Just that quickly Annette Grayson had scurried back to her hole. She'd been out for only a glimpse, grabbed herself a chunk of Jay Morgan, and was gone again. Would she pay for it like the cheese pizza? Could she work off the memory of him on the stationary bicycle?

He stopped walking, looked down at his feet. He'd forgotten his shoes.

thirty-three

One-thirty in the morning, and Morgan had painted himself into the corner of the hotel lounge. He knew he was in for an apocalyptic hangover but couldn't make himself care. He was maxing his Visa card on Sheraton martinis.

After Annette had kicked him out, he'd waited in his room for an hour in case she regained sanity and wanted to call. No call. He'd gone down to the bar in his socks. He'd kept drinking, hunched over the table, eyes going glassy and unfocused.

He stumbled to the house phone, dialed his room.

Reams answered, sleepy, mumbled something that might have been "hello."

"Reams, buddy. Any calls for me?" Morgan heard his own voice loud in his ears. Good. A time to be loud. Let the trumpets sound.

"Morgan?"

"Morgan."

"Glad you phoned." Reams woke up, spoke more clearly. "I scheduled a breakfast with a Professor Klein. That one-year job I told you about. Klein runs things over at San Gabriel College. He can get you on the short list."

"I didn't ask you about that," Morgan said.

"What?"

"Did I have any calls?"

"What? Here in the room? No, no calls."

"Not from—" He almost said her name. That might not be good. They all had to work together in the same department. "Not from a woman? Did a woman call?"

"I told you. No calls."

"Goddammit." Morgan hung up. He almost dialed Annette's room but knew it was a bad idea.

He went back to his table in the lounge. Somebody was sitting there. A man.

"Hey," Morgan said.

The man looked up. A crooked smile. Jowls. A cheap suit, poly-ester and wrinkled. Red eyes. "Your table?" he said.

"Yes."

He stood. "Sorry." He rubbed his chin stubble with hairy knuckles. "Nobody around this time of night. Nobody to talk to. How about I sit down, buy you a drink."

"Sure." Morgan sat.

"I'm Deke."

Morgan gave his name, and they shook hands.

"Here for the conference?" Morgan asked.

Deke Stubbs shook his head. "Other business."

Stubbs bought Morgan a martini. He drank beer from a big, green bottle. Morgan asked about it.

"Grolsch," Stubbs said. "It's foreign. Somebody put me onto it recently."

"That's good. You've got to try new things," Morgan said. "You've got to come out of your groundhog hole."

"How's that?"

"We all live in little holes," Morgan said. He slurred his words, swayed in his seat. He took a swig of the martini. Most of it ran down his chin. "Got to come out of our holes and screw and drink foreign beer and run back in before anybody sees us."

"I have no idea what you're talking about," Stubbs said.

"Something to do with God and life and stationary bicycles."

"Maybe you've had enough."

"Maybe."

Stubbs put a cigarette in his mouth. "You don't mind, right?"

"No. Good idea." Morgan pulled out one of his cigars, bit the end off, and spit it like Jones had shown him.

Stubbs lit his cigarette, then Morgan's cigar. Both men puffed. They sat back in a gray-blue cloud of tobacco. A couple of guys enjoying drinks and a smoke. Sudden chums at the end of a long day. Morgan was seized with an irrational fondness for the man. How friendly to buy him a drink, keep him company during his fruitless brooding over Annette Grayson.

"Let's get some pancakes," Morgan said.

"Is the kitchen open?"

"We'll go someplace, get out of this fucking hotel." Morgan pushed his drink away, stood, almost tumbled over the table. Stubbs caught him.

"We'll find someplace open," Morgan said. "Come on. I got a car we can use."

"Okay, sport," Stubbs said. "You lead the way."

*   *   *

Morgan made a point of verbally abusing the parking valet, then felt guilty and tipped him twenty bucks when he brought Dirk Jakes's Mercedes. Morgan took the wheel, and Stubbs climbed into the passenger's side.

"That way out of the parking garage." Stubbs pointed straight ahead.

Morgan maneuvered the car, circled down a level. His steady hands on the wheel surprised him. He knew he was drunk.

"You don't got any shoes." Stubbs watched him work the pedals.

"I don't need any goddamn shoes!"

He circled the garage, followed the EXIT signs. A red vest caught his eye, a guy walking along the edge of the garage, cute little bow tie pulled loose. It was the prick from the gift shop, off work. He was walking toward the big Dumpster in the corner. Morgan hit the accelerator, bore down on him, teeth clenched, eyes blazing.

Stubbs grabbed at his seat belt. "What the hell's the hurry?"

The prick stopped, turned. His eyes bulged, grew to the size of headlights, mouth pulled tight in terror. He ran.

Morgan followed, honked the horn.

"What the fuck are you doing?" Stubbs yelled.

Morgan swerved, came within two inches of the prick's knee. The prick dove, screaming fear. He landed in a pile of garbage bags. The Mercedes roared by, tires squealing as it made the turn down to the next level.

Morgan's face was a mask of feral joy, wicked contentment. He laughed, and it sounded like the devil.

They didn't go for pancakes.

Deke Stubbs talked Morgan into heading for the Gulf, where

he'd seen billboards advertising titty bars near the beach. Since it was a thirty-minute drive, they stopped at a liquor store and purchased nine small bags of BBQ chips, a six-pack of Busch, and more cigarettes for Stubbs.

Stubbs was having a problem. He liked Morgan. Morgan told him all about the prick at the Sheraton gift shop. Stubbs hated little smart-ass guys like that. Morgan told him about Annette Grayson, the sudden boink, the woman's lightning change of heart. Stubbs hated women like that. So superior. They'd slum with a guy, then try to cover it.

Morgan wasn't a pompous, know-it-all, snob professor. He seemed to be a regular guy just trying to get some action, have a few laughs, live his life like anybody else. Stubbs would feel real bad when he turned Morgan's lights out and made off with the cocaine—if he could find it. It would be a shame since Morgan appeared to be a stand-up guy.

These were Stubbs's thoughts at a dark, corner table at The Shag Hut just outside of Galveston. The marquee boasted 75 Beautiful Women & 3 Ugly Ones. Onstage a woman named Cricket and another woman named Jade seemed unnaturally interested in one another. One of the women—Jade?—was a curvy Hispanic lady, round ass, hanging tits, an enormous pile of midnight hair. The other was willowy, pale, blond, barely eighteen—maybe.

Morgan swayed with the show, chin in hand, elbow on table. His eyelids were heavy. *He's fading fast*, Stubbs thought. *No sleep. Too much to drink.*

"I'd sure like to be in between that," Stubbs said, nodding at the stage show.

Morgan said, "MmmHmmmm."

"I'm going to take the car keys a minute," Stubbs said. "I left my smokes in the Mercedes."

Morgan waved his disinterest.

Stubbs went outside. He smelled the ocean, the Gulf of Mexico actually. It was a good smell. Maybe when everything was settled, he'd move near the ocean. Not right on the beach. He hated the beach, hated sunburn and sand in his ass crack and screaming kids and surfers. But close to the water where he could smell it and get fresh seafood. Maybe near a pier. He'd never fished, but he thought he might like it.

Stubbs tried the trunk first. He went through by the numbers, pulled out the spare tire, lifted the carpeting.

No drugs.

He looked in the backseat. For some reason there was a bunch of tools. He ignored them, kept searching. There was a god-awful odor in the back. Faint but plain.

If he got lucky, if he found the drugs here in the Mercedes, Stubbs could just take off and leave Morgan inside the titty bar. He wouldn't have to bash the guy over the head—or worse. That would make it easier all around.

He took a pocketknife out of his jacket and opened it, shook his head. A shame. The Mercedes was a damn nice car. He plunged the short blade into the fabric, cut a six-inch slit. He reached in and around. Only stuffing.

Hell.

He did the same to the other seats. Nothing.

Stubbs sighed. He'd have to make Morgan talk. But just to be sure, he went through the car one more time.

Morgan couldn't believe naked women could get so boring so fast. The simple fact was that Jade and Cricket didn't give two shits about Professor Jay Morgan. Neither did Amber, Titania, Zoey, Brandi, Jasmine, or Princess Daisy. As soon as Morgan ran out of dollar bills, he'd be just another sucker paying inflated prices for watered-down drinks.

He looked around for his new pal. Deke had been a good sport. Morgan knew he was a textbook sad-sack drunk. It was good of Deke to humor him, keep an eye on him while he destroyed himself. Where was Deke? The rest room? No. Morgan remembered. The car. Cigarettes. But that seemed like a long time ago.

Morgan stood. He felt tired but steadier. He walked toward the exit. The beefy bouncer gave him a long look on the way out. The parking lot was dark, poorly lit. Chilly. His feet especially were cold. He saw the Mercedes and shuffled to it.

He opened the back door and saw Deke pulling the stuffing out of the backseat. Morgan blinked, not sure if he was seeing right. He opened his mouth. He should say something, make Deke stop tearing up the expensive car, but he couldn't quite get his mind around why Deke would intentionally fuck up the interior of a brand-new automobile.

Jakes will go nuts.

Stubbs looked up, met Morgan's eyes. They stayed frozen like that for a long second.

"Shit." Stubbs grabbed Morgan, pulled him into the car, shut the door.

Morgan couldn't resist. He was stupefied. Stubbs pulled his fist back to his ear, held it a moment, then let loose, popped Morgan across the jaw. Hard. A smack of flesh. Morgan wilted into the corner of the Mercedes, the sparks going off in his eyes, bells. He didn't even put up his hands, couldn't fight back. Maybe Morgan didn't understand what was happening. But Stubbs was on top of him. Another punch. Darkness overtook Morgan a moment, a cottony drifting. He shook himself out of it, tried to speak, wanted to know what and why. The salt taste of blood in his mouth.

"Sorry," Stubbs said. "I can't have you yelling for help."

Morgan groped for reality. Was Deke robbing him? He'd had the car keys. It would have been easy to take off.

"I hate to do this, pal." Stubbs had a fistful of Morgan's shirt, hand cocked for another punch. "I tried to find the stuff the easy way, not cause you any more grief than needed, but it just didn't happen that way. You should of stayed inside and watched the T&A show."

Morgan spit blood. It stained his teeth and chin. "What do you want? Take the car." He couldn't find breath. Panic and dread had sapped him.

"Not here for the car, buddy. Maybe some cargo. You truck anything down here from Fumbee?"

Morgan looked blank.

"Come on," Stubbs said. "I know all about your little side deal, snowman. Don't you want to fork over the goods and get all this nastiness over with?"

Morgan shook his head. He didn't know what the man meant. Cargo? What did he think Morgan was doing? There was nothing in Houston for Morgan but the conference. The only reason he'd even left Fumbee was to get away from . . .

"Oh no." Morgan's own voice was tinny and far away in his ears. Cold dread seeped into him, spread down his spine. He shrank in on himself, looked up at Stubbs.

"Oh no." It was all he could say. He thought feebly he should fight or flee or scream, but he could only wait for the end. Maybe Stubbs would kill him quickly. Or maybe he could figure out what the man wanted, give it to him. Mind and muscle surrendered. All Morgan could do was shut his eyes tight, whine like a whipped dog.

"Knock it off," Stubbs said. "I don't want to hurt you. Just tell me where the drugs are."

Morgan sobbed. He was so desperately tired. And ashamed. He

thought of Fred Jones. Frail, emaciated Fred Jones. The old man would never whine. The sudden thought that Jones would see him like this, hear about Morgan's pathetic display made him the most ashamed.

Morgan had to do something—anything—to help himself. He wouldn't go out a quivering wad of jelly. "Drugs?"

"Don't play dumb. I can put two and two together."

It was perhaps a mistake that Morgan now decided to be creative.

"Jakes." Morgan was appalled at the sound of his own voice, a hoarse croak. Fear. It was a start at least. He was trying. He would rage against the dying of his own, sad, little light.

"What? Jakes?" Stubbs's voice took a rough edge. "What the hell does that mean?"

"The guy I came with," Morgan said. "He's the one. He's got the drugs in his hotel room."

"Let's go get him."

"What are you going to do?" Morgan's voice was better. Still scared but no longer jelly.

"Don't worry about it," Stubbs said. "All you need to know is that I'm desperate and committed and if I don't get what I want, there'll be hurt and pain and bad times forever."

Not an eloquent threat but convincing.

"Okay," Morgan said. "Just take it easy."

"Don't tell me to take it easy. You take it easy."

"Right." Morgan's hands shook. He breathed deep, made himself calm. "What do you want me to do?"

Stubbs let him up. "Get behind the wheel."

Morgan reached for the door.

"Not that way." Stubbs jerked him by the shirt. "Over the seat. I don't want you making a run for it."

Morgan crawled into the front seat, sat behind the wheel. He was breathing better. In the rearview mirror he saw Stubbs move, felt the cold metal behind his ear. Morgan didn't need to be told it was a gun.

"I'll stay back here," Stubbs said. "You can guess what'll happen if you pull something screwy. Don't fuck with me."

"I've had a lot to drink."

"Don't give me your mothers against drunk drivers bullshit." Stubbs pressed the gun barrel harder against Morgan's ear. "This should keep you plenty alert."

Deke handed Morgan the keys and Morgan cranked the engine. "You're going to hold that gun against my head all the way to Houston?"

"Yep."

Morgan pulled out of the titty-bar parking lot, turned vaguely toward the highway.

At the light he made a decision. He barely knew he was doing it. Instead of taking the highway on-ramp, he turned toward the water, the Gulf of Mexico.

"What are you doing?" Stubbs pushed the gun barrel into Morgan's neck.

"I missed it."

"I can fucking see that. Don't make this hard."

"I can get on at the next intersection."

Morgan drove along the water, the Gulf glittered in moonlight. Although he knew the risk, Morgan felt strangely calm. There was a certain freedom in doom. He flashed back to his dream, how he'd felt turning the car into the headlights. A giddy liberty in surrendering to oblivion.

Which was maybe why he laughed a little when he jerked the wheel and turned onto the fishing pier.

"Goddammit!" Stubbs's face flushed. He spit when he yelled. "You think I'm kidding? You don't think I'll blow your fucking head off?"

The pier hadn't been built for cars. The boards rattled, creaked. The Mercedes bounced violently. Morgan sideswiped a trash can, debris exploding upward, drifting down again on the Gulf breeze. Morgan hit the accelerator.

Stubbs reached over Morgan, tried to grab the wheel. Morgan pushed him away, steered one-handed. Stubbs went for the keys, and Morgan punched over his shoulder, tried to get Stubbs in the face. They picked up speed.

"Are you crazy?" Stubbs had gone back to waving the gun. He still leaned into the front seat, tried to threaten Morgan with the .45 and grab the wheel at the same time. "I swear to God I'm going to do it. I'll blast a hole in your face. Hit the brakes."

"You're all talk." Morgan swerved between the guardrails, clipped one on the left with a sharp *crack*, splintered wood. The left headlight winked out. The end of the pier sped toward them in near darkness. Stubbs was tossed around in the backseat, but righted himself quickly, shoved the gun against Morgan's neck. He kept with the threats, shouted himself hoarse.

Morgan didn't care. He half expected—*half wanted*—the bullet. Let it come. Bring on the hot flash of blood, fragmented skull. He could pitch forward into sweet, eternal nothingness.

The Mercedes exploded through the wooden railings at the end, slipped the surly bonds of earth, pier, and reality. They seemed to hover. Stubbs screamed something, the pistol gone from Morgan's neck. Neither wore a seat belt. Morgan felt himself float up and away, weightless, breathless.

Then gravity.

The long, awkward plummet.

It wasn't more than twelve feet down to the water, but the Mercedes in freefall took a lifetime to plunge the distance. It smacked the water, the impact throwing Morgan against the windshield. He bounced back into the seat. A blur of water and darkness and dashboard lights. The windshield looked down into the depths, the remaining headlight flailing against the black of the Gulf.

Chilling panic. Morgan saw himself going down with the car, pictured the salty water rising over his head, his lungs burning for air. A strangled cry of fear, desperate. It had come out of his own mouth.

He clawed at the automatic windows, lowered the one on the driver's side. The Gulf poured in. But the water came slowly. The Mercedes floated near the level of the lapping waves. The hood of the car tilted down into the water, but the rear remained above the surface.

Morgan scrambled through the window.

"Morgan!" Anger, panic, rage mixed in Stubbs's voice. "Goddamn you. Come back here, Morgan. I'm stuck. Morgan!"

Morgan paid no attention. Stubbs continued to scream after him.

Morgan squirmed through the window, bobbed on the freezing water. Went under, swallowed water, kicked to the surface, and coughed. Gulped for air. The shore was a smear of fuzzy light. It seemed about two hundred miles away. Muffled screams still came out of the Mercedes.

Morgan kicked toward shore. He wasn't a strong swimmer. Water smacked his face, stung his eyes. He sputtered, stroked. His arms ached with exertion and cold. He was going numb, shivering.

Morgan felt the bottom sooner than he'd expected, stood in the waist-deep water, and trudged to land. Waves pushed him in the right direction. He made it to the beach, collapsed into the sand, chest heaving with burning breaths.

He propped himself up on an elbow, looked back toward the end of the pier. For a second he thought the Mercedes had gone down, the black against the night made it hard to spot. But there it was, the back end still visible, taillights like the eyes of a demon.

Morgan watched. The Mercedes bobbed. It looked to Morgan like the front bumper was bouncing against the sandy bottom. It was pretty shallow, even that far out. Each time it bobbed, more water poured through the open front window, the tide inching it farther out and away from the pier. The car was sinking slowly, and he hadn't seen Deke get out.

Morgan watched, still gasping breath, as the Gulf of Mexico slowly ate Dirk Jakes's new Mercedes.

The son of a bitch had left him. Stubbs had threatened, begged, screamed his throat raw, but Morgan didn't come back.

When Morgan had taken the Mercedes airborne, Stubbs had lost himself. He'd floated, turned, the night sky a tumbling blur. The whole car had shuddered with the impact of water. Stubbs had hit the floor, his hands flying out to protect him.

His left hand had slid under the car seat in front of him. He heard a crack. Something had come apart under the seat. His fingers had wedged between the metal tracks just as the seat had suddenly shifted backward. His four fingers had been crushed, trapped, pain lancing past his elbow, up to the shoulder.

He'd screamed for Morgan to come back.

Now he pulled hard on his hand. If he could, he'd yank the fingers out of their sockets. He couldn't see the hand, but he knew it was ruined. The water was up to his neck. The pain was nothing compared to the water's relentless rise. Stubbs did not want to drown helpless in the dark. He gritted his teeth, pulled, grunted. He felt the skin of his fingers rip and pull away along the bone.

And the cold water still came.

"Oh, God." Stubbs thrashed, tried to work the fingers loose. "Oh, God, please." His free hand groped, tried to find leverage, anything to help get free. His hand landed on the tools. A hammer, some chisels.

A saw.

The water was halfway over Stubbs's Adam's apple. He stretched, craned his neck, gulped air. "Please, God." He grabbed the saw, held it tight. Tears stung his eyes. "Please." He lifted his head for another lungful of air, the water level hovering at his bottom lip.

He put the saw against his arm just above the wrist. The back of the seat kept him from going lower. Stubbs was already halfway through the bone when it occurred to him it might have been easier if he had just put the .45 in his mouth and pulled the trigger. The dark waters closed over him, the Mercedes gently bouncing against the sandy bottom, tiptoeing out to sea.

Part 4

thirty-four

Moses Duncan unlocked the door to his dark little farmhouse, Eddie right behind him. He was tired and pissed and cold and hungry. He felt for the light switch.

Then the hands.

They grabbed him from all directions; Eddie too. Moses tried to twist away and earned a fist on the side of the head.

A voice. "Be still, bitch."

He was thrown to the floor, facedown. A kick in the ribs. Moses *whuffed* air, heard Eddie mumble fear noises. Somebody turned on the lights.

"Damn," Moses shouted. "Take what you want."

"Shut the fuck up." Another kick, but halfhearted this time.

A black man in a purple suit knelt in front of Moses. He grinned, no humor touching his eyes. Moses felt hands and feet along his body, keeping him pinned down. He wouldn't have tried to move anyway. He froze, kept his mouth shut, waited to be told what to do.

"They call me Red Zach. You heard of me?"

"No, sir," Moses said. He chanced a look, swiveled his eyes around the room. A bunch of coons. Hell. Just his luck. Some kind of damn poetic justice maybe to die in the hands of a mob of coons. Maybe they were with that Ellis son of a bitch. Maybe they knew Moses had been looking to splatter some buckshot across Ellis's face, and these coons were here to kill him.

No, that didn't make sense. Ellis was hanging with those two white guys. The mob in his living room was strictly an all-coon outfit. Hell and shit.

"Well, you going to hear a lot more about me real soon," Zach said. "As a matter of fact, we're going to get acquainted because you work for me now."

Moses opened his mouth to protest, but a heavy hand on the back of his head pushed him down. Moses kissed the floor, bumped his front teeth against his upper lip. A trickle of blood.

"Think of this like a hostile corporate takeover," Zach said. "Just how hostile is up to you, but maybe you should consider the perks."

Moses Duncan was not going to work for no goddamn nigger coon in a purple pimp suit. Daddy would roll in his grave. But he shut up and kept his ears open.

Someone dropped a bag next to his head, a suitcase. He looked at it from the corner of his eye. It was his, the one he used to stash his merchandise. They must've gone through the whole house. Maybe even found the sawed-off, single-shot .410 he kept duct-taped to the back of the toilet in case somebody came at him when he was on the crapper.

"The bad news," Zach told him, "is that your freelance days are over. You answer to Red Zach now. That piss you off? I see it in your eyes. Don't try to hide it. Good. I'm glad. I don't want no cunts working for me. But I don't want no fools either. You play it smart and it works out for everybody. You hear what I'm saying?"

Moses thought a second before answering. "I hear you."

"Good," Zach said. "Now here's the part maybe you'll like. Once you start working for me, you going to do a lot more business than what you got in your little suitcase here. We going to talk about some real greenbacks. You got a college town here. Ripe. I'll show you how to work it. Somebody else starts poaching your territory, I send my boys down, stomp it out quicker than a forest fire. You see the potential?"

Moses said that he saw.

"You got any objections?" Zach asked. "Can you see any reason this business arrangement won't be mutually beneficial?"

The hand on the back of his neck tightened just slightly.

"Sounds like a good deal to me," Moses said.

"Excellent. What happened to that guy's face?"

It took Moses a second to understand he'd meant Eddie. "Glass. Cut him all up."

"Uh-huh."

"Can I get up now?" asked Moses.

"Nope. We got just one more thing to talk about first."

"Okay."

Zach softened his voice, friendly, put his hand on Moses's shoulder. "I think a brother maybe came to you recently with a big score. A shitload of premium coke. Why don't you tell me all about it. Start at the beginning and don't leave anything out."

thirty-five

Don't you ever go stir-crazy in here, man? Don't you ever want to stick a gun in your mouth and blast your fucking brains out?" Jenks asked.

Tad Valentine scratched his wild, white beard and considered the question. This Sherman Ellis/Harold Jenks person obviously didn't like being cooped up. He'd offered him the pick of his library, had even suggested some Langston Hughes or Etheridge Knight that Valentine mistakenly believed would appeal to Ellis/Jenks's ethnicity.

But the young man had instead latched on to a copy of Jerzy Kosinski's *The Painted Bird*. The novel's nonstop atrocity fest seemed to hold a special horrified fascination for him. Jenks frequently consulted a *Webster's Dictionary* between chapters. Valentine decided—not for the first time—that he was simply not in tune with the multicultural complexities of today's youth. Ellis/Jenks puzzled him not only for being black, but for being young and part of a world that did not need or want men like Valentine. They wanted MTV and PlayStation and the Internet and soft drink commercials with half-naked teenagers and many other things that scared the hell out of Valentine.

And this young black man made him nervous, on the lam and in some kind of peril from what Valentine could gather. It wasn't that he disliked Ellis/Jenks. But the kid was a bold symbol of everything *out there*, and now he wanted to hide *in here*. Valentine worried Ellis/Jenks would bring the world and its troubles with him.

And just what the hell was the kid's name anyway? Sherman Ellis or Harold Jenks. It seemed there was a halfhearted effort under way to conceal the man's identity. Wayne DelPrego had started with Sherman Ellis and had gradually abandoned it for Harold Jenks.

Valentine had decided to think of the black kid as Sharold Jenkis. It seemed a reasonable compromise.

"Sometimes," Valentine said.

Jenks looked up from *The Painted Bird*. "What?" He'd forgotten that he'd asked Valentine a question.

"Sometimes," Valentine repeated, "I think about putting a gun in my mouth. But it's not because I'm cooped up as you say. It's the thought of going out there." He pointed at the rest of the world through the dirty window. The glass was badly smudged.

Jenks looked out the window. "It's just a parking lot."

"Hmmmm, yes. Where's Mr. DelPrego today?"

"Snuck out," Jenks said. "He's stir-crazy too."

"It wouldn't fit anyway," Valentine said.

"Say what?"

"The gun. I couldn't get it into my mouth." Valentine went to the other window, the big one. A thinly padded bench ran the length beneath it. He flipped the lid, hinges squealing, and pulled out three and a half feet of something wrapped in cloth. He lowered the bench lid again and set the bundle on top, peeled away the cloth slowly, and revealed a long, double-barreled shotgun.

"It's a twenty-gauge," Valentine said. "I wouldn't be able to reach the trigger."

Jenks set the book aside, came over to look at it. "It's pretty."

"My father gave it to me as a graduation present. We hunted duck quite often before I went off to New Haven." He picked up the shotgun, cradled it lovingly, broke it in half, and looked down each barrel. "Still clean."

The darkly polished wood gleamed, ornate silver scrollwork. An expensive firearm. Valentine had not held the weapon in over a year. The cold metal in his hand sparked a memory. A duck blind before dawn, the sun rising pink-orange over the lake. The last morning they'd gone hunting before Valentine had left for the East. His father had wanted him to be an engineer. Oklahoma oil had paid for the shotgun, the private lake, Valentine's education. Father had been bitterly disappointed when his son turned poet. *Poet.* The word had struck his father like a tomahawk between the eyes. Poet was code for communist-faggot-slacker to an Oklahoma oil man. His father had died before the Pulitzer Prize, before the *New York Times* interview, before everything.

Jenks took the gun from his hand. "Cool. Let me see."

Valentine let go reluctantly, watched Jenks sight along the barrel.

"What you shoot with this?"

"Ducks," Valentine said. "Or geese."

"What you use?" asked Jenks. "Slugs?"

"If you want to scatter the bird across the county."

Jenks's eyes shifted back to the bench seat. "Any shells in there?"

Valentine followed Jenks's gaze to the bench seat. He looked back at Jenks and said, "I've made it a point not to pry into your business."

"Good."

"But maybe you'd better tell me what's going on, eh? Perhaps I could even help."

Jenks bit the end of his thumb, looked out the window. After a long pause, he shook his head. "I think you'd rather not know."

Valentine lifted an eyebrow.

"But I appreciate it," Jenks said. "Thanks for letting me and Wayne crash here. And thanks for trying to show me about the books, letting me look at *Painted Bird*. It's wasted on me but thanks for trying."

"Education is never a waste on anyone," Valentine said.

Jenks smiled, shrugged. "Okay, man. Sure."

Valentine nodded. He was a patient man. Perhaps he could pry some information out of DelPrego upon his return.

Wayne DelPrego left campus at a fast walk, looking over his shoulder as he slunk back into the knot of woods that bordered Eastern Oklahoma University. He didn't venture deeply, not like when he and Jenks had hidden from Red Zach's crew. He skirted the edge, stopped and knelt in a thick patch of shrubs when he saw his trailer.

He watched.

Be damned if these gangster shitbags would run him out of his home. He'd been wearing the same clothes—same *underwear*—for three days. And he wanted his truck. It wasn't much, but it was all he had.

Watching the back of the trailer didn't show him anything. Jenks was sure they'd watch the place, but how? Sit in a car on the street, or would somebody wait in the trailer for him with a loaded gun and the lights out? Or both? Maybe this was a mistake. He'd mentioned to Jenks he might try to sneak back for his truck, but Jenks had put his foot down. He'd said just to grab the cocaine and get back quick.

Fuck it.

DelPrego bolted from the shrubs, sprinted, his breaths huffing little clouds into the cold air. He dove under one of the trailer windows, pressed his back against the half-rusted wall. He listened.

Nothing.

He thought about crawling through the gap in the aluminum skirting and getting under the trailer, but shivered at the thought of what might be under there. Oklahoma was lousy with all kinds of spiders and scorpions. DelPrego hated the thought of escaping gangsters only to have a brown recluse scuttle up his jeans and bite him on the gnads.

Voices.

DelPrego held his breath, cocked an ear toward the open window above him. A conversation. He felt footsteps shaking the flimsy trailer, coming toward the window. DelPrego pressed himself as flat and as low as possible.

"What're you doing?" The first voice.

"Mmmpgh Mmbf Mmmmmm." The other.

"No, leave it open. It stinks in here."

"Mmmph. Mmmm."

"Then put your jacket back on, but leave it open."

The footsteps retreated from the window. "Mmmph mmmmmm?"

"Because Red Zach said so. If they come back, we grab 'em if possible or call his boys in for backup."

The other voice uttered a string of garbled nonsense.

"I don't like it either, Eddie. You think I want some coon giving me orders? But once we straighten this Jenks kid out, they'll go back to St. Louis and we'll be sitting on a gold mine. No more small-time."

"Mmmm mmmph mmmm."

"Me too. What you want?"

"Mmmph."

"We had fucking Taco Bell yesterday."

They argued five minutes about lunch. The first voice told the mumble voice he'd be back in thirty minutes. DelPrego heard the front door slam. A few seconds later an engine cranked, vehicle noise fading on the road out front. A second later the TV went on. DelPrego listened. It sounded like a game show.

Anger. Someone was in his home watching his damn television. Probably drank his last beer. He found himself getting up. Some remote bastion of intelligence shouted to the rest of his brain that a truck and a trailer and a ten-year-old RCA television were not worth dying for. But there he was crawling under the window, heading for the back door.

At the back door he stopped, took the little oilcan out of his jacket pocket. The old redneck janitor Brad Eubanks had gotten it for him last night. Even then, DelPrego had been thinking, putting the plan together in his mind. He squirted oil on the hinges, made sure to use plenty. He squirted oil into the lock, anyplace that might make a noise.

He took the back-door key from his pocket. He'd removed it from his key ring so it wouldn't jingle against the other keys. He inserted it in the lock. Slowly. He pinched the key between thumb and forefinger, froze, listened. The game show drifted from the open window. DelPrego made himself breathe. Then he turned the key.

The lock slid back and DelPrego cracked the door an inch. No sound. He put his ear to the crack to make sure the game show was still going. It was. He looked inside but couldn't see very far down the hall. The hall went past a little place where a washer and dryer would go if DelPrego had them. Then past the kitchen and opened up into the living room/dining room combo area. The TV was against the far wall in the living room. The whole trailer was like a cramped miniature version of a real house. A strong gust of wind would blow the whole thing over. It was a flimsy dwelling. The floor creaked. DelPrego would have to step lightly.

He opened the door, stepped into the trailer. He pulled the door closed behind him, each movement in exaggerated, agonizing slow motion. He took one step toward the kitchen and the floor groaned. He took his weight off the spot. He slipped out of his tennis shoes, set them aside. He walked along the side of the hall, inching forward until he saw the kitchen around the corner.

Beyond the kitchen, the living room and the TV.

Someone was in the easy chair, the battered La-Z-Boy he'd picked up from a junk heap and patched with duct tape. He couldn't see who, only an elbow on the armrest, a hairy hand holding the remote control.

The hand was white.

DelPrego frowned. This didn't make sense. He'd been expecting one of the gangsters who had chased him and Jenks into the woods. In his mind, he replayed the conversation he'd heard under the trailer window. One of the voices had specifically mentioned Red Zach.

Okay, never mind. White or black, this guy was in his house, waiting to kill him.

He walked through the kitchen, looked at the counters. No knives in sight, and he couldn't risk the noise of opening a drawer. He grabbed a saucepan. He'd come up behind this guy and bash his brains in.

He started toward the easy chair, careful steps, slow, quiet, get within arm's reach, and let him have it. DelPrego screwed up his courage, gathered it into a tight, hot ball in the center of his gut. He had to crack this dude's skull with everything he had. He didn't want the guy to get up again.

The guy swiveled the chair, looked square into DelPrego's eyes.

DelPrego looked at him and screamed, dropped the frying pan.

The guy in the La-Z-Boy screamed too. It came out ragged and muffled. His head was completely bandaged, only big, frightened eyes showing from slits. The mummy-faced guy had the chair in the recline position. He thrashed in the chair, struggled to sit upright and turn the chair back to the pump shotgun leaning against the wall.

DelPrego regrouped, launched himself before the guy reached the shotgun. He smacked into Mummy-man, tumbled over, chair tipping. They landed on the floor in a clinch, clawing and grabbing.

Mummy-man rolled on top of DelPrego, a hand going over DelPrego's face, pushing. A pinkie finger slid into DelPrego's mouth. He bit down hard. Mummy-man's hoarse scream died in the cotton bandages. He jerked his hand back. DelPrego punched, but Mummy-man twisted away. The blow glanced to the side.

The skill level of the fight went from bad to idiotic. Pulling at clothes, rolling. They bumped against a coffee table, tipped over a lamp.

Mummy-man pulled free, kicked away DelPrego's fumbling hands. He belly-crawled across the dirty shag toward the shotgun. DelPrego lunged and grabbed one of Mummy-man's ankles. Mummy-man kicked. He was two inches from the butt of the shotgun. He reached, stretched, strained against DelPrego's hold.

DelPrego cast about. He needed something to hit with. A large glass ashtray had fallen from the coffee table. He reached. Two inches.

Both men stretched in opposite directions, gritted teeth, grunted.

DelPrego got to his knees, readied himself before letting go of the ankle. He grabbed the ashtray, turned, and leapt back on Mummy-man, who had the shotgun in his hand. DelPrego crashed into Mummy-man hard, pinned the shotgun against his chest. DelPrego landed a knee into the Mummy's gut, heard air burst out of him. He raised himself, the ashtray high over his head. He brought it down hard.

It smacked hard into the Mummy's forehead. Mummy-man jerked.

"Fuck you, King Tut." DelPrego hit him again.

Mummy-man went slack, sank into the shag. DelPrego sat on him, chest heaving, sweat. He shook. His hands especially trembled out of control. He dropped the ashtray, fell off of Mummy-man's body, and lay on the carpet, sucking for breath. Another dead guy. He'd bashed in another guy's head. For the second time DelPrego was a killer. No. Three times. He'd killed the guy with his shotgun when the drug deal had gone bad. But somehow that had been different. Not up close like when you bash a man's skull into jelly.

He stood, knees like water. He'd need to think what to do. He had his truck keys, so he wouldn't have to flee on foot. He ran back to his bedroom, found the stash of 280 dollars he'd been saving for an absolutely life-and-death emergency situation. This qualified. He grabbed a knapsack, filled it with two changes of clothes (four changes of underwear) and his father's Purple Heart from Vietnam. He left the knapsack on the bed and went to put on his shoes.

The sight of Mummy-man's loose-limbed body disturbed DelPrego. Maybe he should do something with the body, hide it somehow. Or maybe just the thought of the dead man in plain sight on his shag carpet gave DelPrego the willies. He didn't want to think of himself as the kind of man who'd bash a guy's skull in, then just leave the body lying around. He bent over the Mummy, grabbed him by the jacket lapels. Touched his chest.

Breathing.

DelPrego gasped, put the palm of his hand over the guy's heart. It beat. Crazy, relieved giggling bubbled up in DelPrego's throat, spilled out of his mouth. Mummy-man was alive, his breathing seemed regular, normal. Of course, he hadn't hit him that hard, not enough to kill him. Mummy-man had only been knocked cold. DelPrego didn't know why he was so happy. The son of a bitch had been waiting to blow a giant hole in him with a shotgun.

DelPrego shook his head. He was glad he hadn't killed the guy. He didn't want the memory, didn't want to see the man's mummy face haunting him in his dreams. He already got chills whenever he thought about the man he'd killed with the golf club.

DelPrego grabbed Mummy-man under the arms, dragged him into the little bathroom. He dumped him into the tub, made sure he was faceup and could breathe okay. He'd need something to tie the guy up. All DelPrego wanted was a head start.

DelPrego heard a car door slam. He froze.

He rushed to the window, peeked through the blinds. It was the other one. *Shit.* The face seemed familiar. He tried to remember. It came to him slowly like a grainy movie slipping into focus. *Holy fucking shit.* The guy from the drug deal. That fucking redneck who'd tried to steal Jenks's coke. And while DelPrego had stood gawking, the guy had reached the front door. *Shit shit shit.*

The shotgun! Too late. DelPrego had left it in the living room. *Think, dumbass!*

He looked at the Mummy-man in the tub.

*   *   *

Moses Duncan was halfway to get food when Red Zach had called him on the cell phone. He'd said to forget about watching the trailer. Get back to the farm quick. Change of plan.

Right. Sure. For the thousandth time Duncan thought about cutting loose, hitting the road. On the one hand, he did stand to make a lot of cash working for Red Zach. On the other hand, the thought of Red Zach moving into the old farmhouse, setting up shop like it was a goddamn Motel Six, probably had Daddy spinning in his grave. So Duncan was going to bite his tongue and bide his time. Someday, in a month or a year or ten, he'd have the last laugh on these coons.

Duncan tried the front door. Locked. He knocked. No answer.

"Come on, Eddie. It's me." Nothing.

"Hell. Now what?" He banged on the door louder, shook the trailer.

Duncan sighed and walked around behind the trailer. The back door was open, and he went inside. "Eddie?"

Duncan heard a flush. The bathroom door creaked open. Eddie came out, tugging at his face bandages.

"What's up?" Duncan asked. "Stitches itching again?"

Eddie nodded.

"Get your shit together. We'll eat later. The coon squad wants us back home." He tossed Eddie the car keys and picked up the shotgun. "I got the twelve-gauge. Your turn to drive."

Eddie stared at him, didn't move.

"Don't just stand there, dummy. Come on."

"Mmmph. Mmmm," Eddie said.

"What?"

"Mmmmph Mmmmm Mmmmph."

"Your tongue must be swelled up or something," Duncan said. "Suddenly I can't understand a damn thing you're saying."

thirty-six

The ride back from Houston was uneventful and unhappy.

Reams's anger at Jay Morgan was of the slow, brooding variety. Morgan realized the professor had gone to some trouble to arrange the morning job interview, but Morgan had simply not given a rat's ass. The police had kept him until nine in the morning.

Dirk Jakes's anger at Jay Morgan was more of the ranting and raving variety. Jakes's brand-new Mercedes had been "stolen" according to the story Morgan gave the police. But more than anything, Jakes seemed hurt and angry that he hadn't been invited to the titty bar when Morgan had "borrowed" the Mercedes for his midnight drive.

All in all, Morgan was damn unpopular for the duration of the cramped ride back in the Geo Metro, the only rental available on short notice. They made it back into Fumbee late Sunday night, and Reams dropped him off without a word.

For all Morgan cared, Jakes and Reams could go fuck themselves. With corncobs. He had no energy left for apology. The night and early morning with the police had left him wrung out. He couldn't tell them the real story without it leading back to Annie Walsh. He'd tried to keep it simple. After the titty bar, he'd gone, so he claimed, to the beach for some air so he could sober up. A bunch of Mexicans had beat him up and thrown him in the water, then taken the Mercedes.

"We found the car ten minutes ago," a big detective had told Morgan.

Morgan had shrugged. "Those crazy Mexicans."

"What about your shoes?" one cop had asked.

"I wanted to walk in the sand."

"Then shouldn't you have taken off your socks too?"

"I told you," Morgan had said. "I was drunk."

Morgan had claimed the whole incident had happened about a mile down the coast and away from the pier. The situation seemed impossible and hopeless. Nobody had mentioned a body. Morgan had watched the car go down. There'd been no sign of the man.

Perhaps Morgan should flee the country. A former colleague made good money teaching English in Asia. Morgan had seen the job listings before. English teachers needed in Japan and South Korea.

But that would take time to arrange. Surely recent events would catch up and overwhelm him before then. At least he was home. For a while, the world could wait. He went to bed, slept like a cold, dead stone.

Monday morning he went to Albatross Hall. He was five minutes late for his poetry workshop. He noticed three empty chairs in a row, didn't have to think too hard about it. Ellis, Lancaster, and DelPrego.

"Has anyone seen our missing comrades?" He gestured at the empty seats.

The class shook its collective head, mumbled ignorance.

"Never mind. Let's get on with it. Tammy, read us your poem."

A thin girl, sandals with socks, dishwater hair, and no makeup. "It's called 'The Aftertaste of Love.'" She stood and cleared her throat, read from a pink sheet of paper. "How he clings, like the orange dust from cheese puffs. How he screams the silent, dog-whistle need of his generation. But nobody hears..."

Ah. It was as Morgan thought. God had started punishing him already.

Morgan closed his office door. It had been a long morning. He switched on the radio, then rummaged his desk drawers. The radio announcer spit out the local news, then switched to the weather. Mild for most of the week, but winter's last hurrah gathered up north and west in Colorado. A cold front. It threatened to slide south by the weekend and dust Green County with a few flakes.

Morgan found what he was looking for in the bottom drawer. A flask of Jim Beam. Not his usual poison, but it would do in a pinch. He unscrewed the cap and took a long swig. The familiar warmth again in his belly. Morgan decided that not only had he officially fallen off the wagon, but that the wagon had also backed over him and parked on his head.

He took another swig.

The phone rang in midswig, startled him. A mouthful of booze spilled down his chin. He grabbed the phone. "Hello?"

"Morgan? It's Dean Whittaker."

Morgan sat up straight. "What can I do for you, sir?"

"Good news, Morgan. Lots of press going to be there all the way from Tulsa and Oklahoma City. We pulled some strings. Going to be great press for the university."

"Uh . . ."

"Also, we have the honors college assigning the poetry reading as mandatory extra credit for their freshman composition and humanities classes. I know these sorts of events aren't generally well attended, but we want to put our best foot forward, eh? I think we can fill up the whole damn auditorium."

"That's fifteen hundred seats."

"Well, the press, faculty, most of the administration, the graduate students from the writing program, the usual collection of community art-fags—you didn't hear me say that—and about a thousand freshmen. I know most eighteen-year-olds don't usually go in for this sort of thing, but the seats will be filled and it'll *look* good. That's what counts. The eyes of the entire university will be on this show. Exciting, isn't it?"

"Sure." Morgan found his hand reaching for the Jim Beam.

"You are going to put on a good show for us, aren't you, Morgan?"

Morgan cleared his throat, picked his words carefully. "I promise a professional reading with excellent and innovative poetry."

"Right," Whittaker said. "Just so long as we get the right message across. You know what I mean." He said good-bye and hung up.

Morgan drank whiskey, rubbed his eyes. He thought about Ginny. Maybe he should call her. He was surprised to wish he could be with her. She had a soothing effect. She'd been right. People who have a secret together need each other. He picked up the phone, put it back down again. No, she might still be with her parents, and Morgan didn't have the spine right now to explain himself.

He called Sherman Ellis at home. The phone rang and rang.

Morgan hung up, bit his thumbnail.

Morgan's phone rang and made him jump. He grabbed for it quickly. Maybe Ellis had *69 and was ringing him back. "Hello? Hello?"

"Take it easy, Professor," Fred Jones said. "You sound like you just ran a mile."

"I'm really pretty busy right now, Mr. Jones."

"Busy my ass. I have four new poems, and we have an appointment."

Morgan rubbed the bridge of his nose, bit off the first reply, and took a deep breath before saying, "You know, Mr. Jones, part of any good poet's education is to accumulate a myriad of poetry experiences. There's a poetry reading on campus tonight. It might be a good experience to give your own work a rest and go hear some other readers."

"Quit jerking me off."

"Okay, I'm sorry. But seriously, there's a guy on campus maybe you could talk to. A Pulitzer Prize–winning poet."

Jones went quiet on his end for a moment, then said, "Who?"

Morgan told Jones how to find Valentine's office. The image of the two strange old men amused Morgan. Let them drive each other nuts. The thought made his mouth twist up in a grin. It had been a long time since anything had made Morgan smile. His face muscles weren't used to it. It almost cracked his face in half.

thirty-seven

DelPrego was sweating hard. The thermostat in the dingy little farmhouse seemed to be stuck on the ultrahell setting.

And the farmhouse was full of black guys with guns. They all seemed pissed off. DelPrego sat in a corner, tried to make himself as inconspicuous as possible. The sweat poured down his back, formed under his armpits, and dripped. The thick bandages on his face were heavy and damp, clung sticky to his face with somebody else's blood and grime.

Duncan had gone to the kitchen with a black man in an expensive yellow suit. It was evident the man in yellow was in charge. He had the hard eyes and easy, cheerless grin of a man used to getting what he wants.

DelPrego's eyes shifted toward the door. It was agonizingly

close, but he was too scared to bolt. Maybe if he simply stood and strolled out like it was no big deal, they'd ignore him. Or maybe they wouldn't.

The drive in Duncan's truck had been nerve-wracking. Duncan had held the shotgun loosely in his lap. DelPrego had thought about grabbing it or leaping from the truck at full speed or a number of other things that ultimately all seemed like bad, bad ideas which would make him horribly, horribly dead.

He waited, closed his eyes. When he opened them again nothing had changed. He was still in a world of shit.

Red Zach sat at the kitchen table and drank Moses Duncan's coffee from a Rebel flag mug. He paged through a J. Crew catalog and wondered how he'd look in a turtleneck. Something subdued. A nice taupe maybe. He liked earth tones. He was supposed to visit his mom at Easter, and he couldn't go dressed up like no Huggy Bear motherfucker from *Starsky & Hutch*.

Duncan entered the kitchen, sat at the table across from Zach.

"Maurice saw Jenks on campus," Zach said.

"Did he get him?" Duncan asked.

Zach sipped coffee, shook his head. "By the time he turned the car around, he'd lost track of him. But we think he must be hiding out someplace at the university. Maybe in somebody's dorm."

Duncan shook his head. "Don't make no sense. If he knows you're hot on his trail, why don't he just leave town?"

"I didn't ask for your peckerwood opinion, but I'll explain. There's only five roads out of this town, and I got them all watched. He's got no car and no money and the next closest town is thirty-five miles. No, he's tucked in someplace, lying low. You're going to find him."

"Me?"

"You deaf or something? You think a gang of brothers can roam your cracker campus without attracting some attention?"

"Eddie looks like a damn freak. You don't think *he'll* attract attention?"

"Good point," Zach said. "You go by yourself."

"Great."

"Go tell your boy you're taking a field trip."

"Right." Duncan left the table.

Zach waved Maurice over. The man stood straight as a blade, hands folded in front of him. "What's the word, Red?"

"Follow that redneck. Make sure he's obeying orders."

"And if he tries to take it on the road?"

Zach's face stretched into one of his trademark, evil grins. "Pull the plug on his sorry ass."

DelPrego saw Duncan coming toward him. Duncan shrugged into his coat, so DelPrego stood. Maybe they were finally getting the hell out of here.

"You stay put, Eddie," Duncan said. "I got to run an errand on my own."

DelPrego's eyes widened. He did not want to wait another minute in the farmhouse.

"Take it easy. I'll be back when I can." Duncan slapped him on the shoulder, then leaned in and whispered, "Just stay out of the way of these boys. We'll get them out of our hair soon enough." And then he was out the door.

DelPrego slowly looked around the room. One guy playing solitaire, two more watching television, and another two in the kitchen. He knew there were more someplace. DelPrego walked toward the bathroom. *Keep it casual.* He went in, shut the door behind him, and eased the dead bolt into place. He sat on the toilet and peeled off the bandages. The air on his skin was welcome relief.

DelPrego looked at the bandages and shivered. They were caked with dried blood, and some kind of slick goo DelPrego hoped was only ointment. The smell almost made him gag. He scrubbed his face in the sink, wiped off with a semiclean towel.

He looked at the window over the toilet. Small, but he was pretty sure he could squeeze through it, and be damned if he was going to wait around there until his luck ran out. He knelt on the toilet seat, pushed the window up. Cold air flooded the tiny bathroom. DelPrego breathed it in, filled his lungs. He'd always had an acute intolerance for heat, and the big gulps of cool air settled his nerves a little. But not much.

He put his arms through the window, wiggled his shoulders through one at a time. He hung half out the window, the drop down was a little farther than he'd thought but no big deal. He wiggled down to his hips and jammed himself in the window. He put his hands on either side of the window, set his jaw, pushed. He was just a fraction of an inch too wide. If he shucked his jeans, he could do it, he could just slither through, he was sure.

He backed into the bathroom, feeling for the toilet seat with his boot. His heel slipped on the slick porcelain and he fell backward, landed hard between the toilet and the sink. It made a good racket. DelPrego held his breath. Waited. Nobody came to investigate.

He grabbed the back of the toilet to pull himself up and his hand ran across something. He looked. A gun taped to the back of the toilet. He peeled it off, examined it. A .410 shotgun, a hack job. The barrel had been sawed almost to nothing, and most of the butt had been cut away, leaving only the pistol grip. He checked the breach, broke it in half. One shell. A fat slug.

Okay. Better than nothing. If he were going to get out of there, the shotgun might come in handy. But he hoped not. He wanted to sneak out without any trouble. He dropped the gun out the window.

He took off his boots, then slipped off his jeans. He remembered the drop and put his boots back on. He didn't want to twist an ankle or land on something in the grass with his bare feet. He was still worried about the tight fit through the window. He'd probably scrape a little flesh. No big deal. As long as he squeezed through.

He shimmied back through the window, wedging himself again at the hips. But this time he detected a little more give. He pulled hard, felt his flesh bunch against the window frame. His flanks burned where they scraped against the wood but only for a second. He popped through, hit the ground hard. He stood, caught his breath and examined his raw, red hips. Scraped and bruised but nothing to worry about. Now all he had to do was put his jeans back on and—

His jeans were still in the bathroom.

"Fuck."

He leapt for the windowsill but could only just grab it with his fingertips, not enough to pull himself back up. His jeans were gone. His ass was very, very cold. A frigid gust of wind shriveled his testicles.

He looked around, didn't see anyone, picked up the shotgun, and ran for the barn. It was still cold inside, but at least he'd escaped the wind. He scanned the barn and saw an old horse blanket thrown over some lumpy machinery. He could wrap it around his waist like a kilt.

He pulled off the blanket, revealing the gleaming motorcycle underneath.

"Whoa."

He wrapped the blanket around himself and knelt to examine the bike. A Harley, fat and low. It looked like it had recently been worked on and cleaned up. He checked the gas tank. Full. The bike was his ticket out, but he knew it would make a roar when he cranked it. He'd have to start the thing and ride fast before all those brothers poured out of the farmhouse to cut him down.

He straddled the bike, put up the kickstand. There was no way to ride the motorcycle and still keep the blanket. He was going to be cold no matter what. His ass stuck to the freezing leather.

DelPrego stood on the kick-starter. The engine sputtered. Smoke. *Come on, come on.* He kicked it again, and the engine howled to life. He twisted the accelerator, made sure it didn't conk out. It sounded good, powerful. It took him a few seconds to figure the gears. The bike leapt forward, through the barn doors. DelPrego felt like he was riding a dragon.

An old memory flashed in his mind, senior year of high school. His only motorbike experience, an old dirt racer. Every weekend out with his cousins, to the bottom of the dried-out quarry and back. It was coming back to him now. He leaned into the turn, coming around the farmhouse. Once on the other side, he'd break for the road. The cold wind bit hard into his naked flesh.

He sped past the front porch, black guys spilling out, white eyes wide. But they didn't have guns drawn. He was going to make it.

A car parked at the end of the drive. The driver's door swung open. Another black guy stepped out. He wore a red suit, black shirt, and no tie. He flicked a cigarette away, and his hand went into his jacket. DelPrego knew it would come out with a pistol.

DelPrego still had the .410 across his lap. He took it in one hand, kept the bike steady with the other. He lifted the shotgun level with his chest, arm outstretched. Even hacked down, the shotgun was heavy. He pointed it directly at the red suit blocking his path. He spurred the bike faster. It shot forward, a thundering mechanical warhorse.

Ivanhoe. I'm fucking Ivanhoe.

The red suit pulled a silver automatic, thumbed off the safety, and squeezed two shots. DelPrego heard and felt the second slug *whizz* past his ear.

He pulled the trigger and the shotgun belched fire, kicked out of his hands, and tumbled back along the dirt driveway. The slug knocked the red suit back across the car, his chest exploding in blood.

Shots behind DelPrego now. But he was already leaning low over the handlebars. He'd found the road and opened the bike up for all she had. A wild, bare-assed streak across eastern Oklahoma.

thirty-eight

For Christ's sake." Jones panted. "You trying to give me a fucking stroke here?"

Bob Smith slowed down halfway up the flight of stairs. "Sorry, Boss. We're almost there. One more flight." Sometimes the boss scared him. Smith didn't know what to do those times the old man overexerted himself, the blood draining from his pinched face. Smith had made the mistake once of suggesting the boss hire a nurse. Jones had chewed him out good for that one.

"Fucking Mount Everest." Jones sucked breath.

"You want a hand, Boss?" Smith reached for the old man's elbow.

Jones swatted him away. "Lay off. I can make it."

They made the fifth floor and Jones took a minute to catch his breath. Professor Morgan had told the boss to listen for the music. It had sounded goofy to Smith, but he cupped a hand to his ear and listened. A faint tune echoed through the halls.

"Benny Goodman," Jones said.

Smith would have to take the boss's word for it. The big man stood quietly with his hands folded in front of him. A minute later, the old man stood straight, nodded at Smith. They followed the music, and Smith let the old man set the pace.

Not for the first time, Smith wondered how he and the boss had ended up in bumfuck, Oklahoma. But it wasn't Smith's job to wonder such things. The boss still had a lot of connections and more than a few enemies. So when it was time for the relocation, Smith packed his bags. There had never been any question that Smith would go wherever Jones went.

They arrived at an office door. Jones knocked, didn't wait for an answer, and pushed the door open. Smith's hand drifted into his jacket, a habit from the old days. He always itched for the feel of his gun butt when they walked through a strange door. Never can tell what's on the other side.

A wild-haired man scribbled fiercely at his desk. He looked like a cross between Santa Claus and Charles Manson. There was a colored kid on the sofa reading a book. Both looked up as Smith and Jones entered the room.

Jones asked, "You Valentine?"

"Who are you?"

"Jones. I'm a friend of Professor Morgan," the old man said. "He said you'd look at my poems."

"He lied."

"What?"

"I don't do that. Look at poems, I mean."

Jones frowned. "Maybe I made a mistake. You're the professor?"

"Yes."

"You won the Pulitzer Prize for poetry?"

"Yes."

Jones threw up his hands. "Then what the hell is this?"

Smith stirred behind the old man. He didn't like it when the boss was unhappy. The colored kid watched the whole thing with big eyes.

Jones said, "Morgan mentioned you enjoyed your privacy. Maybe I should pay the dean a visit."

Valentine blinked. "Hell and blood." He held out a hand. "Let me see the poems."

Jones nodded. Smith handed the folder of poetry to the professor, then stood in a spot where he could see the door and the whole room.

Jones sat on the couch and turned to the colored kid. "Who are you?"

"Harold."

Jones pulled a cigar out of his coat pocket, handed it to Harold Jenks. "Smoke that, will you?"

Jenks shrugged, unwrapped the cigar, and bit off the end. He lit it, puffed. The old man closed his eyes, let the cigar aroma wash over him.

Jones opened his eyes again, looked Jenks up and down. "So what's your story?"

Morgan got Sherman Ellis's address from the registrar's office and drove to his apartment. Nobody home. He called four more times and left a note on Ellis's apartment door.

It was getting down to crunch time, and Morgan was getting desperate. He had no idea where students kept themselves, where they hung out. Blindly roaming the campus looking for Ellis didn't seem too productive. He needed some help.

Morgan parked on campus and went to Albatross Hall. He locked his office door behind him, slumped at his desk. He didn't turn on the light, didn't want people to see it shining under the door and know he was there. He especially wanted to avoid Dean Whittaker.

He got on the phone and dialed the hospital, where some clerical person told him Ginny Conrad had checked out.

His fingers hovered over the Touch-Tone pad, and Morgan realized he didn't know Ginny's home number. It had never occurred to him to ask for it. She'd always just been there, showed up on his doorstep. Another call to the registrar produced her number.

Morgan looked hard at the phone for a long time. Ginny had said her parents were coming. Morgan didn't want to talk to Ginny's father, but he needed somebody to help him track down Ellis. Ginny probably knew all the student hot spots.

Morgan found the bottle in his desk drawer. A few belts would help him think. The booze splashed harshly in his gut. He hadn't eaten anything, and his stomach made little dying sounds.

He grabbed the phone, dialed quickly before he changed his mind or puked.

Morgan was ready to hang up, but Ginny answered after twelve rings. "Hello?"

She sounded good, Morgan thought, voice strong. He wasn't sure what he'd expected. Morgan opened his mouth, but nothing came out. Maybe Ginny didn't want to talk to him.

"Hello? Helllloooo."

"It's me," Morgan whispered. He didn't want anyone walking by his office to hear him.

"Professor Morgan?"

"Yes."

"Are you in the library or something? I can hardly hear you."

Morgan raised his voice slightly. "How are you feeling?"

"The doctors said it looked worse than it really was. A lot of bruising."

"Uh-huh."

"My parents were here, taking care of me," Ginny said. "But I sent them home."

"Uh-huh."

"I mean sometimes my mother can be *so* smothering. And my father has this anal streak. He's always—"

"Ginny, I need a favor," Morgan said. "And I need it fast."

A pause. "What is it?"

Morgan explained.

"Have you tried the Black Student Union?" Ginny asked.

"There's a Black Student Union?"

"Let me make a few calls," Ginny said.

"Great," Morgan said. "What then? Call you back in an hour?"

"No. I'll meet you."

thirty-nine

Wayne DelPrego could not feel his ass. His frozen balls had shriveled and retreated. But he didn't dare stop until he reached Lancaster's apartment. The motorcycle roared.

A few wide-eyed motorists had gawked, but so far no cops. Some luck.

He parked the Harley in front of Lancaster's place, looked around, didn't see anyone. He sprinted to Lancaster's door. His bones ached, teeth chattering. He pounded on the door. "Come on, Tim."

No answer.

He knocked louder, looked over his shoulder. So far nobody had seen, but sooner or later somebody would notice the crazy pervert.

He tried the knob. It turned. He pushed the door open and

darted inside, shut it behind him. He let himself warm up, breathed easy, relieved. "Tim?" Nothing.

He walked through the little apartment, found the bedroom, and pulled open Lancaster's dresser drawers. He found a pair of boxers. Sweatpants. He put them on.

He walked around the apartment, tried to get some idea where Lancaster had gone. DelPrego couldn't remember his friend saying anything about leaving town, visiting his parents, anything. He went to the bedroom closet to see if Lancaster's suitcase was gone.

He slid open the closet door. When the body fell out, it took DelPrego a split second to realize what he was looking at. He screamed, stumbled back, tripped on the corner of the bed, and spun into a rack of compact discs. Scattered them. DelPrego landed hard on the floor, breathing hard, heart kicking its way out of his chest.

He crawled to the body. "No," he whispered.

Lancaster looked like he was made of wax, pale and shiny. His eyes were open, looking up, jaw slack. DelPrego studied his face. It somehow didn't look like Lancaster, the life sapped out of him, no light in his eyes. DelPrego grabbed the body, shook it wildly, without reason. "Tim. Tim." The skin was cold.

"Oh, no."

He gathered Lancaster in his arms, a strained, animal noise rising in DelPrego's throat, coming out a wheezing grunt, the sound of raw, disbelieving pain. His fingers dug into Lancaster's clothes, his skin. He willed this not to be true. But Timothy Lancaster III was dead. Gentle, silly, pretentious, naive, kind Tim. Timothy.

DelPrego leapt to his feet, raged into the kitchen. He flung the refrigerator door open, and it slammed against the counter. He jerked open the lettuce crisper at the bottom where he'd unpacked and hidden the cocaine. Lancaster never had any food in the refrigerator. He'd never used the crisper. He looked at the stash of coke, the throaty, strangled growl still coming out of him. This was the stuff that had killed his friend. And DelPrego had killed him by putting it there.

He pulled out the crisper, went through the house, and flung it into the bathroom. The thin plastic shattered on the tile floor, the little Baggies of white powder spilling. DelPrego started grabbing Baggies. He tore them open, a white frenzy of powder. He dumped them into the toilet, spilling, powder caking the side of the bowl, the sink, getting it all over his clothes.

He didn't stop. He screamed and sobbed and cursed and dumped the cocaine. "You goddamn cocksuckers, you fuckers, fuckers, sons of bitches." The tears and snot ran down his face, left tracks in the white dust on his skin.

He sank against the tub, drew his knees up to his chest. He cried and felt dizzy, his throat raw and dry from screaming, his eyes red and hot.

forty

Moses Duncan sat in his pickup truck in the university's south parking lot thinking about Mexican whores. Duncan preferred blondes, big Swedish honeys with long, long legs and giant milky tits. But Mexican whores were cheap. That is to say, Mexico in general was a cheap place to be. He'd been to Juarez once with his dad. The American dollar went a long way, and a guy could get anything—*anything*—down there if he had cash.

Duncan had been thinking he could still get his hands on the coon's cocaine and split town for Mexico. He could disappear and set himself up good south of the border. On his way down, he could unload the stuff in Oklahoma City or maybe Dallas.

He sort of felt bad about Eddie, but these were desperate circumstances. It was every man for himself. Even as he walked out of the old family farmhouse, he sort of knew he wasn't going back. He couldn't. Too much had changed. Too much was different than he had thought. The world wasn't right, and Moses Duncan didn't know how to live in it. In Mexico, cash and pistols would make him The Man. A system he could work with.

He tucked his dad's revolver into the front of his pants. He popped open the glove compartment, took out the Old-West-style, single-action Colt, and stuck it in the back. The corduroy coat hung low enough to cover both pistols. He put on his Harley-Davidson cap, tugged the bill down to hide his face.

He got out of the truck, walked toward the cluster of buildings at the heart of campus. Nothing to do now but keep his eyes peeled. That was important. He wasn't on an errand anymore for that fucking pimp Zach. He was on his own mission.

Maurice sat in his parked Lincoln Town Car two rows from Duncan's truck. If Zach wanted him to keep an eye on Duncan, then the peckerwood must be up to something or giving off a bad vibe. Anyway, Zach was suspicious. Then again, Red Zach was always suspicious of everyone and everything. Maybe that's how the man got to be boss.

Duncan was on the move, and Maurice watched him. He got out of the Lincoln but kept his distance. Maurice was aware he didn't exactly blend in. He checked his gat, his cell phone. He buttoned his coat and headed for the long yard in front of campus. He lagged behind, but kept Duncan in sight.

Zach hadn't said anything specific, but Maurice knew this peckerwood's time was short. Zach would use him to track down Jenks, then Maurice or one of the others would put a bullet between Duncan's eyes. And if Zach still thought it was worth setting up an operation in Fumbee, he'd pick his own man.

A few of the college kids looked sideways at Maurice, but most simply shrank into their coats, gritting their teeth against the sharp wind that had risen sudden and bitter from the west. Maurice craned his neck. The weather looked bad, clouds collecting low in the sky. But he didn't look at the sky for long, kept his eyes on Duncan.

Duncan wandered without plan, strolling a lazy circle around the campus buildings. Maurice shook his head. Amateur. When you're waiting to spot somebody in a situation like this, the better strategy was to stay put in a good location and let the crowd cycle under your nose. Eventually, whoever you're trying to find will drift by. But this was Duncan's turf. Maybe he knew what he was doing.

Duncan stopped, so Maurice stopped too. Maybe Duncan had seen something. Or maybe the motherfucker was just stupid and lost. Maurice backed up close to a tall bush. Watched.

That guy in the denim jacket and the sweatpants looked familiar, Duncan thought. A white guy, but Jenks had brought a couple of white boys with him that day at the barn. This looked like one of them, maybe the guy driving the truck. He looked harder, trying not to seem obvious. Yeah, he was pretty sure it was him.

The guy was walking fast, not really looking around. Duncan could follow no problem. The guy beelined for a building, and Duncan stopped to read the sign. Albatross Hall.

Maybe this was it. He'd go in, find Jenks, put the grab on the coke, then fill these shits with lead and head to Mexico. It was a perfect fucking plan. He touched the butts of his two pistols through the coat's heavy material. Okay. He was ready.

Moses Duncan entered Albatross Hall, followed Wayne DelPrego to the stairway that led up to the building's dead floors.

*   *   *

DelPrego trudged the steps up to the fifth floor. There was no anger left in him, no pity or sorrow, no grief. His capacity to feel anything at all had burned away in the fire of his rage. He was hollow and exhausted and each step was a test.

He found Valentine's office, pushed his way in without knocking. An old man was there, a giant behind him. Jenks sprang from the couch.

"Where the fuck you been, boy? Where's the bag?"

DelPrego said, "I flushed it. I flushed it all. It's gone."

"Are you crazy?" Jenks blinked. "What am I supposed to tell Red Zach now, motherfucker?"

"Tim's dead."

"What?"

DelPrego stumbled past Jenks. "Somebody got to him." He fell on the couch, waited for Jenks to start yelling. DelPrego didn't care. His eyelids were so very heavy. He felt the long blackness pulling him down. He only wanted to sleep.

forty-one

Morgan sneaked out of his office and drove home. He grabbed the mail on the way in. His house was cold, and he turned on the heat.

His life had somehow spun out of control. Maybe it would be okay. Possibly Dean Whittaker would not fire him on the spot when Sherman Ellis failed to materialize at the reading. Perhaps Ginny Conrad would not be scarred for life. Ginny.

Morgan was hungry.

The kitchen was not a happy place. Cupboards bare. The refrigerator wasn't much better. Some butter. Two eggs left in the door. He took them out, shook them next to his ear. Morgan couldn't remember how long he'd had the eggs. They looked fine on the outside, white and smooth. But he couldn't remember the last time he'd been to the market. It was possible the eggs had been there when he'd moved in.

This was ridiculous. Now he was afraid of eggs.

He popped open a beer and looked at his mail. A letter from Kenyon College.

Morgan had applied for a Visiting Poet position at Kenyon. He read the letter. Although they found his credentials impressive, Morgan should go stick his head up his own ass and die. Other pieces of mail wanted to sell him life insurance, pizza, and seeds.

He drank the beer.

Tired.

He went into his bedroom, kicked off his shoes, and fell on the bed. He could not immediately fall asleep. He kept thinking there was something he should be doing. His head spun with loose ends. But he couldn't tie up any of them. Nothing was in his power anymore.

He slept and dreamed he was at the poetry reading. He had to introduce the poets to the capacity crowd, but he was naked. This was when he realized he was dreaming, naked in front of people. Even his subconscious had run out of ideas. He laughed, started stroking himself in front of the audience. Stroking and stroking and not getting anywhere at all.

When Morgan awoke it was dark. Panic jerked him out of bed. He thought he'd overslept, that the poetry reading had started. But it was only six o'clock. He checked the window. The sky looked serious about ruining everyone's plans.

He flipped on the TV news. The meteorologist's plastic smile beamed at him. The cold front, said the weatherman, had shifted somewhat, and Green County was going to get a bit more snow than expected. However, the heavy stuff was going to pass north.

Morgan showered. He stood under the hot water a long time, trying to compose a poem in his head. He was still thinking about the eggs, about fear of the unknown, but it came out adolescent and silly. Then he tried a poem about dreaming and nudity, but that didn't go anywhere either. The hot water started turning cold, but Morgan stood there pretending it wasn't. At last, he couldn't kid himself anymore. He turned off the water, dried himself.

He looked in his closet. How did one dress for a doomed poetry reading? The blue suit was too formal. A shot of Jim Beam helped him decide. Tan slacks and his brown tweed jacket with a black turtleneck. Now he looked his most professorial. Another shot of booze. He could feel it on his breath when he exhaled.

It was still a little early to meet Ginny, but he didn't want to hang around. He took his long coat and went to the car. It was cold, and he almost went back for his gloves and a hat. To hell with it.

He unlocked his car door, felt a wet pinprick of cold on the back of his hand. He looked up. One or two flakes, then another. It was light but steady, swirling in the wind like ash.

Morgan parked on the street across from the administration building. There was a dark tavern across from campus that catered to professors. The drinks were just expensive enough to discourage students.

The snow was coming heavier. *A few light flakes my ass.*

He went in, took a table in the corner. Morgan no longer cared if anyone saw him with a student.

Morgan ordered three vodka martinis. "Keep them coming." He looked at his watch. The poetry reading started in twenty minutes. He was screwed.

Ginny walked in. Morgan saw her and waved her over. He

looked her over. The bruises around her eyes were already fading. A scab on her bottom lip.

She sat. "I have something important to tell you."

"You found Ellis!"

"Huh? Oh no, I made a few phone calls, but nobody's seen him," Ginny said. "Don't worry. He'll turn up."

Godamnsonofamotherfuckingbitchshit—

"I want to talk about us."

Morgan blinked.

Ginny said, "I don't think we should see each other anymore."

"Jesus."

"I don't want you to take it hard," she said. "But don't worry about me. I'm a strong person. I've always been strong."

"Sure." Morgan wished it were true, but he didn't think Ginny strong. He didn't think himself strong. Nobody he knew was strong. Maybe people weren't strong anymore. In the 1950s maybe folks were strong. Eisenhower.

The next martini arrived. Morgan took half in one gulp. He waved at the waiter and pointed at his glass, a gesture meant to indicate *you're too goddamned slow.*

"It's just that this thing has run its course," Ginny said. "We both knew it couldn't work. We're from different worlds."

Morgan realized he was hearing a prepared speech. He decided to ride it out.

"I just don't think we should be . . . involved."

"I understand." Morgan finished his drink just as the third martini arrived.

"But I want us to be friends," Ginny said.

Morgan was a little slow remembering his lines but finally said, "I want that too."

She stood, dramatic, jaw set. Morgan could almost hear the

music swelling. Ginny looked like a chubby Scarlett O'Hara. "Farewell, Professor Morgan."

Morgan flipped her a wave. "So long."

"Well, you could at least act a *little* upset."

Morgan rolled his eyes. "I'm in a shitstorm here. I don't have time for this."

"Fine." She began to stomp out of the tavern.

"Ginny," he called after her. When she turned around, Morgan cleared his throat, and said, "I'm sorry about that guy. Sorry you got hurt."

Her features softened. She nodded once and left.

Morgan tossed his drink down and took the empty glass to the bar. He took a stool next to an elegantly dressed black man and ordered another drink from the bartender.

Morgan turned to the black man. "Some snow, huh?" A little random small talk would get him back on track.

"I've found the local forecasts to be wildly inaccurate." The black man had a deep, articulate voice. Chin up, bright eyes. He carried himself well. "It will get worse, I think."

Morgan suddenly felt clumsy, his fingers thick and stubby. He reached for his glass and knocked over a bowl of peanuts. "Shit."

"I'll get that for you, sir," said the bartender.

"Yeah, thanks." Thanks came out *thanksh*. The vodka had hit his tongue. "It better not get worse," Morgan said to the black man. "Big dog and pony show tonight. Poetry reading across the street."

"I know."

"Bunch of crap," Morgan said. "A big public relations show."

"I'm sorry you feel that way, Professor Morgan."

"Yeah, well I can't really say— Have we met?" The man did look familiar.

The man stood, dropped a ten-dollar bill on the bar. "I'm Lincoln Truman. President of the university."

Morgan's mouth opened and closed a few times like a trout out of water. President Lincoln Truman walked out of the tavern, his back straight. He didn't look back at Morgan.

Hell.

forty-two

Moses Duncan lost DelPrego going up the stairs. Did the guy get off at the third or fourth floor? Or did he keep going all the way up? Shit.

Duncan stopped on the fourth and drew his dad's revolver. If he couldn't find the guy after a quick sweep there, he'd head up to the fifth to look for him. He thumbed back the revolver's hammer. Be damned if they would catch Moses Duncan with his pants around his ankles.

He listened for footsteps but didn't hear any. He didn't hear anything at all as a matter of fact. The floor looked deserted. Dust. Only one in four light fixtures had a bulb in it. No signs on the doors. He went down one hall, crossed over, found himself in a similar dusty corridor. *Who designed this place, some goddamned retard?*

Duncan heard footsteps behind him and froze. He spun around, pressed back against the wall, pistol out in front of him. *Come on, son of a bitch. Show your ass.*

The steps came closer. Duncan extended his arm, gun aimed at the corner. Soon as that guy came around, he was toast. Duncan had come gunning for the guy, but now the guy was coming up behind him. Maybe he had his coon buddy with him. Wouldn't matter. Moses would get the drop on their sorry asses and blast them to hell.

The guy rounded the corner, and Duncan's finger tightened on the trigger.

It was Maurice.

Duncan pulled the gun back, blew out a ragged breath. "What the hell you doing here?"

"Zach thought you might need some backup," Maurice said.

It occurred to Duncan that Maurice would severely fuck up his plan. He should have pulled the trigger, dropped this sucker when he had the chance. As a matter of fact...Duncan considered the pistol at his side, his hand squeezing the butt, tensing.

But Maurice had his automatic in his hands, brought it up, and pointed it at Duncan's head. "I don't like that look in your eyes, peckerwood. You're looking twitchy. You're not thinking bad thoughts, are you?"

Duncan looked down the barrel of Maurice's gun. Could he get his pistol up in time? Probably not. Duncan forced a weak smile. "If I'm twitchy it's 'cause you're sneaking up on me. Makes a fella nervous, don't you think?"

"I hear you." Maurice held out his free hand, kept the pistol steady with the other. "Why don't you hand me that peashooter? I'll give it back when maybe you ain't so nervous."

Duncan laughed, shrugged. "Okay. No need to get all suspicious." He turned the pistol around, handed it to Maurice butt first.

Maurice took it, put it in the big front pocket of his long coat. Then he looked around, took in the fourth floor, the dust. "This place ain't even being used. What the fuck you up here for anyway?"

"I think he might've gone in there." Duncan pointed at a door across the hall.

Maurice turned his head, examined the door. "Don't look like anybody's been in there for a long—"

The Colt thundered, filled the hall, bucked in Duncan's hand. The .45 slug tore into Maurice's shoulder, spun him around, a spray of blood dotting the walls and floor. Maurice grunted, went down. He struggled to lift the automatic.

Duncan stepped on Maurice's wrist, and the gangster's gun clattered on the tile. Duncan thumbed back the Colt's hammer.

Maurice's face was sweaty, contorted with pain. "F-fucking p-peckerwood."

The Colt roared again and a red splotch bloomed in Maurice's gut. Blood spread over him. Maurice clapped a hand over the gushing wound, warm blood seeping sticky between his fingers. "Oh, shit. Y-you redneck fucking…shit." Maurice's eyes glazed. He couldn't keep his head up.

Duncan hovered over him, kept the Colt pointed at the man's face. Maurice's head sank to the cold tile. He twitched, gasped for breath, then didn't move. Very slowly, Duncan reached into Maurice's front pocket, retrieved his daddy's revolver. He stepped back, watched the body for another moment. For some reason he thought it would spring back up, come after him like in a horror movie. It didn't. He'd finished the dirty son of a bitch.

Duncan tucked his guns back into his pants. Now he needed to find his way off this floor. He looked up and down the hall, trying to remember how he'd come in. All these damn doors and hallways looked the same. He made his decision and set off to find the stairs.

He didn't see Maurice roll onto his side, coughing blood. Didn't see the gangster pull the cell phone out of his pocket with shaking, blood-soaked hands.

"Boss?"

"I heard. Go check it out," Fred Jones told his big bodyguard.

"Shots," Jenks said. "Sounded like the floor below us."

"Right."

"You going to be okay without me?" Bob Smith asked.

"Just go," said the old man. "Find out what the hell's happening."

"Okay."

The bruiser checked his pockets on the way out of Valentine's office. Brass knuckles, sap, the .38 on his belt, and the .44 magnum in his shoulder holster. A British commando knife in his boot. He was traveling light that day.

Smith moved well for a big man, walked easy down the hall, head tilted, listening for approaching footfalls. He took the .38 out of his belt holster and put it in his jacket pocket. He wanted a hand on it without flashing the gun in the open. He held the sap in the other hand.

He positioned himself back against the wall near the corner of the hallway. Anybody on the way to Valentine's office would have to pass right under his nose.

He waited, listened.

It was after business hours, so there was a good chance nobody else had heard the shots. Maybe a couple of professors working late or maybe not. Smith shifted from one foot to the other. He didn't like standing for long periods of time, but often it was part of the job.

He was hungry. Jesus, this was going to be a long night. First he had to wait around twiddling his thumbs while that old professor gave the boss poetry advice. Then he'd have to hang around for the reading, then make sure they got home okay. Probably wouldn't be until midnight that he could build himself a nice pastrami sandwich on rye. Some BBQ chips too.

Smith heard footsteps coming. They were shuffling and irregular. The intruder was maybe looking around, trying to get his bearings. Smith stood rigid, hands in front of him ready with the sap.

He'd thought about ordering a pizza, but no way a deliveryman could find his way up to Valentine's office. And he wasn't about to leave the boss alone to make a Burger King run.

The guy was close now. Smith heard him breathing.

Smith tried to remember if there was still a MoonPie in the glove box of the car. No. He'd eaten it two days ago. He made a mental note to stash some snacks in the car. The boss had been keeping an odd schedule lately, and Smith needed to be prepared. Hunger, after all, caused distraction.

A hand came around the corner. The hand had a gun in it.

Smith brought the sap down hard across the guy's wrist. A snap. The guy yelped. The gun flew, slid across the floor. Smith slapped a meaty hand on the guy's forearm, pulled him around the corner.

He knocked the Harley-Davidson cap off the guy's head, patted his coat down, and found an Old-West-style revolver. Smith smelled the barrel before sticking it in his belt, gave the guy a shake. "Who are you?"

"Jesus, my wrist's busted."

"I asked you a question," Smith said.

"I don't feel so good."

"That's a shame. Hold still." Smith had him by the back of the coat.

The guy sagged, wanted to lie down. He groaned, leaned forward, and vomited.

"Christ!" Smith let go of the coat, stepped back, puke splashing on his shoes. The smell almost made him heave too.

The guy took off, running hunched over, clutching his busted wrist to his chest.

"Shit." Smith took one step after him, planted his shoe square in the puddle of puke. His feet flew out from under him. He landed on his back. Hard. The air knocked out of him. He tried to suck in breath, but it was a long few seconds before he could breathe normally. He sat up. A raw spot on his hip where he'd fallen on his brass knuckles. He'd be sore for a week.

He gathered the pistols, limped back upstairs, wondering how he'd explain this to the boss.

Smith lumbered back into the old professor's office. Valentine and Jenks looked at him expectantly.

But Jones read Smith's face, saw the pistols in his hand. The boss could always size up a situation in no time. "Who was it?"

Smith sighed. "Some guy. He got away." He dumped the pistols onto Valentine's desk. Smith didn't need any more guns.

"For Christ's sake," the old man said. "What happened?"

"I fell down."

"What's that on your pants?"

"Vomit."

Jones stood, joints creaking. "Forget it. I want to hear the poetry reading. Let's go."

Red Zach was sick and tired of Oklahoma, farmhouses, rednecks, and being jerked around. He had to take care of this shit quick, or he'd look weak. He couldn't go back to St. Louis without his property and Harold Jenks's head on a stick.

But it was taking too damn long. How hard could it be to find a man in this two-bit town?

Okay, he was getting tense. He closed his eyes and began his breathing exercises. In through the nose, out through the mouth. Long, controlled breaths. It wasn't working. Damn. He hated being on the road so long. Everything he needed was at home. His yoga workout videotapes, aroma therapy candles, the really good CD with the ocean noises. He needed all of it to keep from going nuts and getting an ulcer.

His cell phone bleated in his jacket pocket. He pulled it out and flipped it open. "What?"

It was Maurice on the other end. He sounded strange, weak, like maybe it was a bad connection. Maurice told him to get a pencil. Zach wrote the words *Albatross Hall* on a paper napkin. A building at the school.

"What is it?" Zach asked. "Dormitory or something?"

Nothing.

"Maurice?" Zach looked at the cell phone's display, made sure he still had battery power. "Maurice, you there?"

Must have lost reception, thought Zach. That happened too often with these cell phones. Hit a dead patch and everything goes quiet.

forty-three

Morgan drank another martini, then walked out of the tavern and into the blizzard. Snow flew sideways, stung his face. He walked across the street bent almost in half against the wind. This was bullshit.

The snow was ankle deep, seeped into his socks. The lampposts along the main sidewalk were fuzzy blurs of light in the driving snow. It took fifteen minutes to trudge to the auditorium, a trip that usually took five. Morgan had to keep stopping and looking around to make sure he hadn't taken a wrong turn. The campus looked unearthly and strange in the whirling mix of snow and pale lamplight.

They'll cancel the reading, thought Morgan. *How can they not?* A sudden, unexpected, freak blizzard. The roads would be a mess. He had heard, in fact, a siren in the distance. Emergency services would be caught back on its heels. Nobody would risk the roads for poetry. Nobody would know Ellis had never even shown.

He finally made the auditorium and ducked into the lobby, stomping his feet and huffing for air. His vodka breath burned up his throat and out of his mouth in a toxic cloud.

He heard the crowd. Morgan cracked the door to the auditorium, peeked inside. The seats were filled. He scanned the throng. Professors and administrators in the front two rows. Bored students packed the rest of the place, chatting among themselves. A paper airplane sailed from the back row. A guy in a university sweatshirt leapt up from his seat and snatched it out of the air to the scattered applause of the adjacent rows.

The freshmen. Morgan remembered what Dean Whittaker had said about filling the seats with honor school freshmen. They'd only had to come from the dorms, didn't need to drive or hunt for a parking space.

Jesus Christ Almighty. Morgan was well and truly fucked. A crowded auditorium and no Ellis. Morgan belched, tasted vodka, felt slightly dizzy.

He had to do something. The dean and the rest of the administration were expecting something special.

Well, fuck them. Morgan hiccuped. It wasn't his goddamn fault Sherman Ellis was missing in action. What was he? A miracle worker? He couldn't find a kid who'd disappeared off the fucking planet.

Still, just to show up empty-handed was pretty feeble.

Morgan scanned the crowd. There, in the back row, just coming through the door, were Bob Smith and Fred Jones. The big bruiser helped the old man into his seat.

Morgan suddenly had a bad idea, but it was better than no idea at all.

*   *   *

Dean Whittaker fidgeted in his seat, tugged at the band of the silk panties through his trousers. He usually liked wearing the panties, red with a little bow, and lace trimming. But he'd been shifting nervously, and the panties had crept into his ass crack. They also had a stranglehold on his scrotum.

Lincoln Truman sat to the dean's right, a random vice president on his left. Various other department heads and community big shots in the front row, and someplace there was a chancellor.

And where the hell was Jay Morgan? The show was set to start any minute.

President Truman looked impatient and cross. Whittaker opened his mouth to say something reassuring to the president, but a young woman in a long, black dress came onstage and modest applause signaled the reading was under way.

Whittaker recognized the woman as one of the graduating MA students in creative writing. She had a pierced lip and eyebrow, bright orange hair pinned elaborately into sprouting tufts of hair that sprang out at odd angles. How the hell did she expect to get a job looking like that? Whittaker thought about his own daughter, who was in her third year at Kansas State. Would she come back pierced, covered with tattoos, trailing some long-haired "dude" who fronted a speed-metal band? The thought made him shudder. What the hell was going on with the world?

He fingered his panties, watched the orange-haired woman approach the podium.

"Good evening everyone, and thanks for attending Eastern Oklahoma University's annual graduate poetry reading," she said. "Usually we give this reading in the big classroom in Albatross Hall, but this year it's been moved to the auditorium, because, as you can see, we've had *one heck of a turnout!*"

She paused for a burst of applause that never came.

She cleared her throat. "Our first reader will graduate with his master's in English this spring. His poems have appeared in *Word Junkie*, *Gas-hole*, and *Pea-Pickin' Potpourri*. Please welcome David Blanding."

The pale young man took the stage amid a sluggish ripple of golf clapping. He began to read, his voice a hypnotic murmur blanketing the audience like a high-tech sleep ray from a dime-store science-fiction novel. He wove his poems like elaborate spells designed by some evil wizard to suck all that was interesting and beautiful out of life. If his poems had been music, they would have been the same note over and over again. If his poems had been a meal, it would have been a plate of wet cardboard.

Dean Whittaker watched Lincoln Truman stick his fist in his mouth to stifle a yawn. Whittaker's panties were so far up his ass, he had tears in his eyes.

Morgan got the old man's attention and waved him into the lobby.

"What's with sending me to see that old loon?" Jones asked Morgan. "Guy's got a screw loose. You know some fucked-up people." Jones sniffed, wrinkled his nose. "You smell like a damn distillery."

Morgan couldn't disagree. "Mr. Jones, I need your help."

"It'll have to be quick," Jones said. "Bob's saving my seat. I don't want to miss the reading."

Morgan took Jones by the elbow, started easing him down the hall. "How would you like to be a little more closely involved?"

"Like what?"

Morgan said, "One of our readers can't make it, and we need somebody to—"

Jones dug in his heels, pulled his arm back from Morgan. "Oh, shit no. Are you fucking crazy?"

Morgan latched onto the old man, started dragging him. "I'm desperate, Mr. Jones. *Please.*"

Jones looked like a little terrier being dragged on a leash. He looked side to side for some help, his eyes round with terror. "There's like a million people in there. I'll piss myself."

"You'll be fine."

"I don't have my poems. Bob has the folder."

"I'll get them for you," Morgan said.

"Oh, God. I can't breathe."

"You'll be fine."

Morgan floundered backstage until he found the girl with the orange hair. He told her about the change. She didn't understand. Morgan said what the fuck was there to understand? The old guy would read instead of the black guy. She looked unhappy but said okay.

Morgan had fetched the old man's poems from the big bodyguard. It had taken much goading and pleading, but Morgan convinced Jones to read. Jones looked pale and terrified. Morgan had never seen the old man afraid of anything. He wished Jones good luck and left him backstage.

Morgan's stomach groaned. He belched acid. *I should have ordered a sandwich.* He went back into the lobby, found the men's room. Inside he bent over the sink and turned on the cold water, splashed his face. He leaned on the sink awhile, took long deep breaths.

Behind him, a toilet flushed. One of the stall doors creaked open. Morgan turned and looked into the bloodshot eyes of Professor Larry Pritcher. He stood stiff, neck still in the brace. The professor had tacked up a "wanted" poster offering a reward for information leading to the person or persons who'd assaulted him with *Finnegans Wake.*

"Oh, hello, Morgan." Pritcher talked through clenched teeth. "Hope you don't mind if I don't shake hands. I can barely lift my arms."

"Did they...uh...ever find out who attacked you?" Morgan asked.

"No. I suspect a disgruntled undergraduate. I was rather free with the F's last semester. My own injuries are of little consequence, but my Italian ten-speed was damaged beyond repair."

"How's the reading going?"

"Every poem feels like a punch in the face," Pritcher said. "I'd go home except for the blizzard. Take care, old boy."

Pritcher left the men's room. Morgan splashed more water on his face, scooped some into his mouth, and swallowed. He dried himself with a paper towel.

Back in the lobby he flagged down two kids, torn jeans, skateboarder haircuts. "Who's reading?"

"Some fag," said the kid. "It sucks. We're leaving."

Wouldn't that be nice, thought Morgan. *To live such a simple life. It sucks. I'm leaving.*

He stopped at the door to the auditorium. Maybe he could. Why not? Why couldn't he just leave? Why should the skateboard kids have more freedom than he? Jones didn't need him anymore. He'd make or break on his own. The dean expected him to make an appearance. Ostensibly, this was Morgan's show. It had been his responsibility to get Ellis into shape for the reading. But there was no Ellis. The show, apparently, was a drag and would go down in history as the most embarrassing thing that had ever happened in Green County.

The hell if Morgan would stick around for that. He headed for the door but stopped when he heard the girl with orange hair back at the podium. The first two readers were done, and she was getting reading to introduce the old man.

Okay, Morgan told himself. He'd stay for one poem, see if the old man fainted or what. Morgan could at least do that.

The orange-haired girl said, "I've been asked to read this before we introduce our final reader." She had a card in her hand. "The national weather service has issued a severe storm warning for eastern Oklahoma and parts of western Arkansas. I've been told that Fumbee city workers are now getting the plows out of the garages, but it will be a while before the roads are safe for travel."

A low, hopeless groan rose from the crowd.

"But not to worry," she said. "We have another fine poet for your entertainment. Originally, Sherman Ellis was scheduled to read, but there's been a change. I'd like to introduce our next reader, Mr. Fred Jones."

It took the old man long seconds to cross the stage. He looked ridiculously small and frail from the back of the auditorium. Someone giggled. The old man reached the podium, shuffled his papers, and wiped sweat off his forehead with a bony hand. Morgan's heart broke a little bit.

He couldn't quite see the bigwigs in the front row, but Lincoln Truman's head leaned toward the dean's. Confused murmurs.

"I'm Fred Jones," he said into the microphone. He cleared his throat. "My first poem—"

Morgan couldn't stand it. He closed the door, turned around, and headed for the nearest exit. He felt queasy, guilty. His hand reached for the door and froze when he heard the laughter. *Aw hell, they're laughing him off the stage. Aw, shit.*

Go, get out the door, he told himself. *You didn't ask for any of this.* But Morgan couldn't move, couldn't leave the old man. He went back, flung open the door in the back of the auditorium.

And the cheers washed over him. Students on their feet, howling.

Morgan blinked, rubbed his eyes to see if somehow Metallica

had appeared and taken the stage. No. It was the old man. He shuffled his papers again and leaned toward the microphone. "My next poem is called 'The Zydeco Gangster.'" He read:

When I came from Philly to the Big Easy in '72
in a baby blue Impala full of smack,
I was already pushing gray around the ears.
And I don't move so quick no more,
and the back gives me trouble,
and the hands are kinkin' up.
The hands are key.
So when the dagos hired me
to work the Quarter,
I got a big moulie shadow to do the bone work.

The old man's narrative unfolded. He read it like a pro, voice spinning its magic over the crowd. Morgan too was mesmerized. Jones was a natural. His gift radiated from him like a beacon.

So I went to hear his song
on a humid night in some bayou shithole,
and Che was huffin' on the accordion,
and another bony moulie
was beating time on a washboard,
and the shuffling, breathless racket
sounded like the time we leaned on Tiny Allen
in the homo bar
at the rotten end of Bourbon.

The poem was sad and sweet and nostalgic, yet comic at the same time. Morgan did not remember this one. It hadn't been in the stack of papers the old man had handed to him weeks ago.

So I'm talking to Little Mike on the phone
with Big Mike on the extension
and they say everything is jake back in Philly.
I try to explain the zydeco shakedown,
and how it's so different from
the tearful, slow Pagliacci pleading
when we'd bear down on the mark
like a lumbering toilet-paper mummy
in a Peter Cushing flick,
but they don't get it.
So I ask Big Mike if he remembers the time
we chopped down the glassblower over on Sullivan the brrrrpt
   da bript brip chingle chingle bript
when we riddled his display cases with Mac-10s,
the nine-millimeter percussion
the tambourine tinkle of broken glass,
and I think he's starting to get zydeco.
And we laughed and laughed
and wondered if the Motor City fellas
do it to Smokey Robinson.

The crowd roared, the applause shaking the building. It was right up their alley. A whole generation who'd thought poetry had to be about flowers and bumblebees. Now they'd heard poetry on steroids. Gritty. Extreme poetry like in a Mountain Dew commercial.

Morgan stayed to hear three more. The old man's voice had found strength.

Perhaps they enjoyed it for the wrong reasons. Maybe there are no right or wrong reasons. It might not have been the reading Dean Whittaker wanted, but Morgan thought it was beautiful.

forty-four

Even over the blizzard, Morgan still heard the kids cheering.

The snow mixed with a little sleet. Morgan didn't care, didn't mind that it stung his face. His smile was a mile wide. Something good and right had finally happened.

Morgan ducked his head into the wind, put one foot in front of the other toward Albatross Hall. He wanted to find Valentine, have a drink, toast to Fred Jones's success.

It was after working hours, and the main doors were locked. His keys jingled in his shaking hands. Finally, he found the slot, inserted, turned the key, and pushed the door open.

They grabbed him by both arms, rushed him into Albatross Hall, and shoved him to the floor. Morgan hit hard. He flipped over, looked up at ten black men in long coats. All had pistols out.

A man in a bright yellow suit pointed down at him. "Stay put, motherfucker."

Morgan nodded. "Okay."

"Anybody else in this building?"

"I don't think so," Morgan lied.

"What's up there?" The black guy in charge pointed his gun at the ceiling. "Dorms or something?"

"Offices."

"What you doing here?"

"My office. I left something. A book." Morgan looked at the guns pointed at him and felt sick. "There's nothing here of any value. What do you want?"

"We're gonna go upstairs and kill everyone we see."

Morgan gulped. *What the hell's going on?*

"What you want to do, Zach?" one of them asked.

The man in yellow said, "Fan out and search the floor. We'll work our way up. If Maurice said they were here, then they've got to be here someplace."

"We ain't seen Maurice."

"We'll find him," Zach said.

"What about this guy?" Zach's henchman indicated Morgan with a trigger-pulling motion to the head.

"Don't shoot. They'll hear it upstairs," Zach said. "Just knock him a good one."

The henchman leaned over Morgan. The butt of his pistol came down sharp and fast across the back of his skull.

Morgan's eyes flickered open. He saw only darkness. He closed his eyes and opened them again. No change. He rubbed the back of his neck, climbed to his knees. He tried to stand and lost his balance. His hand flew out and he grabbed something wooden. It wasn't attached to anything and didn't offer any support. He fell forward into a pile of clattering items, metal and wood. Something fell on him, plastic and heavy.

He didn't try to stand this time, crawled forward, a tentative hand in front of him. He found a wall, no, wait. It was wooden. Hinges. A door. He felt his way up until he found the knob. He twisted it, fell forward into the light, a clattering wad of brooms and mops. An empty metal bucket rolled out in front of him.

He staggered and stood, felt the back of his head again. Swelling. He looked at his hand. No blood.

How long had he been in the closet? Morgan checked his watch. No more than five minutes. They'd expected him to be unconscious longer, out of the way. Who the hell were those guys?

What had the gang leader said? He'd ordered a search floor by floor. If Morgan acted quickly, he could make it upstairs in time to warn Valentine.

Or he could save his own ass and run away like a little girl.

It shamed him a little that he paused an extra few seconds to decide.

He bolted for the stairs, legs still wobbly. He didn't pause at any of the lower floors although he wished he knew where the gangsters were. Possibly they were already ahead of him. Perhaps he would find only bodies on the fifth floor. He didn't stop to think about it, bounded up the steps two at a time.

When he reached the fifth floor, he collapsed, lay sprawled on his back, heaving for air. His lungs ached for breath. His stomach churned and burned with alcohol. His brain spun with the knowledge of imminent death.

He willed himself to his feet, jogged the maze to Valentine's office.

He threw open the door, stumbled in, startled a "whoa" out of Jenks.

"There's a bunch of black guys coming up here with guns," Morgan said.

Morgan leaned heavily against the doorjamb, out of breath, sweat sticking his shirt to him, his heart nearing terminal velocity. His eyes took in Valentine's office, darted around the room, and landed on Wayne DelPrego, who sat in a corner chair with his head in his hands. Morgan frowned. What was his student doing there?

Then Morgan saw Jenks. His eyes shot wide. "You!"

Jenks looked confused. "Yo, Professor. What are you doing—"

Morgan leapt, hands outstretched, a feral scream splitting the air. He hands went around Jenks's throat, and both men tumbled to the floor.

"Where have you been, you stupid son of a bitch? I'm going to get fired because of your sorry ass."

"Get him off me," Jenks yelled. "Get him off."

"Professor Morgan!" Valentine leapt on Morgan's back, heaved him off Jenks.

Jenks rubbed his throat. "He's crazy."

DelPrego had watched the whole altercation unfold, hadn't moved.

"I've looked everywhere for you!" Morgan deflated in Valentine's grip. "Fuck it. Just fuck you."

"These young men have been hiding here with me," Valentine said. "Those men downstairs are killers."

"No time for this story now," Jenks said to Valentine. "We need a way out of here."

Jenks went to Valentine's desk, where Bob Smith had dropped the revolvers. Jenks had been glad to see the guns because he was afraid he'd need them. He tucked the .38 into his belt and checked the load on the Old-West Colt.

Wayne DelPrego sat up from his chair. He looked pale and distracted. In a low, even voice, he said, "Give me one of those."

"No way," Jenks said, without looking at him. "You're not straight in the head."

"I'm not asking you. I'm telling you."

Maybe it was the eerie calm in DelPrego's voice. Jenks nodded and handed the Colt to DelPrego.

Valentine thumbed two shells into the double-barreled shotgun. "I know a way downstairs. Follow me."

They followed Valentine out of the office, zigzagged the crazy turns of the fifth floor, and stopped at a door with the word ELEC-TRICAL on it.

"Here?" asked Jenks.

Valentine opened the door, and Jenks recognized the fireman's pole he'd helped the custodian carry. It descended through a wide hole in the floor. Before Jenks could say anything, Valentine leapt on the pole and slid down.

Jenks followed.

The fourth floor whipped past and the pole ended. There was an alarming second of free fall, and Jenks landed on a dusty mattress. It was the third floor.

Morgan landed on top of him.

"Get the fuck off."

"Excuse me, Batman," Morgan said. "I don't have a lot of pole experience."

They managed to roll out of the way right before DelPrego hit. The four of them were in an abandoned classroom. Valentine cracked the door to the hall, took a peek.

"I don't see anyone," Valentine said. "The stairs are directly at the end of the hall. We go down to the first floor, and there's an exit outside right there."

"Let's go," Jenks said.

They filled the corridor, stalked the hall with long, determined strides toward the stairs, guns at their sides, jaws set, eyes hard.

The door to the stairwell flew open and three gangsters filled the other end of the hall. Jenks recognized Red Zach's men. They saw Jenks and the professors, and their hands went into their coats.

Valentine, Jenks, and DelPrego lifted their guns as one. The gangsters fired at the same time. The hallway erupted, shook with gunfire. Dust fell from the ceiling, plaster flying where lead hit.

Morgan hunched against the wall, arms over his head. He felt his coat jerk where a slug ripped through the fabric. He heard yelling, realized it was him.

Birdshot from Valentine's twenty-gauge sprayed the first gangster. He dropped his gun, screamed. The other two fired back. Jenks fired three times. The first bullet went wide. The next two struck home.

The gangster who'd been sprayed with the birdshot lifted off his feet, a new red hole in his chest. The thug next to him fell back, his head spraying blood. He twitched on the ground a long second before going still.

The last of Zach's men bolted back for the stairs, firing wildly over his shoulder. The door banged shut behind him, and he was gone.

Smoke and cordite hung in the air.

"Dear God," Morgan said.

"We got to move," Jenks said. "They heard the shots."

They ran for the stairs.

DelPrego paused over the bodies of the dead black men. He stuck the Colt in his belt and picked up the two fallen pistols, heavy automatics, one nickel-plated.

Jenks looked back. "Fuck that shit, Wayne. Let's go!"

They flew down the stairs, feet barely touching each step.

The exit led them out to the blizzard. It still howled, wind flinging snow and sleet.

"Where's DelPrego?" Morgan shouted over the wind.

Jenks turned around, saw DelPrego wasn't behind him. "Shit."

These were the men who'd killed Timothy Lancaster.

DelPrego held the pistols like white-knuckled death. He'd scour Albatross Hall, and all would fall before him. Nothing mattered but his white-hot vengeance.

He found them on the second floor. They stood in a cluster, a half dozen of them, one gesticulating the story of the shooting on the floor above. DelPrego ran toward them, picking up speed with each step, arms extended and guns leading the way.

Their faces turned, eyes wide, screaming. They pointed guns back at him. Curses. DelPrego didn't hear. There was only the hot buzzing, blood pressure pounding hot in his ears. He squeezed the triggers as fast as he could.

The hail of lead shredded the group, one gritting teeth, grabbing an arm. Another pitched forward. Two ran. Three returned fire, big automatics spitting fire.

DelPrego caught a slug in the leg, he screamed, went down, but twisted to keep his pistols aimed at the group. He kept squeezing the triggers even after his gun was empty. His head swam, stomach heaving. Another bullet plowed a deep groove into his left shoulder. Blood gushed with each heartbeat.

He lay on his side, dropped the empty pistols, and pulled the Colt from his belt. He cocked it, fired along the tile floor, and shattered the ankle of one of the gangsters. The gangster screamed, collapsed to the floor, squirming to get ahold of his ruined ankle. The puddle that formed under his shoe was thick and red and spread rapidly.

Two more bullets smacked into DelPrego's chest. He no longer felt the pain, only the dull impact. He fired the Colt one more time, but the bullet went wild.

He was shot again. Again. His eyes looked up, dull and unblinking. The smile was faint and oddly peaceful.

forty-five

The three of them huddled against the blizzard, looked back at the door they'd used to escape Albatross Hall. DelPrego did not come out.

"Maybe he took a wrong turn," Morgan shouted over the blizzard.

"H-he was r-r-right b-behind us." Valentine had fled the building with only a light jacket. He was turning blue.

"His eyes," Jenks said. "He had a crazy look. I think he's going to do something."

"Can someone please tell me what in the hell just happened?" Morgan asked.

"Get himself killed," Jenks said, still thinking of DelPrego. "I better find him before—"

"D-don't be a f-fool," Valentine said. "You can't go back in—"

Valentine's head jerked around. Morgan and Jenks followed his gaze.

Distantly, figures took shape. They manifested out of the fog like floating stones, great, hard, square chunks of granite. Shoulders. Hands deep into the pockets of their long dark coats, hats pulled low to cover eyes. A ragged line of them moving forward, taking form as they stepped into the feeble lamplight. They did not heed wind or cold, only advanced like a silent, grim tide. Eight of them; no, ten. A dozen square-jawed ghosts.

"Jesus," Morgan said.

"He ain't going to help you." Jenks's hand tightened on his pistol.

Valentine clutched the shotgun to his chest. "No shells l-left."

They marched toward Morgan, Jenks, and Valentine. Behind the line of men came another figure. He was small, bent against the cutting wind, thin hand holding a cloth cap on his bald head. He held on to the arm of one of the bruisers. The small man came within three feet of Morgan and stopped.

"The reading went well," Fred Jones said. "I should kick your ass, but I enjoyed it."

"Who are these men?" Morgan asked.

A blast of wind sprayed the group with sleet. Bob Smith had to use both hands to keep Jones from flying away. Jones's thugs continued to march past.

"The kid told me about his troubles." Jones nodded at Jenks. "I called a few old pals to come help."

Jones turned to Valentine. "A guy from University of Arkansas Press was there. Asked me if I had enough stuff for a whole book."

Morgan's mouth fell open.

"That's m-most fortunate," Valentine said.

"You're going to freeze your balls off," Jones said. "Bob, bring the car around and pick us up."

"Right, boss." Smith lumbered back into the blizzard.

"The weather's going to keep the cops off our backs for a little bit, but we got to move fast," Jones said. "My guys will finish here. They know what to do."

Jenks yanked on Morgan's sleeve. "Wayne."

Morgan said, "One of my students is still in there."

"I got to look for him," Jenks told Jones.

"Nunzio!" Jones waved over one of the long coats.

The guy had big, red cheeks, black eyes. "Mr. Jones?"

Jones jerked a thumb at Jenks. "Take this guy inside. He lost a lamb. Make sure he ain't shot by accident."

"Right. This way, kid."

Morgan watched Nunzio lead Jenks back into Albatross Hall. The building looked like something out of an Edgar Allan Poe tale—dark stone, windows like vacant eyes, the snow piling at the corners. Morgan looked down, saw that Jones had latched on to his arm. He'd been holding the old man up. Morgan hooked arms with Jones, stood close to shield him from the wind. Jones let him.

Jones craned his neck, lifted his mouth toward Morgan's ear. The old man was trying to tell him something. Morgan leaned forward, cupped his free hand around his ear to block the howling storm.

"You got to help me get my book into shape to show this Arkansas Press guy," Jones said. "He says he'll leave a slot in the schedule open this fall."

Morgan said he'd help.

Dull gun blasts echoed from within Albatross Hall. Blue light flashed in the windows.

"W-what are they doing?" asked Valentine.

"Sweeping up," Jones said.

A sudden flurry of shots like a spurt of microwave popcorn, flashes from the third floor.

Jones's car pulled up on the sidewalk with Smith at the wheel. The big sedan carved dirty furrows in the white snow. Morgan opened the door for Jones. Valentine went around the other side. They climbed into the car, sighed relief at the warmth.

"Are they going to be okay?" Morgan looked at the dark windows of Albatross Hall.

"They'll be fine," Jones said. "I need some soup."

Under the car's interior light, Morgan took a good look at the old man. His lips were blue, breathing shallow.

Morgan took his hands. They were lumps of hard ice. "You okay?"

"I can't feel them."

Morgan put the hands between his own, rubbed hard.

"It was like you said," Jones muttered. "When I knew I had the crowd. They loved it. I could feel them. It was the best I ever felt." His voice was fading.

Morgan pulled the old man close, tried to give him body heat. This little, gnarled poet. Morgan's *deus ex machina* hero.

Jenks knelt on the cold tile next to DelPrego's body. His head ached from holding back the tears. Finally, he gave up, let them roll hot and salty down his cheeks and over his lips. Down the hall, Nunzio dragged a gangster's body by the ankle, pulled him to the edge of the pile of bodies the hoods were making. It had been at least five minutes since Jenks had heard gunshots.

Jenks pushed himself to his feet. He felt tired, a hundred years old, like he'd been awake for a week. He looked at the last body Nunzio had put on the pile.

"You know any of these?" Nunzio's hand swept over the pile.

"A few," Jenks said. "The one on top is Red Zach."

Jenks studied Zach, the slack, expressionless face. Eyes glassy and dull. It seemed impossible that this man had ruled his life. It was a hundred years ago he'd been Zach's go boy, running errands. He had even hoped to be like Zach one day, but now the man was only cold bones and loose flesh and an already fading memory of fear.

The cocaine was gone. Red Zach gone. Even Sherman Ellis was gone, with no family to remember him. It was all gone. For Harold Jenks, only the whole, wide world remained.

forty-six

It took an hour for Bob Smith to drive Morgan home. None of Fumbee's stoplights worked. Power was out in various neighborhoods. Fortunately, the roads were nearly deserted, most folks having enough sense to stay at home.

Jones regained some of his color and his voice was stronger. The sedan had good heat and Smith flipped it to full blast. Jones offered Valentine a spare bedroom and the old professor gladly accepted.

Morgan's porch light told him he was one of the fortunate few who still had electricity. He bid everyone good night, rushed up the steps and into his little house. He found the thermostat and thumbed the heat up until it clicked on. He stood over one of the vents, let it blow warm air up his pant legs.

He moved into the kitchen, rummaged every cabinet until he

finally tuned up a half-full bottle of Cutty Sark he didn't remember buying. He filled a juice glass and sat at the kitchen table still wearing his coat. Valentine had told Morgan about Jenks. That was the kid's name. Harold Jenks. Morgan still wasn't sure he understood what had happened.

He wondered if Ginny were okay, vaguely wished she were with him. He didn't feel like being alone, wasn't really sure how he felt. His night had been a horror of dead bodies, yet Morgan felt relief he wasn't one of them. He'd begun this mess with Jones bailing him out, hiding Annie Walsh's body. Morgan could no longer remember Annie's face. It didn't seem like part of the same life.

Now Jones had bailed him out again, even given him a ride home. A strange, sweet, odd old man. Morgan drained the Cutty Sark.

He was so tired but forced himself to shower. The hot water felt good.

No towel on the rack when he stepped out of the shower. He dripped and shivered as he walked to the hall closet, feet slapping wet on the floor.

Morgan didn't even see the lamp until it was an inch from his nose. It shattered against his forehead, and Morgan went down, blinked blood out of his eyes. He climbed to his knees, shaken, opened his mouth to yell. A fist caught him hard on the jaw, rattled teeth. He bit his tongue, more blood.

Morgan lay on his back, legs curled awkwardly under him. He looked up into the grinning face of the man over him. Stubble. Bloodshot eyes, dark circles. All disturbingly familiar.

The man's left arm ended at a red stub, which had been wrapped in white gauze, blood spots seeping through.

"Oh, no." Morgan heard his own voice, small and without breath. It sounded like fear.

Deke Stubbs laughed, a low wicked mix of scorn and amusement. "I thought you might remember me, Professor."

"I thought..." Morgan rolled over, wiped the blood out of his eyes. His head throbbed.

"You thought I was dead?" Stubbs shook his head. "Nope. But I can see how you might think that since you left me trapped in the back of a goddamn car that was sinking into the fucking ocean."

Stubbs kicked Morgan hard in the ribs, and Morgan *whuffed* air, went into a fetal position. Stubbs kicked again. A third time. Morgan felt something give along his side, wondered if a rib had cracked.

"I want to tell you something, Jay old boy," Stubbs said. "When you're halfway through your own arm with a saw, you really learn how to hate. I've killed you so many times in my imagination, I've lost count."

"Please." Morgan backed away, tried to stagger to his feet but froze when he saw the automatic in Stubbs's only hand.

"In one scenario, I shove broken glass up your ass for an hour before I put a bullet in your head." Stubbs stood close to Morgan, stuck the barrel of the automatic against Morgan's temple. "But that's too quick. After what I been through, everything's too quick for you. You're going to learn about a whole new bright world of pain. There's going to be jagged things and sharp things and fiery hot things, and it's all for you."

Morgan said, "I just wanted out of the car. I thought it was sinking."

Stubbs slapped the barrel of his gun across the side of Morgan's head. Little fireworks went off behind Morgan's eyes. Bells. Morgan felt something cool on his cheek. It was the floor.

Morgan was dizzy, couldn't get his bearings. He lost track of Stubbs, allowed himself the fantasy that Stubbs had left, changed his mind for some reason.

But Stubbs was too in love with vengeance. Morgan felt his wrists being bound together. Some kind of thin cord. Then he was being dragged into the bedroom. Morgan could only get one eye open, the other caked closed with blood. He tried to twist around, see what Stubbs was doing.

Morgan felt himself lifted by his wrists. He was half on his bed, half on the floor. The cord holding his wrists had been lashed to the bedpost. Stubbs's footsteps retreated into the next room, but his voice carried. He was still talking, telling Morgan his gruesome story.

"After I sawed off my hand," Stubbs said, "I think I was in some kind of shock. The memory is a bit hazy, but I think I climbed out of the Mercedes." Stubbs voice was closer now. "I threw up too. My gut was tossing pretty bad. Like I said, shock. Also, I swallowed about a gallon of salt water."

Morgan smelled smoke, heard Stubbs inhale. A cigarette.

"Anyway, I wasn't much good to swim with only the one hand. I couldn't work against the tide. I floated along even with the shore for a while until my feet touched bottom and I trudged ashore."

Morgan felt the white-hot cigarette butt grind into his left ass cheek. He screamed, tried to twist away, but Stubbs held it in place. Finally, he let go.

Stubbs flicked the butt away. "Look at that. My cigarette went out for some reason. Guess I better light another."

The burn throbbed, made Morgan nauseous with fear and pain.

"I had to tie a tourniquet with my belt, pull it tight with my teeth," Stubbs said. "If things slow down, I'll tell you how I cauterized the wound. By the way, as if you couldn't guess, yes it was pretty goddamned awful."

Morgan realized with cold dread that this was only the beginning. Stubbs had nursed his hatred since Houston and wouldn't be satisfied until Morgan suffered every possible agony Stubbs's warped mind could generate.

Morgan filled his lungs with air, screamed as loud as he could. "Help! Help! Police! Call the—"

Stubbs's body crushed against Morgan's. Stubbs forced the professor's face into the mattress. He clubbed Morgan twice more with the butt of the automatic pistol.

"No, no. That's not how we do this." Stubbs's breath was hot on Morgan's ear. "I know what you think. Maybe the police will hear or maybe not, but anyway maybe I'll panic and kill you quick and clean. No way. I got plans for you. You're going to beg for a quick death before this is over. And, buddy, just scream your fucking head off because nobody's going to hear you over that blizzard out there."

Morgan only half heard, was only half-conscious. Black spots claimed his vision. He didn't think he could take any more blows to the head. Maybe that was better anyway than being awake for Stubbs's torture session.

"Session," Morgan said out loud.

"What?" Stubbs lifted Morgan's head off the mattress by his hair. "You trying to say something, Professor?"

Morgan wasn't paying attention. He'd stepped one foot into a dreamland, saw Valentine smoking his bong, DelPrego and Lancaster in his writing workshop. Was this what they meant by your life flashing before your eyes? If so, Morgan was disappointed.

"Disappointed," mumbled Morgan.

"What?" Stubbs frowned. "Dammit, don't you go out on me. I need you awake for the fun."

And this Harold Jenks son of a bitch, thought Morgan. *This is all his fault, getting me involved with drug lords and gunfights and cocaine.*

"Cocaine," Morgan said.

Stubbs shook Morgan, slapped him lightly on the face. "Come on, now. Wake up. What was that about the cocaine?"

Morgan didn't move. Stubbs shook him again. "The cocaine, Professor?"

"What?" Morgan's good eye flickered open.

"Don't play dumb. You were talking about the cocaine. Where is it?"

"I don't know what the hell you're talking about," Morgan said.

"Did I mention I was going to put things up your ass?" Stubbs said. "Now start talking, goddammit!"

Morgan forced himself to concentrate. "You'll let me go if I show you where the drugs are?"

Stubbs laughed, a sick wheezing sound. "Hell, no. But I promise not to do all that sick shit. Show me where you've stashed the coke and I'll kill you clean. No pain."

"Untie me," Morgan said.

"Fuck you."

"Untie me and I'll show you."

"Just tell me."

"No," Morgan said. "I don't like being bent over like this. You'll do something to me."

"Tough shit."

"Untie me."

"Oh, for Christ's sake," Stubbs said.

He unlashed the cord from the bedpost but left Morgan's wrists bound. As Stubbs did this, Morgan turned his head, saw that Stubbs had stuck the gun under his other armpit so he could use his good hand to untie the cord. Morgan saw what was probably his only chance. He wanted to hit Stubbs in the face, make him drop the gun, surprise him, anything. If he could get past him, Morgan would even run out into the blizzard naked, maybe try to flag down a car.

Morgan lurched to his feet and lunged, swinging two-handed at Stubbs.

Stubbs sidestepped easily, popped Morgan in the nose with a right cross. Morgan felt cartilage snap, felt warm blood pour down his face and over his lips.

Stubbs laughed, took the pistol from his armpit, and dropped it into his coat pocket. "What? You think since I got only one hand, I can't take a pussy like you?"

Morgan rolled onto his stomach, tried to crawl under the bed.

Stubbs shook his head. "Now that's just pathetic."

Morgan got halfway under the bed. Stubbs bent over, grabbed Morgan's ankle, and pulled him back.

Stubbs *tsked*. "Looks like we've got to do this the hard way now. Doesn't bother me none, but you're— Oh, fuck!"

Morgan had rolled onto his back, Fred Jones's little revolver in a two-handed grip held out in front of him. Stubbs fumbled for the automatic in his coat pocket, but Morgan squeezed the trigger.

The first shot was unsteady, shredded Stubbs's groin. The private eye went down, his one good hand clutching his balls, blood pooling. Morgan pulled the trigger again, blasted a hole in his bedroom wall. The third shot caught Stubbs in the top of the head, sprayed bone and brain.

Morgan dropped the gun, crawled away from the body. He watched a long time, waited for Stubbs to get up, but nothing happened.

Morgan limped into the kitchen. The adrenaline rush was rapidly leaving him. The aches and pain flooded in, head and ass throbbing, ribs screaming with every breath.

He found a kitchen knife, sawed the cords awkwardly until he was free.

Morgan went into the bedroom one more time. Looked at

Stubbs to make sure he was still dead. He looked at his bedroom, the blood. A mess. He looked at the gun on the floor, the one Jones had given to him so long ago. It seemed like forever.

Then he picked up the phone, dialed.

"Bob," Morgan said. "Is he still awake? Okay, put him on." A pause. "Mr. Jones? I know it's late, and it's been a long day. But there's just one more loose end I need you to help me tie up if it's not too much trouble."

Epilogue

Most of the students and faculty at Eastern Oklahoma University were glad it was the end of the semester. Summer waited, flings and family and a break from textbooks. For Morgan, it only meant unemployment. He'd have to hustle this summer to find something. Otherwise, it was adjunct hell at some community college.

Strangely, Morgan couldn't bring himself to worry about it. Where or when he might get his next job seemed like small potatoes. His capacity to fret had been exhausted. The uncertain future stretching out before him was a parole from his old life.

Since Fred Jones had made the poetry reading a success (it received glowing reviews in the Tulsa and Fayetteville newspapers), Morgan was not immediately fired, and his contract was allowed to run its course until the semester's end. But nobody mentioned anything more about Jay Morgan being hired in a permanent capacity at the university. It was generally understood that Morgan would move on, thanks a lot, good luck, and don't let the door smack your ass on the way out.

His office in Albatross Hall was almost cleaned out. He filled a cardboard box with books and file folders but paused over the newspaper clippings. They were yellow at the edges. In the weeks following the Albatross Hall slaughter, Morgan had collected the clippings obsessively. They seemed to chronicle an episode in his life that had refused to end. Every other day a new article.

Some he liked better than others. The article about the man found wandering naked with cuts all over his face seemed unrelated, but Morgan had suspicions.

But the one about the drug raid at a local farmhouse was clearly the result of Fred Jones's machinations. According to the article, authorities had pieced together the following story after finding the bodies of Annie Walsh, Deke Stubbs, and Moses Duncan. Local drug dealer Moses Duncan had hidden the body of the Walsh girl after she'd overdosed on some of Duncan's merchandise. She was found buried under the house. Tulsa private investigator Deke Stubbs, hired by Walsh's parents, had apparently tracked the girl to the farmhouse. Evidence at the crime scene supported the theory that Duncan and Stubbs had killed one another.

Several gruesome details of the killings were left unaccounted for. Morgan tried to laugh about this but couldn't. The officer in charge of the case, a Sergeant Hightower, promised to keep investigating until authorities were satisfied.

The article also quoted Annie Walsh's parents, who expressed relief that the matter had at last been put to rest. Morgan felt a pang of guilt and regret. He tore up the clippings and threw them into the basket next to his desk.

But he kept the postcard from Harold Jenks. It had arrived two weeks earlier and been addressed to Morgan, Valentine, and Jones. It said he was doing fine and thanks for everything. It also said he wasn't sure what he was going to do next, but don't worry it would be something "straight." When Morgan read the postcard carefully, he thought he could just barely detect an apology. Or maybe that was wishful thinking.

He also kept the letter he'd received three days ago from *The Chattahoochee Review*. They'd accepted the poem Morgan had written about smoking the cigars for the old man.

Morgan had tried to call Jones to tell him about it, but the number had been disconnected. The next day, Morgan had found a note from the old man in his mailbox. Jones had written that his "government friends" had been upset. Jones's picture had been in the paper the day after the poetry reading. Evidently that was a no-no, and Jones had been "relocated."

It made Morgan sadder than he'd anticipated. He missed the old man and wished him well.

Dirk Jakes walked into Morgan's office without knocking. "Hey, hey, Morgo-man. Just wanted to stop by and say no hard feelings on losing my Mercedes."

"I sure am sorry about that, Dirk."

"No biggie," Jakes said. "The insurance check finally came, and I just bought this sweet Lexus. Did I mention they found a severed hand in the back of the Mercedes?"

"It's a crazy world," Morgan said.

"Cops say maybe some kind of whacko gang ritual."

Annette Grayson walked in, put her hand on Jakes's arm. "Come on, Dirk, you're taking me to lunch, remember?"

"Sure, babe. Just let me catch up to you in a minute."

She looked at Morgan. "See you later, Jay." There was a message in her eyes Morgan didn't understand, but he suspected it was supposed to be some kind of joke on him.

After Grayson left, Jakes said, "Just between you and me, Morgo-man, I've been banging her for three weeks. Yeah!" Jakes made hip-thrusting motions and stuck his tongue out. "I'm sure you can imagine what that's like."

"I can imagine."

"Listen, don't sneak out of town until we can grab a beer, okay?"

"Right," Morgan said.

Jakes waved and was gone.

Morgan took his last box of personal belongings out to the car and drove home lost in thought. The old man was gone, Jenks was gone, even Valentine had found a new place to hide. Morgan would leave Fumbee the way he'd come in, alone and a stranger.

But he smiled when he saw Ginny waiting for him on his porch. A week after the blizzard, Ginny had shown up drunk and lonely. They'd fucked for five hours. The next day she'd said it was a mistake, and four days after that they spent a weekend in Dallas. Once Morgan had the pattern down, she'd been easy to cope with.

He stopped in front of her on the porch. "Hey."

The weather had turned warm. She wore a dark green tank top and denim shorts. "Hey, yourself. All packed?"

"Almost."

She took his hand, stood, brushed off the bottom of her shorts. "Did you pack up the bed?"

"Not yet."

"I thought I'd stop and say good-bye," she said. "You know."

"I know."

"But you're leaving town, so, you know, it doesn't *mean* anything." She led him through the front door, past the taped-up boxes and into the bedroom. "I mean it simply can't because you're leaving, right?"

"Right."

She tugged his pants down. He lifted her tank top, cupped her breast.

She sank into him, said, "So this is it for us?"

"Yes. The absolute end." He lifted her chin, kissed her deeply and long.

About the Author

VICTOR GISCHLER teaches creative writing at Rogers State University in Claremore, Oklahoma, where the wind comes sweeping through his pants. His wife, Jackie, thinks he is a silly, silly individual. He drinks black, black coffee all day long and sleeps about seven minutes a night. Victor's first novel, *Gun Monkeys*, was nominated for the Edgar Award.